Her Scottish Keep

DARCI BALOGH

KNOWHERE MEDIA

For my daughters, Taylor and Jodi,

You have been my motivation to strive for something better in life and my reminder that I am already richly blessed. May your lives be full of joyous adventures and may all of your dreams come true.

Love you always,
Mom

Tawnyetta's periwinkle bridesmaid dress was holding her back. Three unopened bottles of champagne in her arms didn't help, and lugging them up a ladder added another layer of difficulty.

The dark green bottles, heavy with their bubbling elixir of happiness, knocked together precariously as she moved. They rolled against one another, the glass sounding both strong and fragile. Every time they bumped together she cringed, afraid one was going to explode before she got to her destination. This concern was troublesome, for sure, but Tawnyetta had bigger problems. The most formidable being the ladder, which was over 20-years old and originally built for children.

Late June in Colorado was beautiful as always. Balmy. The setting sun painted the middle class suburban back yard with brilliant orange, pink and red light. Aside from the rolling champagne bottles, and Tawnyetta complaining under her breath, there was only one other noise punctuating the early evening air–the muffled sound of a woman crying.

Tawnyetta kept a firm grip on the ladder with one hand and held the champagne in her other arm as if she was carrying a baby. An unwieldy, cold, slippery baby. Silently cursing the floor length satin skirt that tangled around her feet, Tawnyetta made her way carefully up the ladder leading to the tree house. One rung at a time.

A heavy perfume of lilacs filled her nose. Maybe the scent came from her parent's lilac bushes that lined both sides of their back yard, or maybe it was from the floral arrangement pinned in her hair that bobbed up and down unsteadily as she dangled five feet off the ground. She wasn't sure. The smell brought back memories. Sweeping her away to summer evenings when she was a kid. The kind that had always made her want to stay outside and play until long after dark. She glanced at the glowing sky to the West. Soon the sun would set behind the purple Rocky Mountains and leave a blank slate for the stars to fill. A perfect night for a wedding.

The low murmur of women's voices floated down from the tree house above. The clanking champagne bottles had not yet captured their attention. Everyone in the tree house was focused on one thing and one thing only. As she neared the top of the ladder the muted burble of Bridget's blubbering grew louder and Tawnyetta steeled herself for the scene she was about to join.

Bridget was the bride. Tawnyetta wondered if that was technically correct. Was she still considered a bride? She had not yet changed out of her $5,000 wedding dress and tonight was her wedding night, but since the wedding had been called off...well, she guessed it didn't matter anymore. She was Bridget and she was always the center of attention. Bride or not.

Tawnyetta made it to the top of the ladder and pushed up on the trapdoor with the crown of her head. She was probably dealing a death blow to the flopping lilac twisted into her hair, but she figured she was safe. No wedding photos to worry about at this point.

The trapdoor pulled open from above and Luna peered down. She reached through the square hole and offered Tawnyetta a hand, who took it gratefully. Luna wore her own periwinkle dress, slightly paler, and it snagged on the rough wood as she helped Tawnyetta into the tree house. Luna's face was creased with concern. Whether she was worried about ruining her dress, the champagne bottles breaking, the unstable ladder, or the bawling bride, wasn't clear.

"How's our patient?" Tawnyetta asked.

Luna gave her a worried smile. Tawnyetta didn't really need to ask. She knew how Bridget was doing, because now that she was inside the tree house the bride's weeping rang in her ears.

"Tawny!" Bridget exclaimed upon seeing Tawnyetta pulling herself, the champagne, and yards and yards of periwinkle satin through a trapdoor built for second graders.

"I brought refreshments," Tawnyetta said, holding up a bottle. She hoped it might lighten the mood.

Bridget's crying grew louder.

"Don't cry, Bridge," Tawnyetta said, grunting a little as she crawled next to Luna and yanked the last of her dress through the trapdoor, slamming it shut with her periwinkle dyed satin pumps.

"But that was for my reception! I was supposed to drink that champagne as a married woman! M-m-married to Christopher!" Bridget wailed.

Tawnyetta looked around at the beleaguered bridesmaids; Luna, Sofia, and Angie. All three of them wore the same dress she wore, but in variegated shades of periwinkle. They sat scrunched against the walls of the tree house, their feet meeting in the middle. This space used to hold all of them with room to spare, but now barely allowed them enough room to crawl around each other, especially in their giant dresses.

As the maid of honor and Bridget's official "best" friend, Tawnyetta felt a responsibility to handle this situation.

"Well," she said, peeling the foil off of the first bottle. "Instead of focusing on the negative, tonight we're going to use this champagne to celebrate your freedom."

"Here, here!" declared Angie, clapping her hands lightly in front of her chest like a little girl.

"Do we have cups?" Sofia asked.

They all exchanged a look. Bridget stopped crying and sniffled. Tawnyetta paused in her uncorking. She hadn't thought about cups.

"Hang on," Luna said. With some difficulty she managed to turn around and rummage through the tiny, child-sized cupboard they had used to store snacks for their club meetings when they were kids. "Ta-da!" Luna said triumphantly as she held up a dusty old package of Dixie cups. "Remember when we pretended Kool-Aid was wine?"

Tawnyetta smiled. She did remember. They all remembered. The five of them had been friends since kindergarten, and had created the Purple Clover Club in second grade when her older brothers and her Dad had built this tree house.

Before anyone could respond, Tawnyetta's phone buzzed. She had stuck it inside her strapless bra for the ceremony, because her periwinkle dress had no pockets. As soon as she felt hers buzz, the other bridesmaid's phones started ringing and buzzing. Everyone reached into their cleavage to pull them out. Everyone except Bridget, whose mouth dropped open in shock.

"You carried your phones into my wedding?" she asked with some measure of indignation.

Ignoring her, Tawnyetta read the group text they had all received. She delivered the message to the phoneless bride, "It's Thomas. He wants to know where we are."

Thomas was a late addition to their group and an unofficial member of the Purple Clover Club. Because, *officially*, boys weren't allowed. Funny they'd never really thought of him as a boy. He'd always been odd, funny, and wicked smart, so they'd allowed him to hang around with them ever since fourth grade.

Though not a bridesmaid, Thomas had been a grooms-man. He had witnessed Bridget's dramatic freak out while walking down the aisle towards her groom only moments after finding out he had cheated on her during their engagement. And now Thomas was checking on them.

"Don't let him bring Christopher here!" Bridget said.

"He wouldn't," Luna responded. "He knows."

Tawnyetta typed in a two word answer to him, 'tree house', and hit send. No other explanation was needed.

Bridget scooted over. Her ice white gown puffed around her like giant mounds of meringue. If she realized the rough wood floor of the tree house was most likely tearing the bottom of her princess wedding gown to pieces, she didn't seem to care. She patted the space next to her and said, "Tawny, sit by me."

Bridget had called Tawnyetta 'Tawny' since she could remember. She had a thing for nicknames and had created one for each of them. Sofia was 'Fifi', Angie was 'Gigi', Luna was 'Lulu', and Thomas was 'Mister'. They had never figured out where she came up with 'Mister', but that's what Bridget had called him for as long as they'd been friends – which was to say, forever.

Bridget had tried to force them all to call her 'Gidget', but it never stuck. It was, in Tawnyetta's opinion, not really possible to create a nickname for yourself.

Tawnyetta climbed carefully across the periwinkle clad feet and billowing skirts of her friends until she could plop down next to Bridget. She kept the almost opened bottle of cham-pagne carefully pointed towards the ceiling the whole way.

"At least I'll have my maid of honor next to me tonight," Bridget said with a dismal smile.

"Sure," Tawnyetta said. "I'm here. We all are. Want a drink?"

Bridget's blue eyes widened with eager consent. Even red rimmed from crying she had the most beautiful blue eyes. It was a shame the wedding hadn't worked out with her being such a lovely bride. With long, blonde ringlets, full lips, and those baby blues made even more noticeable from perfectly applied makeup, she really was stunning. Tawnyetta was surprised to notice that Bridget's mascara wasn't even running. Always well put together, their Bridget.

Tawnyetta looked around at the others as they passed the bottle of champagne, pouring the fizzing drink into their Dixie cups.

Angie looked like a fairy. Her long, curly, dark red hair bloomed wildly around her face. Porcelain skin prone to freckle in the sun made her dark brown eyes look almost black. The contrast was not only gorgeous, but gave a hint at her flair for the dramatic.

Sofia sat next to Angie. She had more curves than any of them. Voluptuous, proud of it, and smart as a whip as well. With her deep brown skin, thick black hair that hung down straight as an arrow past her waist, and wide, almond shaped eyes that shone emerald green behind black rimmed glasses, Sofia was an exotic beauty.

Luna was Sofia's younger cousin and second in many ways to her in the looks department. Where Sofia was bold, strong, and assertive, Luna was soft, slender, and mild. She had lighter, sepia toned skin, pale brown eyes, and rich chestnut hair. Her hair, however, had a natural wave that Sofia's did not. It spilled over her slender shoulders and down her back in a soft waterfall of swirls. She may have been the younger cousin, and she may not have the same arresting kind of beauty that Sofia did, but Luna was just as smart and exquisite in her own way.

Compared to her friends Tawnyetta knew she didn't quite measure up in the looks department. Tall, almost 5' 11", and lanky, she was small chested and had more of a boyish frame than the rest of the Purple Clover Club – except Thomas. That worked for Tawnyetta. She thought of herself as a little sportier than the others. Always up for hiking, water sports, skiing, tennis, fencing, kickboxing, or whatever, Tawnyetta figured her wiry body suited her interests to a 'T'.

Her hair was so brown it was almost black, but not quite, and cut right at her ears into what she hoped was a funky look. She wore very little makeup, like Luna. But her skin didn't have the same gorgeous natural coloring as Luna. Tawnyetta was pale with long arms and gangly legs. She did, however, have one feature that could be considered uniquely pretty. Her amber eyes. Sometimes they appeared light brown, sometimes a burnished gold, but most of the time the golden flecks in her eyes gave them the appearance of glowing amber. Bridget called them her wolf eyes.

"This is nice," Angie said and held her paper cup of champagne up to her nose so the bubbles could tickle it.

"Are you feeling any better?" Sofia asked Bridget.

"I will be," Bridget responded as she tipped the bottle, splashing more champagne into her cup. She let out a soft, shuddering sigh, "I just don't know how I got here, you know?" They all watched her with empathy. "I thought I was going to skate into 30 ready to start a family of my own. I thought he was the one," Bridget said, her eyes welling up with tears.

"I hear you, sister," Angie said as she tilted her Dixie cup toward Bridget in a silent toast.

The comment worked and Bridget chuckled instead of falling into a new bout of bawling.

Tawnyetta put her arm around her friend's shoulder and gave it a squeeze. "We've all been there, Bridge."

And they all had. Well, maybe not this version. But some version of this colossal breakup had played out in every one of their lives at one point. Some of them many times over.

"Remember Antoine?" Angie asked with a giggle.

This sent a ripple of laughter through all of them.

With a roll of her eyes Sofia injected, "And what about Carlos?"

Again, laughter.

Over their decades of friendship each one of them had suffered through every kind of bad relationship. Bridget at least had made it to the altar. Almost.

"Maybe we've been focusing a little too much on men," Luna offered, her voice light and whisper thin.

They all looked at her.

"What do you mean?" asked Sofia.

Luna chewed her bottom lip, which she did when she was about to philosophize.

"I mean...I've been thinking a lot about this lately," she said. "I feel like, for me at least, I've spent a little too much time worrying about dating and falling in love and not focusing enough on myself."

Sofia's eyebrows knit together. "You went to college. You bought a car and a condo."

"Yeah, yeah, I did. That's true." Luna sank back against the wall, unable to fully explain her meaning.

"You're talking about big things," Angie suggested. She arched her eyebrows at Luna who nodded in agreement. "Not just accomplishments, right?" Luna nodded again. "Dreams!" Angie exclaimed, raising her eyes toward the ceiling and the unseen sky above it.

"Yes, dreams," Luna agreed.

"I've always dreamed of having a beautiful wedding,"

Bridget said quietly. Tawnyetta wasn't sure she had meant to say it out loud.

Luna leaned forward again, wanting to make her point. "That's what I mean. Did you ever think much about what you would do after your big, beautiful wedding?"

"My honeymoon?" Bridget answered uncertainly. They all giggled. Bridget sighed heavily. "That amazing Scottish castle we were going to visit."

"You could go to a Scottish castle on your own," Sofia said.

"Yes! That's what I mean," Luna agreed.

Tawnyetta felt something stir in her chest. She, too, had been feeling an unnamed emptiness lately. Hadn't been able to shake it. Every day seemed the same and she moved through it with a lack of direction, a lack of purpose. Apparently she hadn't been the only one.

"It's strange that we're all single now," Tawnyetta mused.

All eyes turned toward her.

Bridget sniffled and blinked at her. "We are, aren't we?"

"Unexpectedly unattached," Luna said. Naming it.

The comment made Tawnyetta smile.

"What if we toasted ourselves tonight?" Angie asked. "What if we didn't toast our freedom from men or our single-ness, but instead toasted our dreams?"

Tawnyetta felt a shiver in Bridget's shoulders. She looked at her friend in her fragile state. "What's wrong, Bridge?"

"What if I don't know what my dream is?"

"We'll help you figure it out," Sofia said. She leaned toward the center lifting her Dixie cup into the air. "We'll all help each other go after our dreams. Man or not. Wedding or no wedding. We deserve to have our dreams come true."

"Here, here!" Angie lifted her cup into the air as well.

Maybe it was the light from the orange and pink sunset pouring through the cutout windows. Maybe it was the memories of this place. Maybe it was because they were suspended above the ground where nothing was solid or certain. As they sat in a haphazard circle just like they had a thousand times as kids, Tawnyetta experienced a pang of bittersweet. She felt as if they had all lost something. Not just Bridget and her ruined wedding, her never to be marriage. But all of them. They had given up something precious in the years since they'd last gathered in this rickety tree house.

Was it really something they could find again?

"What do you dream of?" Angie asked all of them, her red hair seemed on fire in the glowing light of the sunset. "What do you really dream of?"

Tawnyetta's throat clenched and she couldn't answer. Her chin trembled and she was surprised to find that she had to swallow tears.

"What do *you* dream of?" Sofia asked Angie. Tawnyetta wondered if Sofia was turning the question around because she couldn't answer it either.

"I want to be a mermaid," Angie said with a boldness that made Tawnyetta think she was serious. Nobody laughed. The golden hour of sunset, the magic hour, had come and they were aglow in its glimmering shine. A sea of frothing periwinkle and white with Angie staring fiercely at the ceiling, a brilliant smile on her face.

"I want–" Luna began, but her voice choked a little and she stopped.

"What's your dream?" Bridget encouraged her softly.

"I want to write novels," Luna answered, her soft brown eyes shimmering with excitement at the idea.

Tawnyetta nodded. Of course. That was not a surprise at all.

"What about you, Sofia?" Luna asked, quiet and encouraging.

"I want to know everything there is to know," Sofia answered with a wide smile. "That's why I want to be a doctor...a professor. I want to be the wisest person in the room!"

They all laughed in delight. If any one of them could achieve that, it was Sofia.

All eyes turned to Tawnyetta. The light was dimming quickly. She wondered if she didn't speak her dream in this singular magical moment that they had discovered between childhood and their adult life perhaps her dream wouldn't come true. But she didn't have words for it. Not exactly.

"I think I want...I mean I dream about...adventure. I dream about climbing mountains and crossing seas and fighting dragons," she laughed.

"Here, here!" Angie said, lifting her Dixie cup again as if sealing their deal with the fairies that danced at twilight.

"Here, here!" They all answered in turn, and toasted their dreams.

Before the champagne fizz disappeared from the back of her throat the rays of the sun that had set the dust dancing and sparkling through the tree house like so many enchanted wishes, were gone. They sat in silence, as if waiting for something to happen.

A heavy thump sent a tremor through the floor of the tree house and they all squealed. The trapdoor slammed open and Thomas poked his head up from below.

"Are you all right?" he asked Bridget directly then turned his gaze on each of them for an answer.

"Mister!" Bridget declared. "You scared us to death!"

"Are you coming up?" Sofia asked, starting to make room for him.

Thomas glanced warily around at the lack of room. "Naw, I don't know if this old thing can take any more weight."

Bridget gasped. "Are you trying to say something, Mister?"

Thomas shook his head. "No, I'm only saying this tree house has seen better days. I just wanted to check on you. I know it was a rough day." He directed this statement at Bridget and leveled a kind gaze full of concern at her.

Bridget threw her shoulders back and looked as proud as she possibly could while sitting on the floor in her wedding dress. "I'm fine. Well...I'm going to be fine anyway."

Thomas nodded. "Okay then, I'll leave you guys to it." He flicked his gaze to the champagne bottles. "If any of you need a ride home, let me know."

As the trapdoor shut Bridget sighed, "We had a limo booked to drive us around all night. That's been wasted. And now the whole honeymoon will be wasted as well."

All of them nodded sadly in unison, acknowledging her loss.

Tawnyetta reached for the champagne bottle to refill Bridget's cup. She paused when Bridget sucked in her breath sharply. Tawnyetta looked up to catch her friend's big blue eyes staring at her, wide with excitement and a tinge of mischief.

"Unless..." Bridget said.

Tawnyetta waited and when no more words came, asked, "Unless, what?"

Bridget grabbed Tawnyetta's arm. "Unless you go with me!"

Chapter Two

Before the wedding, as maid of honor, Tawnyetta had been sucked into all of the over the top romantic nonsense that precedes every wedding. After the glorious event collapsed into sheer chaos, she and the bridesmaids had rushed a screaming, bereft Bridget out of the church and into the tree house. Almost one full day later Tawnyetta had expected to be facing a few days off work. Nothing but free time stretching out in front of her. No particular plans. Maybe she would clean out her closets or go to a matinee movie or do some hiking in the foothills. She had expected to be bored. Instead, she found herself on an international flight heading to London with Bridget snoring quietly in the seat next to her.

The logistics had been relatively easy. Her passport was already in place. She'd gotten it about four years ago when she thought she and her then boyfriend were going to take a romantic trip to South America. That never happened.

Changing her name with Christopher's on the plane ticket wasn't too difficult, it just demanded a hefty fee, which Bridget happily paid. Other than that the entire trip was already planned and paid for, which seemed to give Bridget an extra vindictive thrill.

"Is Christopher going to throw a fit when he finds out I took his place?" Tawnyetta asked as she grabbed random pieces of clothing out of her dresser and tossed them on her bed.

Bridget's pouty lips tightened into a scowl as she folded the clothes neatly and packed them into Tawnyetta's banged up old suitcase.

"He can complain all he wants to his hygienist," Bridget said with disgust. That's who Christopher had slept with, his dental hygienist. "Besides," she continued, "he's probably still sleeping off whatever bender he went on last night. By the time he figures out what's going on we will be in the air." She wiggled her eyebrows at Tawnyetta conspiratorially.

"Remind me never to cross you," Tawnyetta said with a chuckle.

Thomas and the girls dropped by to check on the progress of Tawnyetta's honeymoon hijack, as Thomas called it.

"It's not a hijacking," she corrected him. "It's a Not a Honeymoon."

"It's an adventure!" Angie said with a gasp. She plopped down on the bed next to the half packed suitcase.

Luna's eyes got wide. "Just like your wish!"

"Naw," Tawnyetta scoffed at the idea. "This is hardly me running off to fight dragons."

"Well, technically you are crossing an ocean," Sofia added, arching one eyebrow at Tawnyetta teasingly.

"And the Scottish Highlands are mountains...aren't they?" Angie asked.

"I guess, but they don't have dragons," Tawnyetta said.

"How do you know? You've never been there," Angie retorted.

Tawnyetta rolled her eyes. "It's not really the kind of adventure I was talking about."

"We will be staying in a castle, so that's something," Bridget added.

"True," Tawnyetta stopped packing toiletries into her suitcase, interrupted by a twinge of guilt. "Are you sure this isn't a really rude thing to do to Christopher?"

They all reassured her that it was not. Especially Bridget.

"Serves the guy right anyway," Thomas said. "Anyone that would do that to Bridget is a complete waste of space."

Bridget smiled gratefully at him. "Thank you, Mister."

With the whirlwind of getting ready, Tawnyetta had little time to think too much more about what she was doing. Once they were through security and waiting at the gate to board, she let her mind wander and couldn't help but wonder what she may have gotten herself into.

Knowing Bridget, the Scottish castle she had booked for her honeymoon was all about romance. What if it was dripping with touristy clichés of the Highlands, or staged, corny honeymoon moments? Or both? Tawnyetta could only hope that there was something other than swooning romantic fair to partake of once they got there. But she had already agreed to go, and it did seem like the best thing to do for Bridget. She couldn't let her best friend go on her honeymoon alone.

Other than a few trips to Mexico and once to Canada, Tawnyetta had never left the United States. She had never flown over an ocean or set foot in Europe.

"Refreshment, Madame?" A stunning blonde stewardess smiled at her. She spoke in a hushed tone with a thick accent that sounded Swedish, although Tawnyetta couldn't be sure.

Tawnyetta glanced at her friend who was still sleeping soundly in the aisle seat. She looked back at the stewardess. "Yes, thank you."

The white noise in the large aircraft had put Bridget into a kind of emotional coma. The flight to London was long, very long. They wouldn't touch down at Gatwick airport until tomorrow early afternoon sometime. Then they would have to take off again and fly to Inverness. She may as well get comfortable.

The stewardess waited patiently for her order.

"Um...wine?" Tawnyetta thought wine sounded sophisticated enough for the circumstances.

"Red or white?"

What would a well traveled American drink? Tawnyetta had no idea. She took a 50/50 shot at it and ordered white.

The wine was cold, bitter against her tongue, but it was good. She sipped out of her plastic cup and looked outside, watching the sky turn a gorgeous violet with tangerine clouds.

The seat in front of her wiggled and jerked, bumping back towards her and causing her lowered tray to shimmy. White wine splashed over the edge of her small cup. A few moments later the round head of a middle-aged, bespectacled man popped up on the other side of the seat in front of her. Instead of facing forward, however, he faced backward, looking straight at Tawnyetta. The funny little man peered down at her and sniffed like a cartoon mouse that smelled cheese.

"My apologies," the man said in a British accent. "I believe my seat is malfunctioning."

"That's okay," Tawnyetta said.

"Oh dear." The man glanced down as she wiped the spilled wine up with her tiny airplane sized cocktail napkin. "Let me buy you another."

"Oh, it's not a problem. Don't worry about it."

"I insist," he said. He twitched his hand into the air, waving down the stewardess. In so doing his seat jiggled even more and Tawnyetta had to lift her cup and hold it mid-air to keep it from spilling everywhere.

The British man's name was Clark. After their initial clumsy introduction they fell into an easy chat. His seatmate was sleeping just as hard as Bridget so they ended up in a lengthy conversation with Clark leaning part way over the back of his chair nursing a scotch.

Clark was a travel writer for a small British magazine on his way back from Denver. When Tawnyetta told him where she and Bridget were going, and how they had come to be going there together, his eyebrows lifted high above the edge of his wire frame glasses.

"That's quite the adventure, isn't it?" he asked.

Tawnyetta smiled at his choice of words and nodded. "I suppose it is."

"Have you been to the Highlands before?"

"Scotland? No. No, I haven't."

Clark gave her a jerky nod and took a sip of his scotch. Then he tipped his glass, pointing at her as if she was very brave indeed. He swallowed and said, "You're in for quite a treat, you are."

Tawnyetta couldn't tell if he was being serious or sarcastic, but soon he was entertaining her with stories of his experiences in the Highlands. She didn't know if she felt better or worse after hearing them, but she certainly found him amusing.

The sky darkened to black outside their small oval windows. Clark fumbled in his shirt pocket and gave her his business card before bidding her good night and turning around to settle into his own seat. Tawnyetta was alone with her thoughts.

Bridget remained sleeping like a rock. She'd slept through dinner, several pilot announcements, and Clark's anecdotes of Scotland. Tawnyetta leaned over closer to her friend's mouth just to make sure she was still breathing. She was. She must have been completely worn out.

Tawnyetta pulled the in-flight magazine from the pocket in front of her, the one on the back of Clark's seat. She flipped through it and came across an article on an arts festival in

Edinburgh. Apparently this was an annual festival held in the Scottish city that pulled in people from around the world. Hungry for more information on Scotland she read the whole thing twice over. She had a sudden sense of urgency to learn as much about the culture and the people of her destination as she could. When she was finished with that article she continued to a piece on French wineries until her eyes drooped. She pushed the button to turn off the light above her, put the in-flight magazine back in its pocket, and stared out the window until she fell into a fitful sleep.

In her dream she was visited by mice wearing spectacles and kilts. They ran up and down the aisle of an ancient stone church while she tried to catch them in her empty plastic wine cup. All of the sudden the mice scattered under the pews, hiding in terror. Tawnyetta turned slowly toward the altar that stood at the front of the church and gasped in surprise. Standing at the altar was a huge, green dragon. Its chest heaved up and down, pulsing spurts of flame and smoke out of its nostrils. The dragon's golden eyes watched her carefully and she dared not move. She could hear the tittering of the mice from underneath the pews. They were talking in British accents telling her that she was going to have an adventure, but not to move or her adventure might eat her for lunch.

Chapter Three

By the time they reached Claymore Castle the next evening it was almost dark. Not completely dark, because at that time of year this far North the Highlands saw close to eighteen hours of daylight. Caught in this near night state, the skies were grey and eerie.

Bleary eyed from traveling, Tawnyetta could barely stay awake. It had been raining since they landed in Inverness. A slow, cool drizzle that added to her sleepiness, making her feel groggy like she'd taken a sedative. From her position in the back seat of the car that had picked them up at the airport, she watched the scenery go by in a blur.

Bridget, having slept most of their time on the overnight plane trip, was bright eyed and engaged in a lively conversation with their driver. She had both elbows propped on the front seat as she leaned forward eagerly, trying to catch everything he had to say.

Bridget laughed. Something had struck her funny. Tawnyetta heard the driver's voice well enough, but she had all but given up on understanding the man's accent. She knew that his name was Allen. Or at least that's what she thought he'd said when he introduced himself. His name was all she had gleaned through his thick Scottish brogue. Bridget relayed parts of their conversation to Tawnyetta to keep her up to speed. Tawnyetta tried to listen, but honestly, she was too tired to care.

Bridget, on the other hand, was happily attempting to understand everything Allen said. When there was confusion she giggled and fell back in the seat grabbing Tawnyetta's arm in delight. Tawnyetta offered a wan smile and tried to keep her eyes open. Drizzle fell on the windshield and dripped down her window. She watched the green and gold and grey landscape pass as they followed a narrow road twisting higher and higher into the hills.

"We're here!" Bridget exclaimed, translating Allen's most recent comment.

Tawnyetta's head ached with fatigue and everything outside her window looked fuzzy. She couldn't make out anything that looked remotely like a castle in the drippy, blurred view.

"Ha-e flook, ick cashtel clemoor," Allen said.

Must be some kind of welcome.

When she stepped out of the car it smelled wet. Wet grass, wet stone, and a dank smell, like rushes along the edge of a pond that have died and are rotting back into the rich earth. Thin rain spattered on the umbrella that someone held over her head. She didn't see who it was. Shallow puddles on a cobblestone drive. Deep green trees and shrubs flanking massive stones that rose out of the ground in front of them.

Finally, she saw it.

Through the dim light and the mist and the rain, Claymore Castle. A gigantic stone structure looming up and up into the grey clouds. Lights were set on the ground in front of the castle to shine up on its huge grey walls. Wide stone steps leading to the entrance. Massive wood doors rigged with thick iron hinges. That's all Tawnyetta could remember of the first time she laid eyes on Claymore Castle. Weariness ensured that her brain could not register much more.

"Isn't it gorgeous?! Isn't it beautiful? Tawnyetta can you believe we're actually here?" Bridget's voice penetrated the fog that wrapped around Tawnyetta's head.

No. She couldn't believe it. And more than that, she couldn't drum up much excitement about it either. All she wanted was to crawl into a soft bed and collapse into sleep forever.

There was a butler. There was a cook. Somebody shoved hot tea in a china cup into her hands, but she couldn't focus on their faces and their Scottish accents may as well have been Greek for all she could understand.

Thankful that Bridget had an ear for their way of speaking, Tawnyetta let her do all of the talking. And talk she did. She praised the decor. She asked about the amenities. She wanted to know if the prince of the castle would be there to dine with them the next day.

When they finally made it to their room, the honeymoon suite, Tawnyetta was beyond exhausted. She located the bed, pulled back the covers and fell face first into her down pillow, plummeting quickly into a deep sleep. This night no mice or dragons disturbed her slumber.

When Tawnyetta's eyes slipped open it was morning. In her first few confusing moments of consciousness she didn't know where she was. A soft groan escaped the pile of comforter and pillows bunched up on the other side of the bed. Bridget. Memories of their long trip here filtered into her mind. It hadn't been a strange dream after all. She was here.

Bridget. Honeymoon. Castle.

Tawnyetta pushed back the covers and sat up on the side of the bed. Her whole body was sore. She felt like she had done serious weight lifting at the gym the day before and was suffering the consequences. Her eyelids scratched when she blinked as if she'd walked through a sandstorm on her way home from the gym. Her mouth was dry, her nose was stuffed up, and she was sure her hair was a wild mess. Still, Tawnyetta looked around in wonder.

Perched on a king-size four-poster bed, her feet rested on a thick rug woven in black and green with gold swirls lacing through the pattern. The rug pooled out around the bed in a giant circle, as if the bed wasn't a bed at all, but rather an island in a small pond. Around the edge of the room the rug ended and she could see the floor was made of polished stone. Stone. Not marble or tile, but ancient, grey stone.

There were no corners in the room. It was a complete circle. And it was huge.

The walls were the same grey stone as the floor, though slightly less polished. They reached up at least 15 feet to a domed ceiling. Heavy wooden beams curved out from the center point of the ceiling like spokes in a wheel. A chandelier hung from the center point. Though it was not turned on, its crystals glistened in the dim morning light.

Windows surrounded them on three quarters of the circular wall. Where there were no windows a cavernous fireplace made of white stone filled the space. On each side of the fireplace was a closed door.

A small fire burned cheerily in the hearth, though it could have housed a much larger one. The fire surprised her. It was June after all. But when she stood and walked across the rug she felt the damp air on her exposed skin and understood the fire was meant to take the edge off of the chill.

Still in her traveling clothes, a pair of black leggings and a long, grey shirt, Tawnyetta hugged herself and rubbed her arms to warm her blood. She stood in front of the fire feeling its warmth and listening to the gentle crackling. Her feet were freezing. That's when she spied two thick, white bathrobes hanging from iron hooks by one of the doors, and two pairs of luxurious slippers on the floor beneath them. She wrapped herself in a bathrobe and slipped her feet into the slippers then padded over to the windows.

The windows were thick glass. Handmade glass. Irregularities created optical illusions, like looking through the bottom of a bottle. The tops of the windows were arched and reminded her of the stained glass in a church. They stretched almost the full length of the 15-foot wall. Strips of hand-hewn iron held together smaller panes, which made up the whole window. Hinged on both sides, an iron latch kept them closed, yet they were large enough for her to open and step through into thin air.

Tawnyetta ran her hand along the windowsill. Smooth wood stained almost black. Outside the weather was still wet. She could see the build up of moisture on the glass and feel a draft of cool air even though the windows were closed. A mist shrouded much of the view, but they appeared to be about four stories high. The edge of a well-manicured lawn was visible on the ground below, hinting at more majestic gardens just out of sight.

She was in a castle. Not a mansion or a hotel, but an honest-to-goodness castle.

A thrill shimmered through her body. Not from the cold. She leaned forward until her nose was almost pressed against the thick glass and peered into the mist. If she looked hard enough, she wondered if she could conjure up a dragon flying toward them.

Tawnyetta chuckled and a girlish giddiness came over her. She hurried back to the bed to wake Bridget.

"Bridge, Bridge, wake up" she said, gently pushing Bridget's shoulder.

Bridget only groaned and turned away, mumbling something incoherent. Tawnyetta located her purse placed neatly on top of her suitcase next to a carved antique dresser. She rummaged through it and found her cell phone. The face blinked red at her, 4:42 a.m. Could that be right? Could she be this wide awake this early in the morning? How did jet lag work exactly? She felt her phone vibrate in her hand then turn off. Dead battery. She shrugged. She was awake now. No reason to fight it.

Leaving Bridget to her sleep, Tawnyetta wandered around the room and studied the elaborate artwork that hung on the walls. The furniture was all dark wood, stained to be almost black like the windowsills. Elegant porcelain vases and knick-knacks were placed neatly on the end tables and the dresser. A set of leather bound books filled a slender bookshelf near two large sitting chairs that were placed facing the windows. In front of the chairs was a small coffee table that held a silver tray, two champagne glasses, and a bottle of champagne partially submerged in what must have been ice and was now water. There was a little note handwritten on fine white stationary.

Congratulations on your nuptials!
- The Staff at Claymore Castle

Tawnyetta cringed. She checked that Bridget was still fast asleep, then she reached down and plucked the note up, tucking it into the pocket of her bathrobe. It was probably best to lessen the number of reminders Bridget would have of Christopher over this Not a Honeymoon. She should rip this note up and flush it down the toilet.

The bathroom was huge, almost the size of a normal sized bedroom. It had been modernized, thank goodness, and was dripping with luxury. Polished marble floors with sumptuous white bath rugs, a shower with three walls of glass and one wall of the ancient grey stone. The same arched floor to ceiling windows as the bedroom.

What caught her attention the most was the two-person claw foot tub set against the wall of windows. There was no worry of anyone outside catching a glimpse of the bath tub four stories in the air. Tawnyetta ran her hand along the edge of the tub and over the fixtures. If they weren't antique, they had been made to seem so. Next to the tub was a basket woven with off white reeds and full of soaps, bath bombs, and bath salts in a variety of scents. A long soak would help relieve her soreness and kill some time while she waited for Bridget to wake up.

Minutes later Tawnyetta sank into a steaming bath that fizzed around her travel worn muscles. She had chosen the white clay, lemon, and sea kelp bath bomb out of the basket and it was divine. From her position in the tub she watched as the sun grew stronger and began to burn off the mist outside. It appeared to her that perhaps the drizzling rain was coming to an end.

A knock sounded on the bathroom door.

Assuming it was Bridget, Tawnyetta called out, "Come in."

To her surprise, in walked a young woman wearing a classic maid outfit, black dress, white apron, hair in a bun.

"Good morning, ma'am. I see you've drawn your bath," the maid said.

Tawnyetta's surprise at the maid's presence was equal to her surprise at understanding the girl's accent. Her mind must have cleared after getting some sleep last night. She had automatically lifted her arms and crossed them over her chest when the girl entered. She nodded mutely in response to her comment.

"I'm Anne." The maid gave her a little curtsy. "I am to tend to both of you ladies during your stay. I'll keep the fire up. I've brought you a morning coffee. And if you need anything at all be sure to ring for me. I'm happy to draw your bath for you, whenever you please."

"Oh," Tawnyetta managed to answer. "I didn't realize."

"That's no problem at all, ma'am. I just want you to know that I am at your service."

"Well thank you, Anne," Tawnyetta said, smiling.

"Breakfast will be in the dining room starting at seven, if you please."

Tawnyetta's stomach woke up. She realized she was starving and couldn't remember how long it had been since she last ate. "Thank you, I will be down. Or we will be down," she added.

"Or, if you please, I'll be happy to bring breakfast to your room?" Anne suggested.

Tawnyetta was tickled at the idea of room service, but she had more interest in exploring the castle.

"No, thank you, not today. I'm happy to come to the dining room."

"As you wish," Anne said. She gave a fast curtsy and left.

After her long soak in the tub Tawnyetta fixed her hair and got dressed. She had brought blue jeans with her, but it didn't feel quite right to wear them. She wasn't sure how formal the dining room was, so she found a pair of khaki slacks and a black, long sleeved cotton pullover and threw on a pair of short black boots. She couldn't be sure if the rain was coming back and even with the fire going the castle was a chilly place, probably from all of the stone.

She scribbled a quick note for Bridget, telling her she was going to the dining room. Then she wrote that Bridget could either join her there or ring for their maid, Anne, to bring her breakfast. She used several exclamation points after that last sentence.

The hall outside their room was not massive as she remembered it. It was actually a rather narrow, circular space that followed the lines of their room and led directly to a spiral staircase that presumably led down into the main section of the castle. They must be in a turret of some kind.

As she made her way down the spiral staircase and paused to peek out each small window that she came upon, she felt as if she had been knocked in the head the day before and taken to a totally new place and time. Somehow, she had moved through a veil that existed between her regular life in America and Claymore Castle.

It was a strange feeling, but everything was so gothic and beautiful. She felt like a princess. Or, better yet, a princess that was escaping from her tower. She smiled again. Her imagination really was on overdrive this morning.

Three stories down she finally entered the massive hallway that she remembered from the night before. The spiral staircase ended, spilling her out into a grand area that stretched for what looked like 100 feet or more, with splendid mirrors and tapestries hanging all along the walls, just like castles of old she'd only ever seen in books. There were doors on the far end and two sets of doors on either side. Tawnyetta realized she had no idea how to find the dining room.

She walked silently through the great hall, her footsteps muffled by another thick rug. This one was red and green with those same golden swirls worked into the pattern. It stretched impressively the full length of the hall. She was glad for her long sleeve shirt as there were no fireplaces in this space and the air was cool and a little stale, like being in a cave.

She decided to try her luck on the first set of doors to her left. She put her hand gingerly on the handle and tried it. It wasn't locked and she pushed the door open carefully, uncertain what she might find on the other side.

The room was dim, though daylight shone through floor

to ceiling windows on the outside wall. What light there was illuminated a large, high ceilinged space with inlaid marble placed decoratively in the center of the stone floor and very sparse furnishings. There were, however, human forms standing stock still throughout. For a moment Tawnyetta thought she had stumbled upon actual people, but quickly realized that they were statues. Or, more precisely, suits of armor standing at attention. Swords and other weaponry hung as decor on the walls, making the whole space feel a little bit like a museum. A weapons room. Definitely not the dining room.

Curiosity filled her, but she didn't want to intrude in an area she hadn't been invited. Besides, her stomach was growling and she wanted breakfast. She closed the door and made a mental note to ask about the room and if she could come here and look around.

She crossed the hall to the next closest set of doors and grabbed the handle more confidently than she had the first one. She tried the handle, jiggling it roughly. It was locked.

Tawnyetta was embarrassed and a little nervous that maybe she had just tried to go into another guest's room. She listened for any sign someone was inside, perhaps another maid or staff person who may be able to help her find the dining room. There was no sound.

A strange feeling came over her. It wasn't a sound exactly, more like a sense. A presence. Tawnyetta wondered how old this building was. Was it hundreds of years old? Or thousands? Surely countless souls had moved through this place over time. The weapons room flashed through her mind. It was probable that the history of this castle was violent. Could there be remnants of the Scottish nobility that had lived here before floating around, watching her?

The door handle she had just tried turned suddenly with a loud click. Tawnyetta jumped back as the door lurched open.

Chapter Four

Tawnyetta gasped as the door jerked open revealing a powerful looking man who towered over her from the doorway. Gloom filled the unlit space behind him. Fierce blue eyes shone from the darkness as he glowered at her, his face wrinkled with ill temper.

She froze like a rabbit about to be chased, but with nowhere to run. There was nothing to duck behind, no door to disappear into, just her in the wide hall standing in front of this ominous man.

He stepped into the hall and peered at her with impatience. "What can I do for you, lass?" he asked in a thick, but understandable, Scottish accent. His voice was deep and gravelly. The question abrupt, irritated. After he stepped into the hall she could see him better, and she found him at once terribly attractive and absolutely intimidating.

Looming over her with his height as well as the breadth of his shoulders and chest, he waited for an answer. He had thick, dark hair, cut short. It was messy as if he had just taken off a hat. His strong nose and wide square jaw, which sported a

29

short beard, was distinctly masculine, a bit unruly. He looked dirty as if he'd been working outside in the wet and the mud.

He must be one of the staff. She must have stumbled upon a staff only door. His brusqueness made it obvious she wasn't welcome. Heat rose into her cheeks at her mistake. How could she tell the difference in this place? There wasn't a 'Staff Only' sign anywhere.

She stood up straighter and gathered herself, refusing to cower in front of this intimidation. She narrowed her eyes and met his gaze directly.

"Excuse me," she said coldly. "I was looking for the dining room."

The man arched his brow and gave her a once over, sizing her up as if she needed his permission to have breakfast. Tawnyetta pressed her lips together and did not look away. After a long moment he tilted his head toward her ever so slightly, a gesture of politeness she guessed, though it was a little too late in her opinion. He swept his arm toward the next set of doors with exaggerated chivalry.

"The dining room is across the way," he said.

Tawnyetta didn't like his tone. It seemed polite, but carried a hint of sarcasm. He was teasing her.

"Thank you," she said and turned on her heels away from him. She stalked towards the doors he had pointed to and had almost reached them when she heard his voice again.

"You are welcome, lass," his thick brogue rolled each consonant with flourish.

Tawnyetta paused and looked over her shoulder. He was standing where she'd left him, a look of amusement on his face that fell just short of a grin. Despite his good looks, his boldness irked her. She scoffed lightly and escaped into the dining room.

~

Besides the impertinence of the gardening crew, Tawnyetta found the rest of the staff at Claymore Castle to be delightful.

The butler's name was Stewart. He was slightly more than middle-aged, slightly taller than average, slightly bald, and slightly round. Kind and not quite as formal as Tawnyetta would have expected a butler to be, except for his crisply laundered grey vest and black tails, Stewart treated her like royalty.

There was the maid, Anne, whom she had already met, and another maid named Erin. The two were practically indistinguishable in looks from one another, except that Anne had blonde hair and Erin had light brown. They were equally sweet and accommodating, willing to instruct Tawnyetta on the general goings-on of the castle, and forgiving of her lack of knowledge regarding proper etiquette.

The cook's name was Doreen. Stewart introduced Tawnyetta to her in the kitchen while giving her a quick tour of the castle after breakfast. Doreen was all one would expect in a castle cook, if one ever expected to meet a castle cook. She was large breasted, stout, joyful, with red hair pulled up into a messy bun, rosy cheeks, bubbly blue eyes and a loud laugh. She invited Tawnyetta to come visit the kitchen if she ever felt hungry or in need of a good joke.

Stewart informed Tawnyetta that the caretaker of the grounds was named Dougie and they also had a general maintenance and deliveryman named Shaun. Neither of them were available during her tour, but she assumed the man she had met in the hallway was one of them. Probably Shaun. He hadn't struck her as a 'Dougie'.

Stewart showed her the library, the ballroom, and a sitting room that was ten times the size of her own living room back home. She found out that the wide hall she had passed through to get to breakfast was called the Great Hall. All of these rooms were open to guests, Stewart explained. He also motioned up a narrow stairway they passed during the tour and told her that it led to the servant's quarters. On their way back to the Great Hall they passed another set of closed doors, which Stewart ignored completely.

Upon seeing her questioning look, he paused and said, "These are private quarters."

"I see." She wondered who lived inside. Were they Stewart's quarters? She thought it might be a pushy, rude, American thing to ask, so she went on with the tour without giving it another thought.

They entered the room she had happened upon earlier and she learned that her guess had been correct. This was the weapons room. Every type of blade imaginable was on display in glass cases or hanging on the walls.

"This is a room of sport," Stewart explained. "The main floor area is kept open for that purpose."

Eyeing all of the swords that came in countless shapes and sizes, Tawnyetta asked, "You actually practice sword fighting here? Like fencing?"

"Yes, ma'am," Stuart noticed her reaction. "Do you fence?"

"A little," Tawnyetta responded. She looked around the room with great interest.

"You are welcome to use this space to practice," Stewart informed her.

She smiled, "That would be really cool."

"Yes," Stewart acknowledged her with a little bow. "Cool."

As she had suspected while taking her bath, this day was turning out to be sunnier and dryer than the night before. Stewart showed her the grounds immediately next to the castle and indicated that she was welcome to explore them at her leisure. Her formal tour ended there and Tawnyetta took her time looking around.

She was impressed. The mist had burned away completely to reveal three pathways of white pebbles leading toward three different, magical gardens.

The center path led directly into a well-manicured flower garden. It contained perfectly pruned shrubs and colorful flowerbeds laid out in a geometric pattern with what looked like an unused fountain in the center. Of the other two paths, one headed directly into a wooded area. The other led into a garden that wasn't as well landscaped as the fountain garden, but looked to be even more beautiful. The path took her up ancient stone steps, under an arch of green boughs, and into a wondrous garden like the kind she'd only seen in fairy tales. Ornamental trees, green lawns, and curving naturally overgrown flowerbeds beckoned her to continue wandering.

Before she got too involved in walking the gardens, Tawnyetta decided she would ask Bridget to join her. She left the Secret Garden to go back inside, but stopped short when she saw Shaun at the fountain in the middle of the geometric flower garden.

He noticed her at once and stopped what he was doing to stare at her. He was even dirtier than when she'd seen him before, a wheelbarrow with an open toolbox sat next to him. He must have come to fix the fountain.

Again she felt like a deer in headlights under his gaze. He was at least 20 yards away from her, with several beds of rose bushes and hedges between them, yet she felt strangely vulnerable. He did not speak or wave. He simply stood there holding a giant wrench in one hand and a dirty rag in the other, watching her calmly.

Tawnyetta felt as if she was intruding. She found herself blushing again and was surprised at the thumping of her heart in her chest. Something about this man made her react. She wasn't afraid of him. Not exactly. But he made her feel nervous, exposed.

The moment and their look went on longer than was comfortable. Tawnyetta decided she didn't owe him any explanation for her presence. Stewart had told her she had free reign of the gardens. It wasn't her fault that he was stuck working on a broken fountain while she was out on her walk. Still, she would feel much better if Bridget was here, too.

Tearing her gaze away from his Tawnyetta hurried past the garden, up the steps, and into the castle. She found Bridget in the bedroom.

Bridget had ordered breakfast in their room and taken her own luxurious bath while Tawnyetta was gone. She had also, apparently, gossiped a bit with Anne.

"Isn't this place glorious?" she asked Tawnyetta.

"It really is," she agreed.

Tawnyetta was seated in one of the chairs by the windows and had a view of the manicured flower garden below where Shaun was still working. Even from this high in the air she could see how wide his shoulders were and sense his strength. She was definitely more comfortable checking him out with four stories of stone walls to separate them. The fact that he didn't know she was looking made it easier to let her gaze linger.

"There is prince here just like I thought," Bridget said. "Or I guess they don't call him a prince. I think of him as a prince, but Anne said he's a Lord. Or 'Laird' is how they say it."

"Really?" Tawnyetta responded, still watching Shaun. She was captured by the way he hoisted what looked to be a very heavy stone off the side of the fountain wall.

"Anne said he lives here all the time, but he hardly makes himself known to guests. I guess he's quite elusive," Bridget said with a twinkle in her eye.

Tawnyetta switched her gaze to her friend's with interest. "What is that look for?"

Bridget shrugged in mock nonchalance. "Oh I don't know. What could be more distracting from one's troubles than trying to track down a handsome Scottish Laird?"

Tawnyetta smiled, "How do you know he's handsome? Maybe he's geriatric."

"Anne says he's very handsome." Bridget grinned. "Are you up for the challenge?"

"What challenge?"

"Find him. Flush him out. Make him dance with us...I don't know! It will be fun!"

"We're going to spy on a Scottish Lord in his own castle?"

Bridget nodded happily then corrected her, "A Scottish *Laird*."

Tawnyetta smiled again, happy to see her friend excited about something and keeping her mind off of Christopher. "Sure. Why not?"

Later, when they were strolling through the fountain garden, Tawnyetta told Bridget about the private quarters Stewart had shown her during her tour. Bridget's blue eyes grew wide with the intrigue of it all.

"Do you think that's where he lives?" she asked.

The fountain gurgled, though not at full force, and Shaun was nowhere to be seen. Tawnyetta supposed he had given up on fixing it completely and moved on to another castle project. There must be a lot to do on a huge estate like this with an ancient building to keep up. She and Bridget were strolling comfortably around the idyllic pathways like ladies from an old novel—plotting.

"Well, he didn't say specifically that's where the Laird of the castle lives, but I don't know any other place to start," Tawnyetta answered.

"Good point. Let's wait until it's quiet and we can slip away from Anne and the others," Bridget conspired, her eyes twinkling with the fun of it all.

"Excellent idea."

The opportunity for their adventure did not arise until right after teatime.

Tawnyetta had never had an official high tea before. It was quite the 'to do'. Scottish High Tea included a savory dish as well as delicious sweet goodies. It was really more like dinner with an extra layer of rich desserts. Not to mention the beautiful bone china in a charming thistle pattern that felt decidedly Scottish.

Afterward, the entire staff must have run off to a meeting or maybe to have their own tea, because the whole estate grew quiet. Though they were both stuffed from all of the good food, she and Bridget decided this was the best chance they would get to hunt down the Laird of Claymore Castle.

Bridget followed Tawnyetta to the Great Hall. They passed the weapons room and went up the side stairway that ended in another long hallway. Tawnyetta wasn't totally certain she remembered how to get to the private rooms, but recognized the doors immediately when she saw them. They were closed, as she'd expected. A tickle of excitement pinged in her belly.

"Do you think it's locked?" Bridget whispered as Tawnyetta reached for the door handle.

"Only one way to find out." She held her breath as she grabbed the door handle and pushed. It moved easily. It wasn't locked. The excitement in her stomach blossomed and she looked at Bridget who stood just behind her. Bridget's cheeks were flushed and she pressed her lips together in an attempt to stay quiet.

"You ready?" Tawnyetta whispered. Bridget nodded. Tawnyetta pushed the door open slowly, just far enough to pop her head inside. She didn't see anyone, just an empty sitting room, much smaller than the one Stewart had shown her during the tour.

She turned to Bridget. "The coast looks clear."

"What if we get caught?"

"We'll just say we got lost," Tawnyetta suggested.

Bridget puffed her cheeks up with air then pushed it all

out of her mouth. She lifted her shoulders to her ears and drew her lips down, meaning 'why not'. "Let's do it!" She whispered.

And with that, they slipped into the sitting room, closing the door quietly behind them.

The space was not even as big as their bedroom upstairs, which was unexpected. It had a casual elegance about it, red leather couch, dark brown leather armchair, a gorgeous fireplace with a carved wooden mantle and a beveled mirror above. Despite the fact that it did display a certain level of wealth, it was cozier than the other formal areas of the castle. The room also had a distinctly masculine feeling, which supported the gossip Anne had told them about the Laird not having a woman in his life.

Tawnyetta noticed an assortment of books in various sized piles filling any and all flat surfaces in the room. These weren't like the antique leather bound books in their room, which were mostly for decoration. These books were normal everyday books that looked as if they were being read. Several of them had bookmarkers of some kind in them, torn paper or used envelopes stuck inside to save a place. Tawnyetta was struck at the sheer number of them. This Laird guy must be a big reader.

There was something comforting about this space and they both started to relax. They wandered around picking up books and knick-knacks to take a look at them, getting a sense of the personality of the man who lived here. They got so comfortable in their surroundings that they had just about forgotten they were not supposed to be there—that's when they heard the sound of singing.

The women froze in place and looked at each other, their eyes bugging out in surprise.

"What is that?" Bridget whispered.

"I don't know," Tawnyetta whispered back. She wiggled

her eyebrows up and down at Bridget mischievously. "Maybe it's him!"

Then, for some inexplicable reason, Tawnyetta put down the book she'd been looking at and moved toward the sound of the voice.

Chapter Five

The singing drew her down the hallway. She felt an intense urge to know if they were right. She wanted to know if what they were hearing was really the Laird of Claymore Castle singing in his private quarters. There was no logical explanation as to why she wanted to know, she simply did. And despite Bridget's frantic whispers of warning, Tawnyetta couldn't stop. She stepped out of the sitting room into a hallway that led deeper into the living quarters. The singing grew louder.

It was definitely a man's voice. A man singing joyfully. A man singing off key. As she drew closer she could hear that the singing was accompanied by the sound of music playing. He must be singing along. A man who sang so boldly out of tune would probably not be too furious if he found two women wandering around his private rooms, would he?

The hallway was dignified enough, artwork depicting what looked like the Scottish countryside hung on its walls along with a few ornate decorative mirrors. They passed two entryways to other rooms as they crept along. Glancing inside, Tawnyetta saw the first one was the kitchen and the next was another sitting room, or maybe a small library. The singing was coming from the end of the hallway.

The closer they moved toward the sounds the clearer they could hear other details. The man's voice was a baritone. He was singing with abandon at the moment, unaware that any other ears were listening. The song he was singing along with became clear, too. *Quit Playing Games With My Heart* by The Backstreet Boys. Tawnyetta smiled. It was an impossibly silly song for this situation. It seemed that he knew every word, which was funny. But his deep singing voice with its distinct Scottish accent mixing with the youthful sound of The Backstreet Boys made it beyond charming. It was absolutely beguiling.

There was something else. Another sound she couldn't quite make out until she was standing directly next to the open door of what she saw was a bedroom. Bridget pressed up against the wall directly behind her trying to stay hidden. The indistinct sound became distinct. Splashing water. It took just a few moments before Tawnyetta realized what that sound meant. The Laird of Claymore Castle was taking a shower.

"Tawny!" Bridget hissed and grabbed Tawnyetta's arm to pull her back. "He's in the shower!"

Tawnyetta put her finger to her lips to shush Bridget. That tiny kernel of excitement she'd felt earlier was now a full-blown thrill fest pulsing through her body and she couldn't stop smiling. She realized that she might burst out laughing if she wasn't careful.

The familiar bridge of the song came to an end and the last chorus started, prompting the singing Laird to really belt it out. Tawnyetta couldn't hold it in any longer. She fell into a fit of giggles, which prompted the same reaction in Bridget. It was like they were in elementary school again, their hands pressed tightly over their mouths as they tried to silently laugh, hushing each other the entire time.

Just when Tawnyetta was about to motion that they leave, the sound of running water stopped abruptly. They froze, their eyes opened wide with the possibility of discovery. He was done with his shower.

The next logical thing for him to do was to leave his bathroom. From their position in the hallway they were completely exposed if he were to step out of the bedroom. Tawnyetta's mind clicked quickly through their choices. They could make a run for it, but if he came out of the bedroom immediately they may not have time to make it down to the end of the hall. They risked being seen escaping into the front sitting room. The two options remaining were to hide in the kitchen or the small library. Would someone more likely go to their kitchen or their library right after a shower?

In a split second Tawnyetta made the decision. She grabbed Bridget and pulled her into the small library. They jammed into the space behind the open door and waited.

The song ended and they heard the Laird humming in his bedroom, then the humming got louder as he left his bedroom. Still with her hand pressed hard over her mouth, Tawnyetta squinted to see into the hallway through the thin sliver of an opening from their vantage point behind the door.

The next song started. Another Backstreet Boys song, *I Want It That Way*. She knew this song. It had a long, slow intro. She only hoped it was loud enough to cover up the sound of their breathing as well as her heart beating fast and hard in her chest.

Suddenly, they saw him.

Still dripping water from his shower and completely naked, the Laird of Claymore Castle walked past the door where they hid, blissfully unaware he was being observed.

Tawnyetta sucked in her breath. The view was minimal and he had his back to them, but the sight of his body was staggering. He was like a wild animal, muscles rippling under his skin, wide shoulders, a brawny back that flexed as he moved, a round, toned bottom, so virile she could not have averted her eyes even if she'd wanted to.

Bridget, too, was affected by the sight of him. She gasped out loud and he stopped abruptly.

Tawnyetta wanted to run. Burst out the door and fly past him, dash down the Great Hall and out of the castle before he knew who she was. Or, better yet, escape through the library window so he would never know they had been here at all. She glanced at the window, but they were two stories high. That wasn't an option.

The Backstreet Boys kicked their song into the rhythmic section. The long, slow intro was over. The Laird of Claymore Castle moved his hip to the side and lifted his bent arms into the air as he started to sing along. Relief washed through her whole body. He had stopped to do a dance move. He had not heard Bridget at all.

There was a pause in his dancing and an energy filled the air around them. The music was pumping through the hall so loudly that it sent tiny tremors through the door. The Laird moved his hips back and forth with the song, then stopped again. Tawnyetta watched in glorious anguish, knowing exactly what was about to happen. She could sense it. So could Bridget.

To their delight and horror the Laird did a full 360-degree turn on his heels as part of his Backstreet Boys dance routine. Both Tawnyetta and Bridget watched in sublime shock as they were given a full frontal flash of his family jewels. It took every ounce of self-control they possessed not to squeal at the sight.

Smashed behind the door, the two women doubled over in an attempt to contain their laughter. When the Laird disappeared into the kitchen, Tawnyetta tried to keep her wits about her enough to watch through the slit and wait for an opportune moment for their escape.

That moment came when they heard the unmistakable sound of a coffee grinder erupt from somewhere inside the kitchen. Tawnyetta yanked a furiously giggling Bridget out from behind the door and they made a break for it down the hallway, praying that he was not facing the entryway while making his coffee. Neither of them was brave enough to look into the kitchen as they passed, terrified that they might be seen and equally terrified of what they might see again.

They stumbled out the front door and Tawnyetta had the sensibility to close it as quietly as possible. Pulling the door slowly until it clicked into place, she winced as the sound echoed through the empty hallway. Luckily, there was nobody else to hear it, or to witness them exiting.

Laughter bubbled out of Bridget in spite of her struggle to keep quiet. Under pressure, her mirth made its escape in a long-winded snort, which made the moment even funnier to both of them.

The two women ran as fast as they could up the stairs to their bedroom. Several times as they climbed the spiral staircase one of them would let out a peal of laughter and they would both collapse into the stair railing, overcome with merriment to the point that they were unable to breathe.

Once safely in their room they fell onto the bed, weak with laughter. Flushed with excitement from their excursion and their near brush with the naked Laird of Claymore Castle.

"I can't believe we just did that!" Bridget exclaimed.

"I can't believe those dance moves," Tawnyetta retorted.

This sent Bridget into a new fit of laughter and she rolled over, shoving her face into her pillow to mask her squeals of delight. Tawnyetta couldn't even do that much, her abs were contracted in a silent guffaw. Bridget lifted her head from the pillow and crowed, "The Backstreet Boys!"

This sent them howling again until their cheeks were wet due to crying from laughter.

"Wait, wait." Tawnyetta wiped her eyes and chuckled. "Didn't they do a video where they were half naked in the pouring rain?"

Bridget nodded, smacking Tawnyetta's upper arm with acknowledgement. "They did!"

Tawnyetta had to wipe her eyes again. "That was too good."

Bridget chortled as she looked at Tawnyetta with mischief in her eyes. "Did you see him?" She asked, obviously impressed.

"Oh, I saw him." Tawnyetta arched her eyebrows and nodded, showing she had taken note of the Laird's generous gifts.

"He was incredible looking," Bridget said.

"That he was."

Bridget crinkled her brow in a delicate expression of curiosity. "Was he handsome?" she asked.

Tawnyetta gave her an incredulous look and said, "I didn't see his face."

"Me neither!" Bridget blurted out and they broke into laughter again, flopping onto their backs side-by-side on the bed.

As Tawnyetta giggled uncontrollably she could not get the vision of the Laird's muscled, masculine body out of her mind. It was true, she had not seen his face. But honestly, he could have the homeliest face she'd ever seen and it wouldn't matter. The man was built like a Greek God, and he wasn't a bad dancer either. An intense, hot spike of energy shot through her stomach and made her shiver, like a rush of adrenaline.

Her laughter dying down, Bridget sighed and wiped her eyes. "This is the best Not a Honeymoon ever."

Tawnyetta turned her head sideways on her pillow so she was looking at her friend and grinned. "Good."

Bridget smiled back then let her gaze move lazily across the room, fully relaxed and soaking in their surroundings. Something caught her attention and she pointed. "Look, look, look!" She scrambled off the bed and moved hastily to the corner of the room where the champagne they'd never touched was in a fresh bucket of ice.

"They've re-iced the champagne!" Bridget declared with pleasure.

"Perfecto!" Tawnyetta sat up on the bed. "Let's celebrate!"

"Let's!" Bridget agreed.

While Bridget opened the bottle and poured them each a glass Tawnyetta looked up the Backstreet Boys on her phone. She turned her speakers up as far as they would go and played *Quit Playing Games With My Heart*. Bridget giggled, her eyes sparkling as she handed Tawnyetta a flute of champagne.

"To the best damned Not a Honeymoon in the history of Not a Honeymoons!" Tawnyetta exclaimed and they toasted. Then they danced around the room doing impressions of the Laird of Claymore's best move that was now burned forever into Tawnyetta's mind.

Early the next morning, Christopher called and ruined everything.

Chapter Six

Tawnyetta slept through the sound of Bridget's cell phone ringing as well as the motion of her getting out of bed and answering it. What did finally wake her was the sound of her friend's agitated voice. Bridget was speaking in a controlled rage with a touch of a tremor, which hinted that she was trying not to cry.

What time was it? Tawnyetta peered at the tall windows and knew it wasn't dawn yet. She had not yet grown used to the slow light of morning and lingering sunsets caused by the extra hours of daylight here in the Scottish Highlands. So it was difficult for her to guess at the time of day.

"I'm not going to apologize," Bridget spoke harshly into the phone.

Apologize? Tawnyetta, still groggy from waking, wondered who she was talking to.

"And, no, I am not paying you back for taking this trip," Bridget continued.

Christopher. Of course. Seriously? He was calling to harass the woman he cheated on about paying him back for taking their honeymoon without him? Anger bubbled up inside of her belly.

Men. Tawnyetta was disgusted.

As miffed as she was at the audacity of Christopher's phone call, as well as the inconvenient timing of it, she understood that Bridget needed her privacy. She threw on a pair of jeans, a black cotton t-shirt, and a light sweater. She had learned from her experience so far in the Highlands that always having a light sweater on hand was probably a good idea. Not too different from her hometown in Colorado.

Tawnyetta made her way down the spiral staircase. Once again she thought how eerie a place like a castle could be when it wasn't quite daylight and there was nobody around. When she got to the Great Hall she wondered how early the staff actually rose in this place. She could go to the kitchen and see if the cook was there, maybe get some coffee. Or she could go for a stroll in the gardens.

She stepped to one of the tall windows that looked out across the front of the estate and saw that a heavy mist still lurked in the dawning light. She delighted in being outside most of the time and was an avid hiker in the Rocky Mountains where she grew up, but something about these ancient grounds covered in a thick fog made her wary of being alone on this estate.

With a sigh she turned back and decided to go for the coffee. Then she noticed the door to the weapons room and her interest was piqued.

Stepping inside, Tawnyetta turned on a few of the standing lights instead of the giant chandeliers hanging from above. It seemed like a waste of energy to light the whole room just for her.

Avoiding the suits of armor, because she had a lingering childlike fear that they may start moving, Tawnyetta meandered through the room admiring beautifully forged long swords, sabers, and daggers in the display cases. There was a rack of various weapons along one wall. She assumed these were used for practice instead of the antique specimens in the displays.

Just for fun she picked up one of the svelte slicing sabers from the rack. The weight of it felt empowering in her hand. Still annoyed at Christopher, and men in general, she held it out in front of her and pointed it at one of the suits of armor across the room, slashing the air.

That felt good.

Maybe she could burn off some of this negative energy with a little swordplay exercise. Tawnyetta held the blade between her thighs to free her hands. She took off her light sweater and placed it on a nearby display case. Then she took hold of the saber properly and walked to the center of the marble floor in the middle of the room. She slashed the air a few more times before settling into an attack stance.

Imagining Christopher standing in front of her with his dental hygienist, Tawnyetta lunged and stabbed the air. She grinned. Then she did it again, this time allowing herself to imagine flicking each button off of his shirt and slicing his cheek with a 'Z' like Zorro always did in the movies. Caught up in her imagination, Tawnyetta decided to play out a similar scenario with every obnoxious date she could remember and both of her ex-boyfriends.

She lunged and attacked, retreated and parried, shuffling her feet back and forth as all of her fencing training came back to her through the movements. She threw in a few moves she'd seen in pirate movies and switched from her right to her left hand and back again, exercising both arms.

After a short time she worked up a decent sweat in her T-shirt and jeans, but she was not deterred. She could take a bath later. Right now she was fighting with the demons from her past.

Losing herself a little bit in the moment, Tawnyetta starting grunting hard whenever she lunged and calling out the names of each of her imaginary foes as she vanquished them.

"Christopher!" She called out as she stabbed him in his belly and relished his stunned expression. Twirling around using both hands to slash at an oncoming ex who approached her from behind, she cried out, "Benjamin!" With two quick moves she had relinquished good old Ben of his sword and cut his hands so badly he could not fight back. "Freddy!" She yelled and stabbed with gusto at a particularly vile blind date who she suspected had tried to drug her drink. With a wide sweep of her saber she cut off Freddy's head and watched it roll across the marble floor.

Ready for her next opponent, Tawnyetta threw her arm up and over her head in a wide arc, then whipped her body to follow, intending to bring the bade down hard and lunge towards the nearest suit of armor now that she was feeling brave. Instead, her blade came down with a loud smack on the forearm of Shaun. He was standing behind her in real life and had lifted his arm up in defense of her oncoming attack.

Tawnyetta screamed and dropped the saber as soon as she felt it make contact with his arm. The blade clattered to the floor, the sound of it echoing through the largely empty room. She covered her mouth with both hands.

"Oh my God!" she exclaimed.

Shaun brought his arm down so she could see his expression, a mixture of surprise and amusement. He had been standing behind her watching her attack invisible opponents and shout out their names.

He looked down at his intact work shirt, a thick black and green tartan print, and said, "I think I'll live."

The shock of seeing him was quickly followed by embarrassment at the fact that he had been watching her. Her annoyance at all men came boiling up and bound together into a singular annoyance at this one man standing in her presence.

"What are you doing sneaking up on me like that?" She leaned over to pick up her saber, her face flushed from the workout and the humiliation.

"I heard a wee bit of racket in here," he replied. He stooped at the same time and swept the saber up before she could reach it. Then, with a smirk, he offered it to her, hilt first.

She snatched it from his hands. "And so you just barged in? Do you always interrupt guests when they're in the middle of an activity?" She tried to sound as important and affronted as possible.

Shaun arched an eyebrow at her, his eyes twinkling at her outburst. "I try not to interrupt guests if I can help it."

It wasn't quite an apology. She scowled at him.

Ignoring her disapproving look, Shaun moved past her to the rack where she'd gotten her blade. The lamplight didn't reach everywhere in the room, so he stood partly in shadow as he looked at her then at the rack of weapons.

"You fence?" He asked.

She nodded, still glaring. Then she shrugged a little bit and admitted, "I was just messing around, though. Kind of a mix of everything."

He gave her a cocky half-grin, "Yes, I gathered."

"Shouldn't you be fixing a fountain or something?" She asked. Shaun didn't say anything, just watched her calmly like he had in the garden. And just like it had in the garden, standing under his gaze made her feel exposed. She needed to fill the emptiness so she asked, "Do you fence?"

He nodded. "Yes, I do." His words rolled off of his tongue, making everything he said sound roguish.

Tawnyetta watched as he bent his head and admired the weapons, running his finger along one of the saber handles.

He was about 6'3" she would guess. And his dark beard, cut short against his chiseled features, accentuated his strapping good looks. Tawnyetta swallowed and focused on keeping up her glare.

Shaun looked up at her, the light illuminating his deep blue eyes just enough she could see they were still twinkling. His grin turned to a mischievous smile that sat slightly crooked on his lips.

"Fancy a duel?" he asked.

She wasn't sure she'd heard him correctly. "Excuse me?" She tried to sound haughty.

"Would you like a partner...to practice?" He gestured towards the marble floor where she had been fighting pretend men.

"You mean me and you? You and I?"

Shaun glanced around the room then back at her. "I don't see anyone else here, do you?"

His tone at once infuriated her and sent a shiver up her neck. She moved to the center of the marble floor and swished her blade a few times in front of her, making the shape of an 'X' in the air.

Lifting one eyebrow at him, she answered, "Why not?"

Before choosing a blade Shaun took off his heavy tartan shirt, revealing a navy blue V-neck cotton T-shirt underneath. His arms were tan and roped with muscle. She watched the thick muscles flex as he pulled a saber off of the rack and whipped it through the air a few times, warming up. He walked towards her wearing a cocky smile. She wanted to best him at sword fighting so bad she could taste it.

He paused. "Shouldn't we be wearing face masks?"

"We're just messing around," Tawnyetta answered, thinking that maybe she sounded tougher than she felt. "We'll go slow...and be nice," she warned.

"I'll be nice," he answered. Then, under his breath and

with a low chuckle, he added, "It's you I should be worried about."

As he took up his position opposite her they held each other's gaze. He had amazing eyes and she had to remind herself to stay focused on the task at hand. They both took the on guard stance and moved slowly back and forth with each other. It had been a while since she had sparred with any kind of opponent, and this one was particularly intimidating in both size and intensity.

She thrust at him and he knocked her blade to the side easily with his. He was strong that was for sure. But she was small and quick, and she had a feeling he may underestimate her abilities because she was a woman.

He jabbed and she parried. Blades sliding against each other sounded slick and sharp in the echoing room. Morning rays of sun spilled gently down through the tall windows, creating large chunks of light across the marble floor. Tawnyetta and Shaun kept their attention completely on each other as they moved in a circle, kicking up tiny dust particles that floated through the sun's rays. As if dancing, they moved in and out of shadows, thrusting and parrying carefully at each other then backing away. Never breaking their gaze.

Tawnyetta's arm was getting tired and she wondered how much longer she could keep this up, but she refused to quit. She didn't want him to win. She didn't want to give him the satisfaction. The air between them sizzled with a kind of competitive sexual tension. Another reason she didn't want to stop.

Her breath was coming more quickly now, partly from fatigue and partly because of the low-key excitement of their duel. She could see Shaun's chest moving up and down more rapidly, too. With each breath, a salty sheen of sweat across his exposed chest muscles glistened. Her own T-shirt clung to her back where sweat had started to trickle down the length of her spine from the exertion.

Tawnyetta decided she couldn't keep up this pace much longer. She had to make a move. Her chance came when he swept his blade across his body and at an arc as if to bring it down on her in a cutting motion. She quickly ducked under his arm, turned in a circle so she was now standing at his side, and pointed her blade roughly at his kidney.

Shaun's reaction was automatic and not only displayed his agility but also his skill at swordplay. He leaped up and turned midair so as he landed he was facing her again. Right as his feet touched the ground he swung his blade down into hers to knock her off balance, whipping his saber in a circle around her blade, he thrust to the side. This move broke her grip on the handle and flung her saber up into the air and down with a crash about ten feet away.

Tawnyetta was stunned. The move brought him towards her so fast that they were now standing less than two feet from one another, breathing hard, staring into each other's eyes as the clamor of her disarmed saber echoed through the room. For a split second she imagined him tossing his saber to the floor and taking her in his arms, pulling her into his wide chest with those strong, muscled arms. She couldn't move. She just stared at him, and he at her, their breath coming rapid and shallow.

The next moment Shaun dropped his gaze from her eyes to her empty hands then to his own hands still clutching his blade. His face softened, brows furrowed in concern.

"Did I hurt you?" He stepped closer, the question cracked in his throat.

Tawnyetta felt a rush of attraction. He smelled good, like fresh earth in the springtime with a hint of spices–cloves to be exact. She still couldn't move. Her heart beat fast in her chest.

Shaun dropped his blade on the floor and grabbed her

hand. His fingers and palm wrapped around hers, rough and warm. His other hand caught her waist as if he was afraid she may be about to faint and he was trying to steady her.

His touch brought her out of shock and she pulled away, taking a half step back.

"I'm fine," she managed.

"Are you sure?" He didn't look convinced.

This was inappropriate. She didn't need to be manhandled by the gardener. She was fine. She had just been a little surprised when her saber was ripped out of her hand.

"I'm perfectly fine, thank you," she said curtly.

Shaun's concern dissipated and he looked her up and down as if checking to see if she was bleeding or broken, ensuring she wasn't lying. Then he gave her a half nod and amusement settled back into his eyes.

"I'm sure your wife would have something to say to me if I sliced you up on your honeymoon," he said.

Once again a look of surprise struck her features. She opened her mouth to speak then closed it again. What was he talking about?

"My wife?" she asked.

"The wee lass upstairs." He looked at her as if she was dense.

Suddenly his misunderstanding became clear and she chuckled, shaking her head. "She's not my wife. We're not married."

"You're on your honeymoon, are you not?"

"We are on a *Not a Honeymoon*." Tawnyetta saw that he didn't understand. She didn't owe him an explanation, but still felt compelled to relay that she and Bridget were not a couple. "My friend, Bridget, well, her wedding was canceled at the last minute. And she already had this trip planned so I came with her instead of her husband."

As her explanation penetrated his mind, Shaun's face

shifted from confusion to something more like embarrassment. He shook his head as if clearing cobwebs, then gave her a puzzled smile.

"You're not married?" he asked.

Tawnyetta shook her head 'no' and found herself blushing under his gaze. He looked at her with renewed interest and started to say something, then stopped himself. He flicked his gaze toward the wall with the rack of weapons as if searching for words. His weight shifted from one foot to the other, then he chuckled and looked back at her with a glimmer in his eyes.

A ridiculous thrill shot through her body. His eyes on her created a visceral reaction that she could not control.

"You don't say?" he said.

She wasn't sure how to answer. She wasn't sure how personal she wanted to get with this man. He was attractive. Scratch that, he was gorgeous. There was no real doubt about that. But wasn't she here for Bridget? How would Bridget feel if Tawnyetta had a vacation fling with the hired help while she was suffering through a massive break up?

Shaun opened his mouth to say something, but Tawnyetta interrupted him.

"In fact, I should be getting back to see how she's doing."

And without another word she stalked out of the room, forcing herself not to look back, although she knew without a doubt that Shaun was watching her leave.

Chapter Seven

T he next night they dined in a different dining hall. The castle had three separate dining halls, and the one they had been using up to this point was the smallest of all three. New guests had checked in and this necessitated a change in dining arrangements.

When she and Bridget first arrived there were two other couples staying in the castle, but they had left the following morning. Tawnyetta had never even seen them. Up until now she and Bridget had enjoyed full run of the castle and gardens without the possibility of running into anyone except for the staff. A party of six were now booked into the West Wing of Claymore Castle. They were a family from London. A middle-aged mother and father accompanied by their grown daughter and her husband as well as their son and his wife.

James and Tilly Prescott had been married almost 45 years. Whether by habit or design they dressed in color coordinated outfits and tended to finish each other's sentences. James was tall with a large frame. He had the look of a man that used to be hefty, but didn't carry much weight anymore, which gave him a decidedly droopy appearance. With thinning hair on top of his head, bushy eyebrows, a large nose, and sagging brown eyes, he liked to take the reins in conversations, discussing a wide variety of topics whether or not anyone was interested. Tilly Prescott was a fine looking woman with pale blue liquid eyes and soft gray hair styled short and classy. Extremely polite with a large vocabulary, she was eager to notice and point out anything crass or uncouth. Their daughter, Tabitha, had thin, fine hair like her father, her mother's dim eyes, and a wilted expression. Tabitha's husband, Lawrence, was as nondescript as a human being could be, barely taking up any presence in the room or in the minds of his dining companions. Tabitha's brother, James Travis Prescott III (everybody called him Travis), looked identical to his father except he had more hair and less droop. Travis's wife, Bea, was short, round, and dark, except for small, bright blue eyes. She was the complete opposite of the women in her husband's family, both in looks and personality. Perky, talkative, and always ready for a laugh, Bea was Tawnyetta's favorite.

On the first night of the Prescott's stay a formal dinner was served to all eight castle guests on a long table in what was called Stag Hall. With towering coffered ceilings crafted from dark wood high above them, stained-glass windows stretching to the ceiling, solid wood wainscoting eight feet high with the walls above it painted ox blood red, Stag Hall was an impressive space.

The dining table could fit twenty, but tonight was set for eight. Taking up the center of the room, the table was flanked by windows on one side and a large fireplace on the other. It was set with off-white bone china that had a delicate pale green Celtic knot pattern and heavy silverware with carved bone handles. Crystal goblets glistened in the candlelight. Deep red candles glowed steadily from their positions in silver cande-labras whose bases were made from deer antlers. Tawnyetta had never seen a table dressing so bold. It was magnificent, almost formidable.

The Prescott's were courteous, if a little dry. At times throughout the evening their comments came off snooty, but Tawnyetta seemed to be the only one who noticed. Mr. and Mrs. Prescott senior took the task of making conversation with Tawnyetta and Bridget very seriously. As if they'd been personally assigned as ambassadors to the American girls by the Queen.

"Colorado?" Mr. Prescott asked, his grey bushy eyebrows raised in surprise. "That's quite the Wild West isn't it?"

"Well, we're from Denver. It's not as wild as you might think," Bridget explained.

She looked well, at least better than she had since her argu-ment with Christopher. The whole mess had sent her into a bit of a depression that Tawnyetta had worked hard to help her overcome. After some sleep and a few long walks in the Secret Garden she had recovered nicely. With any luck she would be back to her bubbly self soon enough.

Tawnyetta, on the other hand, was feeling a little drab. After her one-on-one with Shaun in the weapons room she had found it difficult to get him out of her head. When she and Bridget went on walks in the gardens she was distracted by the hope that they would run into him somewhere. But they never did. In addition to that disappointment, she had grown accustomed to the less formal dining area and wasn't comfort-able in Stag Hall. Perhaps she didn't particularly enjoy dining with the entire Prescott clan. Or perhaps her hastily packed clothes weren't quite up to snuff if they were going to be eating this formally every evening. Either way, Tawnyetta found it all a little tiring.

The main topic of conversation at dinner was Laird Michael MacBrody. According to the Prescott's, his avoidance of them and lack of attentiveness was to be expected.

"I thought we might have seen him by now," Bridget complained with an airy sigh.

Mr. Prescott senior spoke again, his deep British accent lending him an air of authority on the subject. "It isn't uncommon for any nobility who rents out there estate to remain distant or even off the property during their guest's stay. I'm not sure we will see much of Laird MacBrody at all while we're here."

Bridget glanced at Tawnyetta, forcing them both to smile as they suppressed their recent memories of the Laird dancing in his birthday suit. Bridget kept her composure and said, "I'm pretty sure he's on the property. I just assumed he might join us for a meal during our stay."

Mr. Prescott senior grunted. Tawnyetta wasn't sure if it was a positive or negative commentary on that assumption.

Near the end of the meal Stewart approached and stood at the table to make an announcement.

"Laird MacBrody requests your presence at a spring ball he will be hosting this Saturday evening," Stewart said.

Small gasps of delight escaped the Prescott women. Bridget and Tawnyetta shared a look while Mr. Prescott senior nodded his approval.

"Ask and ye shall receive," Mrs. Prescott said, smiling at Bridget.

The surge of excitement at the idea of a ball and finally meeting the evasive Laird MacBrody was quickly overshadowed by Tawnyetta's realization that she had nothing to wear. As if reading her mind, Bridget raised her hand like she was in school and Stewart was the teacher.

Stewart looked at her and nodded, "You have a question, Miss Bridget?"

"I was wondering if there is some place we could go shopping? I'm not sure what one wears to a ball," Bridget admitted.

The Prescotts all shared a mildly disdainful look at the American's lack of experience on the subject. But they didn't say anything out loud.

"It is a formal event," Stewart replied. "I will send you information and inform the chauffeur that you wish to make some arrangements in town before the ball."

The next morning they went to Eldin.

Bea escaped with them, because she also needed to find a dress for the ball. Her mother-in-law and sister-in-law already owned formal wear, of course. But apparently Bea didn't travel with formal evening clothes, unlike the rest of the Prescotts. Tawnyetta sensed Bea was happy to get away from the lot of them and spend some time with the boisterous and outgoing Americans anyway.

Allen drove them and this time Tawnyetta was able to decipher about one-quarter of what he said. She sat directly behind him and watched his large ears wiggle when he spoke then looked to Bridget for a translation, although little words like 'wee lass' and 'Laird MacBrody' stood out to her ear.

With the castle's medieval walls behind them they made their way down a curving road that opened up to a stunning Highlands landscape. Tawnyetta didn't know if she'd ever seen anything quite that green. Thick grass blanketed rolling hills that lifted higher and higher until they turned into sharp peaks of rock and stone. The scene looked like a bright green ocean with undulating waves broken occasionally by yellow flowers bursting forth to soak up the sunshine while it lasted.

"Tec och noo in te heather 'ills," Allen said. Something about heather. There were smatterings of lavender in some areas and she imagined when the heather bloomed these hills would be even more gorgeous. As it was right now, Tawnyetta could barely pay attention to the conversation in the car as her eyes soaked up the scenery.

Eldin was a tiny place. To get to the center of the city they drove through modern housing, two story boxes with stone walled front gardens that looked like blocks that a giant had stacked up in rows on the edge of town. The city center of Eldin looked exactly like the Renaissance Festival Tawnyetta had gone to in high school. Two story shops built out of the same stone used to build Claymore Castle. As if the original builders were only given one option of building materials. All of the shops matched each other with quaint wood paned windows and doors on the front of each and individual wooden signs announcing what one could find inside. The signs sported names like 'The Granary', 'Room to Bloom' and 'The Ditzy Teacup'.

There was no Wal-Mart here or Target or shopping mall of any kind. Tawnyetta wondered where they got their groceries if there wasn't a name brand grocery store within the town limits. As far as a dress shop, she was not convinced they would be able to find anything formal enough for a ball in this little town.

"Ech for doo lasses no," Allen said, slowing the car and pulling it to the side of the brick laid street. Translation—they had arrived.

"This is a dress shop?" Tawnyetta asked.

The sign above this door read 'Sadie Sews' and Bea spoke up knowingly. "A seamstress' shop. She probably provides this service to many guests who come to the castle."

Walking into Sadie Sews was like walking into a fairy tale. Tawnyetta half-expected a group of singing mice to run out with needles and thread and start whipping up a Cinderella style ball gown around her where she stood.

Bolts of fabric of every conceivable color lined the walls. A huge table in the center of the room held scissors, pin cushions shaped like tomatoes, strawberries, and ladybugs with needles sticking out in all directions, and sturdy wooden racks with wooden pegs where spools of thread in every color waited to be used. There were dress forms, some empty, some clothed in a variety of dresses in different stages of completion. Floating, floral chiffons that looked like they were from the 1940s, svelte cocktail dresses with low cut necklines, and a few of what must have been prom dresses for high school girls in the area. Did they have high school proms in Scotland?

"This place is darling!" Bridget exclaimed as she walked along the bolts of cloth admiring the colors and textures.

Sadie herself was strong and stocky. She wore a heavy cloth apron that stretched from her ample bosom to just below her knees. She moved quickly on her feet for someone of her stature. Faded jet-black hair that was beginning to show signs of grey fell in layers to her shoulders. Sharp green eyes that were at once pretty and intelligent peered over the top of her wire-rimmed glasses.

"Three gowns in three days?" she asked. Her curtness did not imply the task was impossible, merely that she was getting her facts straight.

"Yes, if that's possible," Bridget answered for all three of them. Tawnyetta and Bea nodded in agreement.

"Anything's possible if we have light left in the day," Sadie muttered more to herself than to her new clients. "Who's first then?" The seamstress yanked a soft tape measure from her apron pocket and let go of one end so it unrolled quickly until the end hit the floor.

Bridget went first. Sadie whipped the tape measure around her with precision. She called the numbers out to her assistant, Isla, who was equally efficient and looked very much like a slimmer, younger version of Sadie. Tawnyetta wondered if they were related. As soon as Sadie was done measuring Bridget, she ordered her to go to the wall of fabrics. They were to pick out the fabric they wanted for their ball gowns.

Tawnyetta was next. Quick as a wink her measuring was complete and Tawnyetta was turned loose to look for fabrics. She was overwhelmed. There were so many colors and textures to choose from she found it difficult to even make a preliminary decision. She watched Bridget out of the corner of her eye to see what she was leaning towards.

Bridget, who had been hovering around the pastel pinks and blues, asked, "What do you think about this?" She held up a pale pink bolt of satin that rippled in her arms.

"It's lovely," Tawnyetta answered.

"There's a darker pink if you're interested," Bridget suggested, laying her hand on a deep pink taffeta.

Tawnyetta shook her head, "No, I'm not really one for pink."

Bea was released from her measuring and joined them, offering her opinion with a polite smile, "With your coloring, you should pick something darker perhaps?"

"But it's a spring ball," Bridget complained. "Shouldn't we be the colors of Easter?"

Sadie interrupted their conversation. Done making her notes on their measurements, she looked each of them up and down intently. Her eyes darted over their bodies, taking in their curves, their height, their hairstyle and color, their bone structure and skin tone, as well as their eye color.

"Pink will do well for you," she told Bridget. Turning to Tawnyetta, "Not you." She peered at Tawnyetta's eyes, furrowing her brow as she considered their unusual color. She glanced at Bea almost as an afterthought and declared, "Pale gold or blue."

Bea looked down to her hands where she held a pale gold bolt of fabric that shimmered in the light. She beamed at having chosen correctly.

Sadie turned away and perused the wall of fabrics. For a moment Tawnyetta thought perhaps the seamstress had forgotten about her dress. Her natural inclination would have been to choose black fabric and have an elegant black gown. But her tendency towards dark colors wasn't very spring-like. Since this was a once in a lifetime experience, so different than anything she'd even done before, Tawnyetta wished she could find a color that would make her look and feel beautiful.

Sadie turned from the wall, a bolt of green silk in her hands. "This. This will be perfect on you."

Green?

"That's so unique!" Bridget spoke up.

The fabric in Sadie's hands was not as dark as emerald green and not as bright as kelly green. The closest color Tawnyetta could compare it to in her mind was the shade of spring grass. The fabric appeared liquid, as if jewels had melted into a glimmering pool.

"What color is that?" Tawnyetta asked, reaching out and running her finger along its cool, slippery surface.

"I call it the Highlands," Sadie said. She smiled brightly at Tawnyetta for the first time since they'd arrived. Then the seamstress held the end of the bolt up to Tawnyetta's neck and laid it across her chest so the others could see. Sadie's smile grew even wider.

"Oh my God," Bridget said.

"What?" Tawnyetta asked, a little insecure.

"It just makes your eyes look amazing...and your skin...and your hair!" Bridget stared at her as if she hadn't seen her in a long time.

"That's a good thing?" Tawnyetta asked.

"It's a very good thing," Bridget responded.

With an 'I Told You So' look, Sadie proceeded to determine the cut of each of their gowns. She and Isla used muslin forms cut in various styles to piece together what each woman wanted and what would look good on their frame.

Tawnyetta's would be a scoop neck that dropped off of the edge of her shoulders with a tight bodice. The bodice led into a 'v' shaped waistline that blossomed into a full billowing skirt with a short train. Bridget's dress would be a Greek style gown with a halter top and a more fitted bodice that dropped over the roundness of her hips then flourished into a dramatic skirt that kicked around her feet. Bea, who was a little shorter and rounder than the other two, opted for a trimmer, narrower cut gown with a sweetheart neckline and three-quarter sleeves. Her shimmering gold dress was also fitted with a small bustle to add drama and flare to her form.

"It's too bad we don't have diamonds and emeralds and rubies," Tawnyetta said. The excitement of their new elegant gowns triggered her imagination.

"That would be divine," Bridget sighed.

"Is there a jeweler in town?" Bea asked.

"Yes, there are two," Sadie answered.

Tawnyetta and Bridget exchanged a look, slightly confused.

"Unfortunately that won't help. I'm afraid I can't buy expensive jewelry just for this party, even though it is a ball," Tawnyetta said apologetically.

"You don't have to buy it," Sadie responded. "Both places in town are happy to rent fine jewelry for special occasions at the castle." She observed the looks of astonishment on their faces. "How do you think all of those fancy ladies get their jewels?"

"It's true," Bea explained. "Most of the time the wealthy don't wear their own jewelry to big events. They borrow it from an even wealthier family member or rent it for the night from a jeweler."

Bridget and Tawnyetta's surprised expressions turned quickly to smiles.

"That would be great!" Bridget exclaimed.

"You may want to visit the jeweler right away," Sadie suggested. "This Saturday is the ball and anyone who's going is probably shopping now. Even Laird MacBrody is in town today, I hear, getting fitted for a new kilt."

Brows raised, Bridget and Tawnyetta shared another look. This one full of playful mischief.

Chapter Eight

Minutes later, all three women were traipsing down the street under the guise of going to the jewelry store then getting a cup of tea at The Ditsy Teacup. Bridget filled Bea in on their wish to get a glimpse of the elusive Laird MacBrody, stopping just short of informing her that they had already glimpsed the Laird in all of his glory once.

"I've heard that Laird MacBrody keeps himself to himself," Bea said.

Bridget, eyes gleaming with the excitement of the chase, said, "It's just so mysterious. I can't help but be intrigued by him."

It was good to see Bridget so full of exhilaration. Her face was bright and she showed no hint of the low mood she'd been in. After ball gown shopping and then heading to a jewelry store to pick out shiny baubles, this day was definitely hitting all of Bridget's fun buttons.

"Sadie said the tailor shop was right next to the first jewelry store." Bea cocked her head. "Interesting placement of shops don't you think? It's as if they're trying to give the men in this town a lesson on relationships."

Tawnyetta chuckled. Bea had a wry sense of humor. Plus she was down for a little adventure. It was nice to have her along.

They came across the first jewelry store. It was called 'Fine Gold and Gifts'. The three of them stopped to admire the display in the front window while they developed a plan of action. As they stared at the glittering rings and necklaces Bea tilted her head toward the tailor shop. The wooden sign above its door read 'Abernathy's'.

"I'll slip over to the tailor's window and see what I can see," Bea suggested. "You two stay here. If the Laird sees me he'll be less likely to recognize me since we only just arrived last night."

While Bridget and Tawnyetta pretended to admire the jewelry, Bea sidled about ten feet down the brick sidewalk and glanced nonchalantly into the front window. Tawnyetta caught Bridget's eye in their dim reflections in the glass. They had to bite their lips to keep from laughing.

Just as the jeweler, a wiry little man with thick spectacles and a shock of greying red hair, noticed Tawnyetta and Bridget at the window, Bea re-joined them.

"Did you see anything?" Tawnyetta asked in a loud whisper.

"There is a man, handsome devil, talking to the tailor," Bea said, her voice low and conspiratorial. "I realized too late that I can't identify Laird MacBrody because I don't know what he looks like."

They all fought the urge to crack up.

"We need to work on our spy techniques," Tawnyetta said.

The jeweler came out from behind his counter and started toward them, eager to invite them in and get a sale.

"We've got to check this out," Bridget said to Tawnyetta.

She gave the jeweler a brilliant, dismissive smile and small wave then grabbed Tawnyetta and Bea by the elbow and steered them swiftly away. Tawnyetta had half a second to give the jeweler an apologetic nod before they disappeared from his sight.

They stood in a line with their backs against the stone wall between the windows of 'Fine Gold and Gifts' and 'Abernathy's', hopefully out of sight of anyone in either shop. They took a few moments to gather themselves before Tawnyetta, who stood closest to the tailor's window, leaned over to peer through the very edge of the window and see what she could see.

Immediately she made out who she assumed was the tailor. A tall, thin, nervous looking man dressed in a fine suit and wearing a measuring tape around his neck like a doctor might wear a stethoscope. He was engaged in tentative communication with a well built, dark haired man. The man wore a tuxedo jacket and a dark grey and black tartan kilt. Though his back was to her, his size and shape was familiar, wide shoulders, thick, muscled legs. She had definitely seen those legs before, bare and dancing.

Bridget tugged at her elbow, "Do you see him?"

Tawnyetta turned her head quickly and whispered, "I think so." When she turned back and took another peek, her purse erupted with sudden vibrations and a ringtone. The interruption was so unexpected that Tawnyetta yelped and jumped, startling the other two women who let out small shouts of surprise. The sound got the attention of the tailor and he shot a look her way. The man in the kilt turned toward the window to see what all the commotion was about and Tawnyetta ducked out of sight before he could see her, or her him.

Caught in the middle of the sidewalk trying to spy on Laird MacBrody, Tawnyetta cursed under her breath as she shoved her hand into her purse to retrieve her phone. The other two women were dissolving into giggles and Tawnyetta was afraid the whole jig was up.

"Go, go, go!" She hissed at the other two. "I think they're coming."

The three women hurried down the street. They could hear the sound of an ancient door squeaking open, but they didn't turn around to see if it was the tailor or the jeweler or Laird MacBrody.

Tawnyetta managed to get to her phone and hit the answer button. It was Sofia.

"Hello?" Tawnyetta said, out of breath.

"Hey, what are you up to?" Sofia asked.

Tawnyetta started laughing, but managed to answer, "You have no idea."

"Come on!" Bridget wanted them all to hurry. "We'll have to use the other jewelry store."

Tawnyetta told Sofia to hold on as they made their way around the corner. When she was certain they were a safe distance away from Abernathy's, she put the phone back up to her ear.

"What's up?" Tawnyetta asked.

"I thought I would check in on you guys and see how Bridget's doing. How's the trip?" Sofia said.

"It's been pretty fun so far."

"Who is it?" Bridget asked. Tawnyetta mouthed Sofia's name. "Fifi!" Bridget exclaimed. "Tell her hi!"

Tawnyetta nodded and waved Bridget and Bea on toward 'The Ditsy Teacup', indicating with a flick of her hand that she would stay behind and finish her conversation on the phone before joining them. She wanted to talk to Sofia privately.

"Bridge says 'hi'," Tawnyetta said.

"Is she doing okay?" Sofia asked again.

"She is for the most part. Christopher called the other day and put her in a bad way for a while."

"Jerk," Sofia said.

"Not to worry, we have found a distraction." Tawnyetta explained how they had been trying to find Laird MacBrody and had, so far, found him once in all his glory. "I've been kind of encouraging her to crush a little bit on the Scottish Laird. I think it's a fun distraction for her from Christopher and that whole mess."

"That does sound distracting," Sofia laughed. "And how about you?" She asked.

"Me? I'm fine," Tawnyetta answered.

"We were all just kind of hoping that you were having an adventure, you know? Following your dreams and all that."

Unbidden, Shaun's face popped into Tawnyetta's mind. She thought about the sword fight dance they had shared and felt a twinge of curiosity, wondering where he was today and what he was doing. She shook her head as if she could discard the thought of him through the movement.

"Are you still there?" Sofia asked.

Tawnyetta nodded then realized Sofia couldn't see her and answered, "Yes, I'm here."

"So, is anything exciting happening for you in Scotland?" Sofia pressed, not one to be ignored.

"Oh, not a whole lot." Tawnyetta glanced up and down the street at the charming stone buildings and thought of the rolling hills surrounding the castle and the ball gown that matched the green Highland grass. "It is beautiful here, though," she responded. "And there's going to be a ball, so that will be fun."

"A ball? When?" Sofia asked, obviously delighted at the idea.

"This Saturday night."

"An honest-to-goodness ball?"

"Yes, isn't that cool?" Tawnyetta asked. Again, an unbidden thought entered her mind. Sadie had said something about other people in town being invited to the ball. She wondered briefly if Shaun was one of those people.

"Well it sounds like an adventure to me!" Sofia said.

"Yes," Tawnyetta responded, a smile tugged relentlessly on the corners of her mouth, making her smile at nobody in particular on the street. "I suppose it is."

Chapter Nine

The next morning Tawnyetta set out on her own. It was early. Bridget was still sound asleep in their room. The sounds and smells of cooking came from the kitchen, but no staff could be seen and all was quiet in the castle and gardens.

The sunshine of the previous day had not yet reappeared this morning. Tawnyetta found the now familiar dreary morning weather more welcoming today. She had spent enough time in the gardens at the castle that she was no longer uncomfortable exploring them alone in the mysterious morning. In fact, the Highland mist gave everything an otherworldly feel, especially the Secret Garden.

After entering through the archway she followed a grey stone path that was so embedded in the ground it appeared to have grown there. The path led to an equally ancient and semi-dilapidated stone stairway. A wide fence of the same stone, but covered in deep green moss, flanked each side of the stairway and Grecian urns sat at the top, one on each side. Thick, pale green ivy overflowed from them, spilling and twisting down the railings and along the wall that continued into the garden.

Great iron trellises, almost twenty feet tall at their highest, held darker green vines that grew so thick in some places, no light pierced through. At least a dozen of these trellises were lined in a great row over the pathway, which created a living tunnel. More climbing plants sprung up from the black earth at the base of the trellises and claimed sections of the tunnel for themselves, snaking and roping their way up through the vines and draping the organic walls with pink and white and red flowers.

Tawnyetta was enchanted. She paused to lean down and smell the sweet scent of the flowers. She peered through openings between the climbing plants where daylight winked to see what might be on the other side. More greenery, more flowers, more places to explore.

At the end of the ivy tunnel was an iron gate set between two partially collapsing white stone pillars. The gate was overrun with climbing flowered vines. So much so that much of the ornate iron work was hidden, but it was still functional. She could see where it had been opened and closed recently. The pebbles and debris scattered across the pathway had been swept aside by the movement of the gate.

She pulled the gate open and it let out a defiant squeak. When she stepped through into the next section of the garden she heard the distinct sound of metal on rock. A thumping, cracking sound from just around the corner. She followed the sound, curious to find its source.

She came to a halt when she saw Shaun.

He stood on the opposite side of yet another low stone wall, a sledgehammer in one hand. He was pounding a metal bracket into the hard stone. He looked up, noticing her motion in the otherwise still space.

Tawnyetta's skin tingled at the sight of him. His heavy work shirt was off and draped on the wall next to him, leaving him in a white T-shirt. His forearms flexed where he held the hammer, worn leather gloves covered his hands. Standing in the dewy morning, a fine mist melting on the ground around him, his eyes were electric blue. He stood up from his half bent position and stared at her for a long moment. Her heart jumped into her throat and she found that she could not speak or move. Then, suddenly, his expression changed, as if he'd woken from a daydream. He tipped his head in her direction, breaking the strange spell between them.

"Good morning, lass," he said.

Shyness flooded through her and she couldn't think of what to say. She hadn't admitted to herself that she hoped to see Shaun this morning. Alone and away from everyone. Now that he was right there in front of her, she couldn't look away. As he gazed at her, waiting, embarrassment slipped over her and turned her cheeks pink.

"I'm sorry," she took a few steps back and turned to leave him alone.

In one swift move he dropped his sledgehammer on top of the wall, placed his gloved hand on it to balance and hopped easily across, like someone might hope over a turnstile at a subway station.

"Don't go," he said as he landed and straightened.

"I don't want to bother you while you're working," Tawnyetta finally found her voice.

Shaun dismissed his sledgehammer project with a back-handed wave. "You're not interrupting a thing." He glanced around behind her. "Where is your friend?" He put emphasis on the word friend and grinned as he pulled off his work gloves.

"She's still sleeping. She's not much of a morning person."

"But you are?"

Tawnyetta relaxed a little at the question. Glad to have something to talk about. "I am. I like to get up and get things done."

"Me too." He placed the work gloves on top of his work shirt on the wall.

Tawnyetta stepped closer to the stone wall. She peered at where he had been pounding on the side of the rock to try to determine what he was working on.

"I see that," she said, smiling back at him. Something in the way Shaun held himself shifted. He ducked his chin and leaned on one foot then the other. Her praise pleased him.

"Are you enjoying your room in the keep?" He leaned against the wall, settling in for a talk.

"The keep?" She wrinkled her brow.

He indicated the castle towers with a quick nod of his head. They were visible just over the tops of the surrounding trees.

"Aye, that's where your room is. Inside the keep."

"What's a keep?"

He seemed to be enjoying his role as instructor. "The keep is the stronghold of the castle. It's where Laird's of old kept their most precious possessions."

She knew he was speaking about the fortress aspect of the castle. But the look in his eyes made her cheeks redden again. She considered his comment and thought about their room in the uppermost floor. The spiral staircase had a few tiny windows in it for light, but not anything that a human could fit through. The large windows at the top floor were too high for anyone to get in using a ladder. With its un-scalable walls, lack of windows, and the single door entry at the bottom, she could see how it would be quite a stronghold.

"I suppose it would be difficult to get in if nobody wanted to let you in," she said.

"Aye, it's the safest part of the castle. The most protected. The most difficult to enter."

Tawnyetta looked at him, but he wasn't looking at the keep. His deep blue eyes were trained on her. Gazing at her face, the lines of her jaw, her full lips, he seemed lost in thought. Tawnyetta cleared her throat. This brought him out of whatever reverie he had been in and he thought of something polite to say.

"Is this your first visit to the Highlands?" he asked.

"It's my first visit to Scotland. To Europe, actually."

His eyebrows raised a fraction of an inch. "We're honored to have you."

"Well, it was Bridget's...my friend's choice actually. I filled in when it was decided that her fiancé, or ex-fiancé I guess, wasn't coming." Tawnyetta smiled sheepishly.

"Ach, that's right, that's what you said before." He folded his hands in his lap and cocked his head at her. He seemed amused, but he didn't say anything. Tawnyetta felt as if she should fill the void.

"You've always lived here?" she asked.

His eyes moved unconsciously toward the castle, then down to his hands in his lap. He sighed. "I was away at Uni in Edinburgh for a while. Then I came back."

It was strange to her that someone who studied at a university would become a gardener. She furrowed her brow at him. "Would you have rather stayed away? Done something else besides this?" She indicated the surrounding garden

He stiffened, almost imperceptibly. Something like a frown flickered through his eyes. "I used to want to stay away. But we don't always get what we want, do we?"

Realizing her faux pas she tried to think of another subject. Being a gardener wasn't such a terrible job and she hadn't meant to offend him, but it was obvious she had hit a nerve. She opened her mouth to apologize for being too personal and stepping over a line when the iron gate squeaked and caught both of their attention.

A tiny, fragile old man teetered through the gate. He was dressed in layers, navy blue pants, a hunter green vest, a dark grey sport coat that looked like it was made of wool, and a red scarf that matched the red cap sitting askew on his head. He was gnarled and wrinkled and looked like he lived in the garden. She wouldn't have been surprised to find out he was some kind of elf or troll and not an actual human being. She glanced at Shaun for his reaction and saw that his expression had softened considerably.

"Dougie," he said, giving the little old man a warm smile.

Shaun left his seat on the stone wall and went to Dougie, offering him his hand to help him walk over the rough ground.

Dougie waved him away with a curt look. "Off with you, lad. I can still handle myself."

His brogue was thick, but Tawnyetta had gotten better at deciphering the Scottish accent when she concentrated. When he got closer, which took a few long moments, Dougie zeroed in on Tawnyetta with sharp blue eyes. His body was thin and stooped, his face held deep wrinkles and spotty, salt and pepper stubble, but his eyes were clear and focused, unchanged since his youth, she imagined.

He pointed a crooked finger at her and shook it in mock scolding. "And who is this bonnie wee lass?"

Shaun shot her an amused glance and cleared his throat before answering, "This is Miss Tawnyetta. She is a guest at the castle."

Dougie nodded his approval. He came to an uneven stop in front of her and offered her his hand. She took it. Dry cool skin covered fragile old bones. He patted the top of her hand with his other palm and leaned in toward her to get a better look. He smelled like pipe tobacco and moss, exactly what she would expect a gnome to smell like.

"Welcome, lass. It's good to have such a bonnie face in the garden."

"Thank you, that's very kind. It's nice to meet you."

"This is Dougie, the caretaker of Claymore Castle. He's been here as long as anyone can remember," Shaun explained with another amused smile and a gracious half-bow.

Dougie dismissed the bow by raising his palm in protest and shaking his head once. Shaun stood straight again, politely obeying the elderly caretaker.

"Are you familiar with the MacBrody's, lass?" Dougie asked her.

"No, not really. I came here with a friend on short notice. I did not have time to look into the history of the place before we left," she responded.

"Look no further, lass. I know all there is to know about Laird Michael MacBrody."

Shaun shifted on his feet and turned his gaze to the ground. Dougie gave him a sideways look and leaned in to speak to Tawnyetta conspiratorially.

"I've known Laird Michael since he was a wee bairn. The very day he came screaming out of his mother," Dougie said.

Tawnyetta smiled. "Really?"

Shaun cleared his throat, fidgeting. He looked uncomfortable, embarrassed. He must be feeling guilty talking about his employer while taking such a long break. He probably wasn't supposed to stop and fraternize with the guests on a work day.

Dougie paid him no mind and continued, "Do you know that he wasn't even supposed to be Laird? He had other plans. Big plans! He was going to be a big man of academics in Glasgow or Edinburgh." Dougie nodded for emphasis. "His older brother was Laird first. Laird Greg. Laird Greg was the first born and the heir to Claymore Castle."

Shaun cleared his throat again, pushing some loose pebbles at the foot of the stone wall around with his toe. He mumbled something.

"What's that?" Dougie asked.

Shaun picked up his sledgehammer, work shirt and gloves, and said, "I'll be getting back to work now."

Dougie waved this comment away, but Shaun took off toward the iron gate anyway.

Dougie turned his attention back to Tawnyetta. "Laird Greg inherited this whole place." He indicated their surroundings with a feeble sweep of his arm. "But he was taken too young from this world. Died in a terrible accident."

Shaun glanced back at her and Dougie for a brief second, one hand on the iron gate, a scowl in his eyes.

"That's terrible," Tawnyetta said to Dougie, though her attention was on Shaun.

Dougie shook his head with dismay. "Laird Greg was a wild one, and his wild ways overcame him too young." The old man hung his head and made tsk-tsking sounds.

Shaun's blue eyes held hers for an instant and Tawnyetta saw a flash of anger shoot through them. She didn't understand why he would have such a profound reaction to the tales told by this harmless little old man. Before she finished her thought, Shaun pushed on the iron gate and disappeared. The squeak it made echoed through the garden.

Tawnyetta turned her attention back to Dougie. "That's terrible. I had no idea."

"Aye, it's an awful sad story. But Laird Michael came back to us, thank the heavens. He is a hard worker, smart as a whip, and the best Laird for Claymore Castle."

Dougie continued to regale Tawnyetta with stories of Laird MacBrody. He told her about the late Laird Greg's heavy drinking and wild ways. How he was a fighter, a strong man, and though he had a good heart overall, the elderly man explained that Laird Greg had been impulsive and sometimes the selfish older brother to the young master Michael. Greg and Michael were the only children of the previous Laird and Lady, the aristocratic couple that had hired Dougie to be the head caretaker. Though he had loved both young men since they were born, Laird Michael had always been the kind one. Dougie bragged on Laird Michael's wonderful sense of humor and generous nature.

"It was a heart breaker to be sure when young Michael went off to University to make his own life. There was nothing for him here, just being the younger brother of Laird Greg," Dougie explained.

They were walking arm-in-arm. Dougie had her by the elbow and she had her arm linked in his. Partly because he was being a gentleman, but also she felt better holding on to him as she was worried he might totter over. The mist was burning off and it would be a sunny morning at least. Strolling with Dougie through the beautiful gardens listening to his Scottish brogue as he told her many stories of the family and the young brothers that grew into men here at the castle, Tawnyetta couldn't help but feel like she had gone back in time.

Even though she was enjoying herself, a small thought needled her as they strolled along. Why had Shaun reacted to Dougie's stories with such guarded hostility? Every time she got caught up in flirting with him it seemed that the assistant gardener who had captured her eye slipped into dark moodiness. What did it say about him that his moods shifted so quickly from light to dark? And more than that, what did it say about her that she found him so intriguing?

Chapter Ten

Claymore Castle had no spa.

Ladies preparing for the ball with manicures and pedicures, facials and exfoliation, waxing and mud treatments, were forced to go into Eldin for a spa day.

Two vivacious young redheads, sisters, ran the only spa in town. Sandy and Rochelle were darling, bubbly, round-eyed young women who prided themselves on pampering their guests. Today those guests included not only Tawnyetta and Bridget, but all three Prescott ladies. They bustled all of the women into various areas of the spa so they each received every treatment available. Offering all of the normal expected services, plus tea, red or white wine, fresh-baked shortbread cookies, and the main staple of any good spa, gossip.

Tawnyetta and Bridget sat high up on pedicure chairs, their feet and calves coated with a sea salt cream and wrapped in plastic so the mixture would soak into their skin. Sandy worked on doing their nails while Rochelle took care of the Prescott ladies on the other side of the room. Bea, her sister-in-law, Tabitha, and Mrs. Prescott were getting facials.

"You will have a lovely time at the ball," Sandy informed them. "Claymore Castle throws nothing but the best kind of parties."

"Does it?" Bridget asked, giving Tawnyetta an exuberant smile.

"And Laird Michael, he's such a charmer, and so handsome," Rochelle interjected from across the room where she was placing slices of cucumbers over the Prescott women's closed eyes.

"Is he?" Bea asked from under her cucumbers. "We haven't had the chance to meet him yet."

"Yes," Tabitha said with her thin, whiny voice. "I'm beginning to wonder if that really is polite? For the Lord of the castle to ignore his guests?"

"Well, my best friend, Anne, is one of the maids up there," Sandy said.

"We know Anne," Tawnyetta injected.

"She says that Laird Michael inherited a terrible mess when his brother died. She says he's working all the time on practically everything at the castle just to get it back to normal. To where it was when their father was alive," Sandy told them with a knowing nod.

"His brother died?" Bridget asked with some surprise.

Sandy nodded solemnly. "Yes, a terrible accident. He was driving after having a wee bit too much to drink and drove his car off of a high road. Smashed it to bits. When they found him he was already dead. It was an awful shock to everyone."

Rochelle made a clucking sound with her tongue. "It wasn't a shock to everyone," she stressed the word *everyone*. "We all knew Laird Greg lived dangerously. The whole town knew. It wasn't a surprise to some that his wild ways ended badly."

"That's true," Sandy agreed.

Mrs. Prescott spoke up from under her face mask, "It's a shame when someone is handed everything in life and they fritter it away."

Tawnyetta didn't want the gossip fest to go too sour. Mrs. Prescott was the kind of person who could say something judgmental and suck all the fun out of the room.

"But Laird Michael is different, isn't he?" she asked Sandy.

Sandy's round eyes grew rounder, "Aye, yes. And he's a handsome one as well. Laird Greg was handsome in his own way, but Laird Michael." She sighed, not able to finish her thought completely she was so overcome at the thought of Laird Michael.

Bridget's eyes sparkled.

Rochelle piped up, "I danced with him once."

"Laird Michael?" Bridget asked.

Rochelle nodded with enthusiasm, "Yes." She sighed. "He is dreamy. It was at the Daffodil Festival when he was home visiting, the year before his brother died."

"Will you all be coming to the ball as well?" Tawnyetta asked, curious as to how the social structure in this little town worked.

"Not this one," Sandy explained. "This is a private affair. The castle does have public affairs, dances and festivals and the like, that everyone attends."

Tawnyetta and Bridget shared a look. The classist setup offended their American sensibilities.

Sandy read their expressions and shook her head at them, "Oh, don't you worry. It's not an offense. After all, if everyone was invited to the private ball, who would serve the drinks and the food? It's a good job for those that have it."

"I suppose that's true," Bridget said.

Tabitha snorted. Tawnyetta glanced at the Prescotts and couldn't read their expressions under all of the face mask goop.

Bea wasn't a snob, but Tawnyetta could sense snobbery oozing off of the other two.

Sandy continued chatting, unfazed by any attitude coming from Tabitha and Mrs. Prescott. "Anne and Shaun, that's her boyfriend who works in the gardens, have been able to save up plenty of money from working the parties at the castle. Enough that they're planning a huge party for their own wedding."

Tawnyetta was wrapped up with being annoyed at Tabitha and her mother. So much so that what Sandy had just said didn't register right away. Then Bea asked Rochelle if her face mask was supposed to sting. While Rochelle came to Bea's rescue there was a few moments lag in the conversation. Enough time for Sandy's comment to sink in.

Humiliation and anger rushed through Tawnyetta. Heat pumped into her stomach and chest. Had she heard correctly?

Bridget and Sandy chatted about the hot pink nail polish Bridget had picked out. Tawnyetta watched their mouths moving, but was having a hard time focusing on the words.

"I'm sorry," she interrupted. Bridget and Sandy stopped talking and looked at her. "Did you say Anne was dating Shaun? The Gardener?"

Sandy nodded. "Yes, though I think he's more than just the gardener. He has other duties as well, running errands and such." Sandy dipped the tiny brush into the hot pink bottle of polish and pulled it out. A big fat droplet held on the end and she expertly smoothed the color onto Bridget's waiting nail. "Anne thinks that he has a fine future there, because the head caretaker is very, very old. There's no reason Shaun can't take his place when he retires."

The heavy chemical smell of fresh nail polish filled the air. Tawnyetta felt sick. Had it gotten warmer in here? She wanted to take off the light sweater she'd worn to stave off the morning rain, but her fingernails were still wet. She wanted to go outside and stand in the drizzle to cool off, but her feet were still wrapped in plastic. She was in a mani-pedi trap.

"Are you all right?" Bridget asked.

Tawnyetta realized that both Bridget and Sandy were looking at her peculiarly. She didn't know how long they'd been watching as she overreacted to the town gossip.

"I'm fine," she answered.

Sandy frowned. "Let me get you a drink. You look a wee peaked." She pronounced 'peaked' in two distinct syllables.

"I'm feeling a little warm," Tawnyetta said. "I'd like to go outside for a minute and get some fresh air." She looked down at her half done pedicure.

"Of course," Sandy responded right away. She twisted the cap firmly back on the hot pink nail polish and jumped up, quickly unwrapping the plastic from Tawnyetta's feet and legs. With a firm but gentle touch, Sandy rubbed the remnants of the thick body cream into Tawnyetta's calves, ankles, and toes.

"You look pale," Bridget told her, a small knot forming between her eyebrows as she watched Tawnyetta with concern.

"Too much wine, maybe." Tawnyetta shrugged it off.

Sandy grabbed Tawnyetta's sandals and slipped them on her feet. "There you go!"

"Thank you," Tawnyetta said as she stepped down off of the chair and made her way to the front door.

"Don't touch anything, your nails are still wet," Sandy warned.

Tawnyetta nodded in understanding. Keeping her fingers splayed out she used both palms to push down on the door handle and her hip to apply pressure so it would swing open far enough she could slip through.

Outside, a cool, refreshing spray hit her face. Grey clouds had settled over the area and a continual fine rain fell. More than drizzle, less than drops.

She kept her back to the spa window, not wanting

everyone to watch her face as she processed what she had found out about Shaun. On the narrow street, a few pedestrians made their way along the brick sidewalks. Tawnyetta took a deep breath of the cool, damp air and let it out slowly, closing her eyes as a mild breeze sent a fresh spritz of misty rain across her skin.

Her heart felt like a stone in her chest. Every time she thought about Sandy's comment, about the fact that Shaun was not only dating someone else but engaged to them, her stone heart sank a little lower. Another breath through her nose. The cool air filtered into her lungs and fought back the hot anger in her chest.

Why did she care so much? How could it possibly matter to her that the gardener, the guy that went around taking apart fountains and hammering stone walls, had a fiancé?

Bridget's laughter muffled through the window. Glancing back through the window to look at her best friend having an animated conversation with Sandy, Tawnyetta knew the answer. After all of the humiliation and heartbreak Bridget had so recently experienced with her cheating fiancé, Tawnyetta was shocked and angry that they had encountered yet another cheating fiancé while on their Not a Honeymoon.

"Unbelievable," she mumbled to herself.

She shook her head as if she could discard the entire situation from her mind and fling it far away. What a jerk. What a colossal jerk. He had openly flirted with her, giving her that smoldering, sexy look. And the whole time his sweet, innocent fiancé was upstairs serving her and Bridget tea and making their bed. The whole situation was infuriating.

"I'm not taking part in that," she said out loud.

A young couple walking past the spa gave her a questioning look. Tawnyetta closed her mouth and offered them a tight smile. This wasn't the place to cause a scene and she didn't want to get Bridget all upset again, so Tawnyetta decided she would keep her mouth shut.

But the next time Shaun even looked in her direction she vowed to give him a piece of her mind.

91

Chapter Eleven

The castle held several sitting rooms, the smallest of which was known as the blue parlor. Small was a relative term, however, as the blue parlor was bigger than the entire first floor of Tawnyetta's childhood home. Stuffed full of uncomfortable ornate seating, sluggish dark blue drapes, large oil paintings of nobility standing in awkward poses, and a life sized, white marble statue of an angry young woman posed in the corner, this room had a strange vibe.

Half dressed, the conspicuous statue was draped in folds of marble fabric that barely covered her breasts. She was a beautiful woman with curls piled on top of her head and a clutch of arrows strapped to her back as well as one in her hand. In her other hand she held a bow. She was positioned with her back to the room, showing off her curvy bottom. But her head was turned in such a way that she looked as if she was peering back over her shoulder seeking prey. Her expression was not the normal demure look you found on many half naked statues of women. She looked fierce.

Tawnyetta couldn't decide if she liked the statue or not,

but she was certain that the room in general brought her no pleasure. They had chosen to wait here because of the blue parlor's placement at the front of the castle. From its windows you had a perfect view of the front drive.

"Aren't you excited?" Bridget asked, interrupting Tawnyetta's contemplation of the statue.

"Sure, I'm excited." That wasn't totally true. Tawnyetta was looking forward to their ball gowns arriving for their fitting. However, she wasn't exactly feeling excited. Her mood had been soured by her realization that Shaun was a cheater. But she couldn't tell Bridget about any of that, so as far as Bridget was concerned she had to stay excited.

"You're just staring at that statue," Bridget said.

"Am I?" Tawnyetta was standing close to the statue scrutinizing her realistically carved eyes. They hinted of revenge and danger.

Bridget, on the other hand, stood at the window watching the drive anxiously, waiting for the delivery van.

"I don't think staring at the road is going to make the dresses arrive any faster Bridge," Tawnyetta teased.

"You're right," Bridget tore herself away from the window and chose one of the uncomfortable blue couches to sit on. She patted the spot next to her and Tawnyetta joined her. From that position they both took in the gaudy decor of the room.

"This room is ugly," Bridget said.

"It really is."

"I wonder why? I mean, the rest of the rooms we've seen have been quite nice."

"Maybe they needed a place to store all of the ugly things," Tawnyetta suggested

Bridget laughed. "Probably! It's weird that all of the ugly things would be blue, though."

This time Tawnyetta laughed.

Bridget let out a heavy sigh. "I'm hungry. I'm going to go get a snack." Tawnyetta moved to get up as well. "No," Bridget said as she gestured for Tawnyetta to sit back down. "You stay here and watch for the dresses. I'll bring something back for you."

"We could ring for Stewart or the maids to bring us something," Tawnyetta suggested.

Bridget shook her head 'no'. "I want to stretch my legs. Besides I can't quite get used to having servants."

Tawnyetta had to agree. It was nice having everything taken care of, but she didn't like the feeling of doing absolutely nothing productive all day long either.

As she waited she tried to keep her eye on the drive as closely as Bridget had, but it didn't take long for that to become boring. To avoid dozing off she stood up and wandered around the room. Looking more closely at the large oil paintings of nobility she wondered what their lives were like so long ago and why they had to wear such ridiculous aristocratic outfits. Their clothing looked hot and restrictive. She stared into their beady little eyes and wondered if these were all ancestors of Laird Michael. If so, she wasn't sure how he could have turned out as attractive as everybody said he was.

She returned to the statue. Perhaps this woman was a legend or a goddess of some kind, like the goddess of war. She ran her finger along the smooth, cool, stone bow trying to remember the name of the Greek goddess of war.

"Do you like her?" A deep familiar voice asked from the other side of the room.

Tawnyetta whirled around, startled at the interruption. Her stomach flipped at the sight of Shaun smiling at her.

He was not dressed in his normal work clothes. In fact, he was dressed up in comparison to how she was used to seeing him. In a pair of black jeans and a tailored white business shirt he didn't look much like a gardener at all. His short beard was freshly clipped, his dark hair combed and in place. Even cleaned up like this he possessed a kind of animal magnetism with his square jaw, mischievous smile, wide shoulders, and well formed muscled chest. A memory of his chest, sweaty and flexing, as they danced with sabers in the weapons room popped into her mind.

She was immediately disgusted at herself for thinking about how attractive he was and decided to turn that anger towards the person who rightfully deserved it–Shaun. Tawnyetta narrowed her eyes and glared at him.

He walked towards her. His movements were casual and bordered on seductive. That sexy half smile on his face and the way he watched her with his ocean blue eyes sent her stomach into a series of flips. Heart pounding, she cursed herself for these feelings. That's probably how all of these types of men got away with cheating, by being so damned attractive.

"It's Artemis, the goddess of the hunt."

"I knew that," she spat the words at him, irritated that she had not known.

He had already crossed the room and stopped just a few feet away from her. He wore cologne. It smelled nice. Really nice. Wasn't cologne a bit overkill for a gardener? Tawnyetta looked away from him as she rolled her eyes, not really concerned if he noticed. He was using the statue as a reason to get as close as possible to her no doubt. She dropped her hand from the marble bow and turned on him. She wanted to face him square on.

"Did you know she was a virgin?" He asked, his eyes twinkling just a little bit.

The question surprised her and she couldn't remember what she was about to say. This way he had of rendering her mute just by looking at her was infuriating.

"What?"

"Artemis was a virgin. I guess maybe she was too scary for

most men." Shaun shifted his gaze from Tawnyetta to the face of the statue.

Tawnyetta scoffed, "Yeah, well, most men are wimps."

He tilted his head and gave her a small nod of agreement. "Indeed."

She wanted to tell him that many men were also cheating creeps who got engaged to one woman and then went after whoever else happened to be around. She opened her mouth to say just that when he spoke again.

"She was also the goddess of childbirth, which I always thought was a wee bit of a strange combination. Don't you?"

Once again his words jarred her enough that she forgot the tirade she was about to unleash on him. A sigh of frustration escaped her lips.

"I don't know." She hoped her irritation about the subject was clear.

"I just never saw the connection." He turned his attention back to the fierce expression on Artemis' face. "Virginity, hunting, and childbirth. They just don't seem like they go together."

"Maybe you just don't like the idea of a strong woman, or the idea of raising a family," Tawnyetta said, arching her brow.

"Do you think that's what it is?" He rolled the thought around as he let his eyes wander over the statue. "I don't think so." He looked at Tawnyetta, then back to Artemis, then back to Tawnyetta again. "I've always thought this statue was beautiful."

The word 'cheeky' came to mind. She had been listening to too many British and Scottish people in the last few days. His attitude was definitely cheeky, but the word didn't quite cover the insolence.

"Are you excited for the ball tomorrow night?" he asked. Once again directing her thoughts into a totally new direction.

The hackles rose on her neck. For someone who was a

member of the staff, and engaged to be married to someone else, he certainly was forward. She wasn't necessarily all about sticking to convention, but his confidence in this conversation seemed like it overstepped a line.

"I am going to the ball. I've been invited as a guest of the castle," she answered haughtily. Maybe if she pointed out her place he would realize that he was perilously close to being so unprofessional that his job could be in jeopardy.

"Of course. I'm glad to hear it."

"I've brought your drink." A voice sounded from the other side of the room. A woman's voice this time. Tawnyetta and Shaun turned at the sound. It was Anne.

Tawnyetta felt a blush rush into her cheeks. Anne had caught them in a conversation that was a little too comfortable for a gardener and a guest. To her credit, Anne seemed unperturbed. She held a tray with a tall glass of what looked like iced tea.

When she caught Tawnyetta's eye, she did a small curtsy, "I'm sorry Miss, I didn't know you were in here."

"Maybe you could get Miss Tawnyetta a drink?" Shaun suggested. He turned back to Tawnyetta. "What would you like?"

Tawnyetta's mouth dropped open in amazement at the gall of this man. Was he serious? He was ordering his fiancé around like she was his servant? All of the attraction she had previously felt for him swept away on a wave of self-righteousness.

"I'm not thirsty, thank you," she said icily, hoping he could feel the heat of her glare.

"Are you sure?" He asked.

"I am absolutely sure, thank you," Tawnyetta said with growing hostility.

Anne looked slightly confused. As if she did not know whether she should bring the drink she held to Shaun or go get Tawnyetta a drink of her own. Tawnyetta thought that maybe Anne should throw the drink into Shaun's face and break up with him. But that didn't happen.

"You can leave mine there," Shaun said indicating a side table. His impersonal attitude toward his fiancé was so brutal that it hurt Tawnyetta's heart to see Anne's reaction. Anne nodded and smiled and set the drink down. "Thank you, Anne," he said as Anne removed herself from the room.

Tawnyetta's mind was no longer foggy. She knew exactly what she needed to say. "I can't believe you just did that!" she said, her eyes shooting daggers at him.

Shaun looked around the room in confusion. As if he could see the problem with his eyes.

Not finding anything, he looked back at her and asked, "What did I do?"

"I think you know exactly what you did," Tawnyetta sneered. "And I am not taking part in any of it. You can forget about that!"

Confusion clouded his face.

Outside the parlor windows the delivery van pulled in front of the castle. Tawnyetta heard Bridget calling to her from the Great Hall to come and see their dresses. Happy for an excuse to leave the presence of such a total chauvinist pig, Tawnyetta pushed past him and hurried out the door.

Chapter Twelve

The ball took place the very next day.

Tawnyetta did not see Shaun again after the episode in the blue parlor. That was fine with her. She did, however, see Anne. In fact, Anne and her mirror image, Erin, were responsible for helping Bridget and Tawnyetta get dressed for the ball.

Tawnyetta didn't feel close enough to Anne to tell her about her fiancé's actions. She was completely uncomfortable being pampered by the blissfully ignorant maid. She tried to make up for it by treating the young woman with great kindness and affection, showering her with praise and thanking her graciously for every little assistance.

Bridget was radiant. She loved dressing up. After the disappointment of her wedding, having this event where she could pretend she was a princess and be the belle of the ball put life into her eyes. It warmed Tawnyetta's heart to see it. She decided to put all of the ugliness with Shaun aside and focus on the night ahead of them. Tonight would be wonderful. Tonight they would live like royalty. Tonight they would finally meet Laird Michael. And who knew? Maybe Bridget would fall in love with someone a thousand times better than cheating Christopher.

The schedule for the evening required the castle guests to arrive at Stag Hall at 6:30 pm for dinner. It was a formal dinner and part of the ball, so they were expected to be dressed for the evening. At 8:00 pm dinner would be complete and the castle guests would join Laird Michael and the other guests he had invited in the main ballroom.

To be ready for a ball by 6:30 p.m., Bridget and Tawnyetta decided they needed to start immediately after lunch.

They took turns soaking in the luxurious bathtub. They washed their hair with fragrant shampoo and smoothed thick creams and rich lotions over their skin. Their gowns had been fitted to them perfectly the day before and waited under heavy plastic protectors on a rolling hanger that had been moved into their room.

They pulled on their finest bras, undies, and stockings then draped the luxurious robes provided by the castle over them to start the next wave of preparations. Since they had already had manicures and pedicures the only thing remaining was their makeup and hair. But before they got started on that task Anne brought them a fruit and cheese plate with some tea as refreshment.

"I have some items for your hair, combs and pins and such," she told them as she placed the tea tray down on a serving table. "Laird Michael told me to gather the items from his mother's collection for you ladies to use if you desire."

"Thank you, Anne," Tawnyetta said while looking the maid directly in the eye. "We really, really appreciate that."

"I'll send your thanks to Laird Michael, Miss," Ann responded with a curtsy. "I'll bring the collection with me when Erin and I come back to do your hair."

After Anne left, Bridget turned to Tawnyetta. "Are you feeling guilty or something?"

"No, why?" Tawnyetta popped a red grape into her mouth.

Bridget gave her friend a knowing look. "You're being extra friendly."

"Friendly's not bad, is it?"

"I guess not." Bridget poured the tea while eyeing Tawnyetta.

Wanting to change the subject, Tawnyetta brought up a tidbit she knew Bridget could not ignore. "Have you decided which lipstick you're going to wear tonight?"

Bridget's eyes sparkled with delight. The distraction worked like a charm.

After they had applied their makeup with the utmost care, they complimented each other's looks. Each of them had done up their eyes with some extra drama and had new shades of lipstick for the evening. Bridget had chosen a deep pink that complemented her blonde, blue-eyed complexion and her pale pink dress. Tawnyetta had opted for a medium coral. With her amber eyes and the green in her dress she thought it added enough color without clashing.

Anne and Erin arrived, bringing with them a wide, shallow box with a heavy wooden lid inlaid with silver. Inside the box was a plush, red velvet interior where bejeweled hair combs, hair pins, barrettes and hair bands were carefully placed. Anne informed them that the items were from the personal collection of the late Lady MacBrody. Tawnyetta was stunned at how beautiful they were.

"How kind of Laird MacBrody to let us borrow these," Tawnyetta said. She picked up a set of hair pins that sparkled with diamonds and dark blue sapphires.

"He's very generous that way," Anne said proudly. It was clear she had a lot of respect for her employer. Tawnyetta felt a twinge of sadness for her again. If only Anne could see the truth in her fiancé and perhaps seek out someone more kind and generous like Laird Michael who she admired so much.

"Oh, Tawny," Bridget exclaimed, reaching for two large hair combs. "These would be gorgeous on you."

The combs shone silver and were encrusted with jewels. Diamonds and Peridot, a pale, almost lime green colored stone, shone as if they were lit from the inside.

"Those would look perfect with your dress," Anne said. "If you don't mind me saying so."

Tawnyetta watched in the mirror as Anne and Erin worked magic on her short, spunky locks. They used hairspray and pins, adding the gorgeous Peridot combs, sweeping her hair up and giving it extra body. Their skill made it look like Tawnyetta had longer hair than she truly did and showed off the elegant lines of her neck and shoulders.

They went to work on Bridget until her long, blonde hair was a resplendent pile of curls sitting high on her head. When their hair was perfect, the maids helped them carefully into their dresses and then their shoes. Once they were completely dressed, Anne and Erin stood on their toes to drape the necklaces from the jeweler around their necks.

Bridget had chosen a lacy diamond collar that stretched from the middle of her neck down to her collarbones. Tawnyetta had chosen a simpler, solid diamond encrusted necklace in a circle shape that held a huge diamond teardrop pendant in the center. The matching triple teardrop earrings fell gracefully along her bare neck.

When they were finally ready and stood looking into the full-length mirror, it was quite astonishing how regal they both looked.

"My goodness," Bridget smiled at their reflection. "We clean up nice, don't we?" She took Tawnyetta's elbow in her arm.

"Let's go to a ball," Tawnyetta said.

They made their way down the spiral staircase from the castle keep to Stag Hall. Inside they found the Prescotts donned in their finest. The table was set with glittering white china, silver and crystal.

The Prescott men all wore tuxedos in the same droopy, unassuming manner that they wore their normal clothes. Still, Tawnyetta had to admit that they looked nice. Bea was beautiful in her brand new golden gown. Her hair had been done up as well and her sapphire and diamond necklace that she'd chosen at the jewelry store sparkled around her neck. Tabitha wore a mint green gown that completely washed any color she did have out of her face. The resulting chartreuse pallor of her skin gave her the appearance of someone who was mildly ill. Mrs. Prescott wore a light mauve gown that was cut well and obviously well made. But beyond being functional as a formal gown, it lacked a certain romance and gave her the air of an out of date duchess.

As they stood in the entryway to Stag Hall, a picture of flowing pink and green, Tawnyetta felt Bridget's hand tighten around her arm. She glanced over and saw not only excitement in Bridget's eyes, but a hint of anxiety as well. It made sense. Bridget had suffered recent public humiliation at her last formal affair–her wedding. Being all dressed up and on display again might cause her some trepidation.

Tawnyetta put her hand over Bridget's hand and gave her an encouraging smile. "Shall we?" she asked. Bridget nodded, her crown of curls bobbing up and down as she did. Then they entered the room.

Stewart, looking crisper than ever, stood like a gentry staring somewhere into the space near them, but not directly at them, waiting to move until he was needed. Beautiful violin music pumped into the room. Or that's what she thought at first. Scanning the room, Tawnyetta was pleasantly surprised to see a live violinist in the corner of the hall playing a light, beautiful tune.

"You two look positively scrumptious," Bea said as she came to them, all sparkly and smiling.

Bridget reached out to her and took her hand. "You too, Bea. You look divine."

They proceeded to the table where they were seated by servers Tawnyetta did not recognize. Several more young men stood straight as rods against the walls of the dining hall. They were dressed in starched black, grey, and white livery that almost matched Stewart's butler uniform, but not quite.

When Tawnyetta sat at her place she had to take a few moments to think back to the etiquette she'd learned during her middle class upbringing in the suburbs of Denver. Not too surprising, there hadn't been much. Several plates of the thinnest, whitest china she'd ever seen were stacked delicately in front of her and topped with a small porcelain crock pot complete with an elegant lid shaped like the head of a deer. There was a heavy crystal goblet full of water and three additional wine glasses of varying sizes. If that didn't intimidate her, she counted three knives, three forks and five spoons at her place setting–five!

Tawnyetta was no longer worried about Bridget's anxiety, because she was busy trying to suppress the butterflies in her own stomach. What had her Aunt Jeannie always said? Start with the silverware on the outside and work your way in? That's what she would have to do and hope for the best.

As soon as they started the first course Tawnyetta lost track of her concerns about using the correct silverware. Eight of the servers, one per guest at the table, approached them so silently that when a white gloved hand appeared to whisk the deer head lid off of her dish, Tawnyetta jumped a little in her chair. Bridget let out a little squeal that she managed to disguise as a hiccup. Still, they could barely contain their giggles.

Inside the exposed dish was a pale orange soup, thick and surprisingly toasty warm despite having been sitting on the table for more than a few minutes while they were seated. Tawnyetta dipped into the first course with what she was fairly confident was the soup spoon and took a bite. Shallots, potato, cream, carrots and thyme. Delicious.

"I hear Claymore Castle has procured a Michelin starred chef for special events," Mr. Prescott announced to the table.

"Mmhmm," Mrs. Prescott agreed, eagerly swallowing her first spoonful. "This is very good. I wonder who the chef is?"

Tawnyetta found it a little insulting for hard working, fun-loving Doreen, the cook, that she wasn't getting credit for the soup. It wasn't impossible to believe that Doreen could have cooked up such a wonderful dish, but Tawnyetta didn't want to argue. She wanted to eat her soup before it got cold.

Once they all finished the first course the eight servers approached the table and removed the top plate that held the soup dish from the stack of plates in front of them. The servers then disappeared from the room soundlessly. In less than a minute they returned, each balancing a single dish on their upturned gloved fingertips. They positioned themselves just behind and out of sight of each guest, one server per every seated diner. On an unseen cue they all leaned forward and slipped the next course in front of the guests like some coordinated dance move. Tawnyetta almost laughed out loud at the formality of it all. She caught herself before that happened, however, and instead shared an astonished look with Bridget.

By the time their dinner was only halfway done, Tawnyetta was too full to eat another bite. She had lost count after the fourth course, but thought they may have had eight full courses before a fruit and cheese plate was offered. She could only nibble at the delectable items put in front of her. The food was wonderful, but rich, and more than she was used to eating at one time. Besides, she didn't want to get too full before the ball even started.

"Dessert will be served in the ballroom," Stewart announced.

It was time to go.

Tawnyetta's hands were sweaty and damp. She used her cloth napkin to dry them before placing it in what she hoped was an elegant looking pile next to her empty wine glass.

She leaned closer to Bridget and whispered, "I'm so nervous."

"I am, too. But it's exciting, isn't it?" Bridget responded in a low voice. "It's a real ball in a real castle. It's like we're Cinderella...times two! Plus we get to meet Laird Michael–and maybe dance with him!" Her face flushed pink.

The servers stood at the backs of their chairs and pulled them out so they could stand gracefully.

"Absolutely delicious meal," Mr. Prescott said to the room.

Mrs. Prescott perked up at the comment. "May we inquire as to the name of the Michelin chef who provided this fine cuisine?" The question was directed at Stewart.

Stewart lowered his head in a partial bow. "Of course, ma'am. The chef Laird Michael procured for this evening is Mrs. Marjorie Marston."

'Oohs' and 'Aahs' came from all of the Prescotts, but Tawnyetta didn't believe for one second that any of them knew who Marjorie Marston was before Stewart said her name. Especially Mrs. Prescott. She just liked to pretend she knew all of the best people.

As they left the table and were ushered out of Stag Hall and toward the Great Hall, Bridget and Tawnyetta walked arm-in-arm. It helped Tawnyetta's nerves to move around a little bit.

The violinist continued to play but his music faded as they moved into the Great Hall and toward the doors of the ball-room. They strolled past the entrance to the kitchen then past the weapons room. For a fleeting moment her memory of Shaun in the weapons room fluttered through her mind, then she pushed it aside. Tonight was not about reliving her past indiscretions with the unethical gardener. Tonight she would start fresh. Tonight marked the mid-point of their Scottish vacation and she had a feeling that it was more than that. This night was definitely a turning point of this trip, yes, but there was a strangeness in the air that made her think it was the beginning of something big. Having this experience was just the first adventure in a long line of adventures that was going to take her places she'd never imagined. She felt as if she was moving at a new vibration. Slow motion through the world.

They drew closer to the huge double doors of the ballroom. Tawnyetta had seen this room on her tour with Stewart, but it had just been a wide open space, unlit and uninhabited, echoing and lonely.

That was not the case tonight.

Music streamed out of the double doors as Stewart opened them with aplomb, finally drowning out the violinist in the distance and giving Tawnyetta her first view of the extravagant gala inside.

Chapter Thirteen

Great crystal chandeliers cast light that looked like so many diamonds tumbling down from the ceiling. The walls, nearly 30 feet high, held towering mirrors along one whole side of the ballroom. Windows on the opposite wall, the only outside wall in the room, looked out across the back of the estate that was lit with lamps along the pathways. The other two walls were covered with a golden wallpaper that had a dark green pattern of what might have been a family crest, Tawnyetta couldn't tell as it was just dark enough for the pattern to be seen with clarity. Wall mounted lights shimmered. Flickering candlelight behind their heavy cut crystal scattered the light across the gold and green walls and reflected on the massive mirrors so that droplets of light flew in all directions.

Stewart stepped through the doors and took up a position facing the crowd just to the left at the top of four steps that led down into the ballroom. All eyes turned toward them. From what Tawnyetta could see from her limited view behind all of the Prescotts, there might have been over a hundred people in the ballroom already.

Mr. and Mrs. Prescott, being the eldest, stood arm-in-arm next to Stewart. It appeared they had done this kind of thing before because they were perfectly calm as they looked out across the attentive crowd and waited for the butler to speak.

"Mr. and Mrs. James Prescott the second," Stewart announced in a booming voice that pushed its way into the room despite the orchestra's fervent playing.

Bridget squeezed Tawnyetta's arm and leaned over to whisper in her ear, "This is just like in the movies."

Tawnyetta nodded and smiled and tried not to be nervous, although the formality of everything was a bit overwhelming. Luckily, they were last in line and she had a chance to study the process as Stewart introduced each of the Prescott couples in turn and they moved down the steps into the waiting crowd. There, the other guests greeted them warmly and shook their hands.

Finally it was her and Bridget's turn. Since they did not have escorts, they were announced individually. Stewart indicated Bridget should step up next to him. So she did.

"Miss Bridget Long," Stuart boomed.

Tawnyetta watched the faces of the other guests as they gazed at Bridget in her form fitting pink gown and abundant blonde curls. They weren't used to seeing someone as unapologetically gorgeous, Tawnyetta realized. In fact, they looked literally stunned, which is why the word so often used to describe Bridget was 'stunning'. Tawnyetta could only see the back of her friend, but Bridget must have smiled at the crowd because several women and all of the men smiled back, some of them bowing their heads slightly in her direction.

Tawnyetta watched as Bridget moved down into the crowd. Now it was her turn. She threw her shoulders back and smoothed the green silk on the front of her dress. Taking a deep breath she stepped as gracefully as possible next Stewart.

She smiled at him nervously. He caught her eye and tilted his head in an encouraging gesture.

"Miss Tawnyetta Campbell," Stewart announced, his voice pressing against the swelling waltz that filled the room.

Her nerves took over and she was unable to smile. She simply tried to make eye contact with as many of the guests as possible and not look afraid. Quickly, her moment in the spotlight was over and Stewart gave her the slightest tilt of his head to indicate she could join the others. With relief washing over her she turned to join the crowd and forgot about the four steps she had to walk down to get there. She took one great stride forward, but her foot didn't find solid ground and she hung in the air awkwardly, alarm shooting through her body. Her arms flew out as she tried to catch her balance. Despite this reflex and every muscle in her body straining to lean back and steady herself, Tawnyetta knew with sickening certainty that she was about to fall down the stairs.

A strong hand grabbed her elbow and pulled her to the landing. She glanced back to find Stewart holding her arm, still averting his eyes and acting as if nothing at all had happened.

"Watch your step," he said quietly.

She got her balance quickly and said, "Thank you." Turning to look over the crowd she saw that they were either politely ignoring the fact that she had almost fell on her face or they hadn't seen it happen. Deciding to focus on the latter, Tawnyetta stepped into the ballroom, gratefully taking Bridget's hand. Soon they were lost in the sea of music and people.

Voices rose around her in greeting. Some were definitely Scottish, some had British accents, but there were no other Americans that she could hear. It was difficult to discern exactly what people were saying to her over the music. But she nodded and shook hands when they were offered and tried to look as receptive and poised as possible.

Being in the midst of the ball was even more magical than

seeing it through the doorway. Men in black tuxedos, some wearing kilts of various reds and greens and black tartans where their trousers would normally be, and women in bright, flowing gowns and glittering jewels, filled the room so Tawnyetta could not see the floor. The crystallized light from the chandeliers shimmered through the air over them. Tiny sparkles seemed to be floating on the sound of the music, moving with each note. The experience was all encompassing and Tawnyetta thought she might lift into the air on the energy in this room.

She felt him before she saw him.

Warmth on the nape of her neck like a hot summer sun burning into her skin. Air moving and trickling across her shoulders, sending a shiver along the length of her spine.

She turned and locked eyes with him through the crowd. He wore a short, tailored, black tuxedo jacket and vest, a crisp white shirt with a charcoal silk tie, and a grey and black kilt with a black fur and silver sporran positioned so that it hung several inches below his waist in the dead center of the front of his kilt.

The orchestra started a darker waltz with a deep rhythm. The heavy thrumming rippled through her body. Twinkling lights moved slowly in a circle over the walls and orchestra and crowd, as if pushed by the sound of the song, like they were riding on a carousel and there was no way to get off.

Tawnyetta held her breath and could not look away from those deep blue eyes that were glued to her own. Shaun. In a kilt. Moving toward her with the rhythm of the waltz as if they were already dancing. As if they'd never stopped.

Her heart beat madly, but she didn't move. There were too many people surrounding her for her to escape without pushing and shoving. Worse than that, she didn't want to escape. Curse him and the quiet upturn of his mouth, the damnable fullness of his lips, the mesmerizing twinkle of mischief in his eyes. How was she supposed to tame her attraction to this devilishly handsome man? His eyes captivated her. The voices around her disappeared and all she could hear was the dramatic waltz. All she could see was Shaun moving steadily toward her, his gait unbroken by the crowd. Tawnyetta must be imagining things because it seemed as if the crowd parted in front of him and the tiny floating lights swirled and danced more feverishly through the air as he got closer.

Then he was there, standing inches away from her, looking down at her with such intensity she was sure he was going to kiss her.

"May I have this dance, Miss Tawnyetta Campbell?" His brogue was low, rolling over his tongue. Another shiver went down her spine.

"You've met already?" Mrs. Prescott said, sounding slightly put off at the idea. She and Bea stood on one side of Tawnyetta, Bridget on the other. Bea's eyebrows were raised in surprise. Bridget looked both impressed at the sight of this tall, dark and handsome Scotsman, and confused at his attention to Tawnyetta.

Tawnyetta pulled back from Shaun, realizing that their interaction must look bad considering he was an engaged man. "Yes, we've met, in the garden," she explained.

"We haven't met, yet," Bridget said brightly. She shot Tawnyetta a teasing glance, silently berating her friend for not telling her about her escapades in the garden. Bridget extended her hand toward Shaun.

He tore his gaze away from Tawnyetta and stepped back. Gathering himself, he stood up straight and looked politely at the other ladies.

Then, taking Bridget's hand and bowing, he said, "Please forgive me for not introducing myself, m'lady. I am Laird Michael MacBrody."

Chapter Fourteen

Tawnyetta's mouth fell open, but the shock of his words only lasted for a few moments before she let out a guffaw of disbelief. Her laugh was so course and loud it drew the attention of many people around them. Shaun seemed surprised at her outburst as well, which was ridiculous. He knew it was a joke. But when Tawnyetta took in the expressions on the faces surrounding her she could see that they did not believe he was joking at all.

"He's joking," Tawnyetta made an accusing gesture towards Shaun. "Or lying," she added with a tinge of snipe. Nobody moved.

Bridget blinked several times switching her gaze between Shaun and Tawnyetta. Mrs. Prescott pursed her lips together in a silent reprimand of all Americans and their ridiculous outbursts. Shaun, still holding Bridget's hand, looked back and forth between the two of them, baffled.

"I thought you said you'd met?" Bea interjected, trying to restore decorum to the situation.

Shaun let go of Bridget's hand and turned back to Tawnyetta. "We have. Several times," he said.

Put out by the calm way in which Shaun was impersonating Laird Michael and how everyone seemed to be going along with it, Tawnyetta shook her head. "You're not Laird Michael." The words blurted out of her at a volume that she didn't intend.

Shaun's eyebrows arched and one side of his mouth twitched up. "Am I not?"

"Of course this is Laird Michael," Mrs. Prescott scolded her.

Bridget's eyes moved down Shaun's body to his strong, muscular legs showing under his kilt. She considered those legs for an instant then shot Tawnyetta a look that said everything. They had both seen those legs before.

"I–I–" Tawnyetta was at a loss for words. Her disdain for Shaun and his antics turned to confusion and then mortification. Heat rose in her cheeks and she clamped her mouth shut to avoid saying anything else. Shaun and Laird Michael were the same person?

Laird Michael seemed to find the entire situation amusing. He reached his hand out to her, palm up. "Perhaps we can clear this matter up while we dance."

Tawnyetta looked down at his hand, wide and calloused in places. For lack of any better way of escaping the strange looks she was getting from everyone else, she placed her hand in his. His fingers, warm and strong, wrapped gently around hers.

Immediately, Shaun–or Laird Michael–turned and led her through the crowd, which indeed parted for him as he walked. Tawnyetta blushed furiously at her misunderstanding. Of course they had made way for him before, he was the Laird and this was his castle.

When they reached the edge of the dance floor, he turned to face her, slipping one hand around her waist and lifting the hand he already held into the air in a waltz position. Tawnyetta silently thanked her parents for forcing her to learn how to ballroom dance. At the time she had thought they were ridiculous, but her feet found the steps easily and she was able to move with some modicum of grace across the dance floor. At least if everyone thought she was a fool, they wouldn't think she was a fool who didn't know how to dance.

Sha—or Laird Michael, kept his gaze on her, a half crooked smile on his face. The corners of his eyes crinkled as he watched her and she knew he was enjoying her discomfort.

"If I'm not Laird MacBrody," he finally asked. "Who is it that you think I am, lass?"

Tawnyetta clenched her mouth shut and jutted out her chin, holding her head up high. She averted her eyes from his amused expression and stared fiercely at nothing nearby.

When she didn't answer, he grinned and cleared his throat to try again. "I take it you don't wish to talk about it?

She snapped her eyes back to him and said, "I don't like being teased. And I don't like being lied to."

"Ho ho," he chuckled as he turned her expertly around the far end of the dance floor. "And what did I lie to you about, exactly?"

Frustrated, and slightly out of breath, both from the shock of her realization of his true identity and the dancing, Tawnyetta answered, "You never said you were Laird Michael. You never introduced yourself."

Once again his eyebrows arched in amused surprise. "But who else would I be?"

She scowled in frustration. He let her think about her next move as he guided them through a particularly busy section of the dance floor. She wondered how long this song was and if, perhaps, she could get out of telling him anything else by just staying silent for the rest of their dance.

In those long moments of silence they moved across the floor as if they had waltzed many times together. He was an excellent dancer. All she had to do was hold her form and keep her feet in time to the three-step rhythm of the music and he took care of the rest. By applying barely perceptible pressure with his hands, the Laird of Claymore Castle twirled her across the floor. Their bodies were perfectly in tune with each other. As he gazed down at her Tawnyetta slipped under the spell of his deep blue eyes. It was difficult not to. He was so handsome, and dark, and masculine, with his short trimmed beard and tuxedo jacket. Their bodies were very close, though not touching. Still, she could feel the warmth of him. He smelled good, too. Like spring run off in the Rocky Mountains and rich spices.

She sighed inwardly. May as well admit her mistake. "I thought you were the gardener, Shaun," she told him.

It took a few beats for this information to penetrate Michael's mind. When it registered, he asked, "The caretaker's assistant?" She nodded. Michael threw back his head and laughed out loud, gaining the attention of the others on the dance floor.

"Shh," she said, glancing around apologetically. "You don't have to make a scene about it."

"Oh, sorry," he said, a twinkle in his eyes. He wasn't sorry.

They made another turn around the floor while Michael pondered the situation and Tawnyetta tried to focus on dancing.

"I suppose you wouldn't expect to see the Laird of the castle working in the garden," he conceded.

"Exactly!" she exclaimed, delighted he understood. "That's what I'm saying."

Michael chuckled again and shook his head. "Shaun. He's a wee scrawny lad. I've not been mistaken for him before."

"Is he? I wouldn't know, I guess." Tawnyetta's brow puckered. "I don't think I've ever seen him." Michael laughed out loud again. "And," she added, "He's engaged."

"That he is, indeed, to Anne." She could almost see the

wheels in his head turning. He looked at her with sudden understanding. "Is that why you were angry at me yesterday by Artemis?"

She blushed again then nodded.

Michael MacBrody, Laird of Claymore Castle, laughed out loud for the third time during their waltz, an unequalled event in some people's eyes. But he wasn't paying attention to anyone's eyes except for the amber eyes in front of him. He pulled Tawnyetta closer to him, just barely, so the chance of their body's touching increased tenfold as this song ended and the next began.

Four waltzes later he led her back to where he'd found her where Bridget and the others waited. Walking hand-in-hand, with the crowd once again parting to make way for them, Tawnyetta thought how odd it was that you could become so comfortable with someone after only 30 minutes. Dancing did that to people.

"Did you get everything straightened out?" Bridget asked. Her eyes flicked to their hands clasped together, then back to their faces.

Suddenly self-conscious, Tawnyetta slipped her hand out of his grip. "I think so. Apparently I mistook Laird Michael for the gardener." She shrugged as if this was an everyday occurrence.

"Get out!" Bea exclaimed.

"In her defense," Michael explained. "I do a lot of the outside work here. It relieves a wee bit of stress."

"I see," Bridget responded. Again her gaze switched between Tawnyetta and Michael. Tawnyetta felt uneasy, on the spot.

"Are you ladies enjoying the ball?" Michael asked politely.

"We are, thank you," Bea answered with a half curtsy. "My mother and father-in-law are burning up the floor."

Mr. and Mrs. Prescott could be seen moving stiffly, yet efficiently, across the dance floor.

"Have you had a chance to dance yet?" Michael asked Bea.

She flushed. Her face turned all red and splotchy under his attention. "Oh no, my husband is not one for dancing."

"I would be honored if you would dance with me." He held out his hand to Bea, whose splotches turned even brighter and a decidedly unladylike giggle bubbled out of her throat. Michael ignored her reaction and took her hand. "Please excuse us," he nodded to Bridget and then to Tawnyetta, holding her gaze for just a moment longer than was necessary.

As they disappeared into the crowd Bridget turned on Tawnyetta. "Oh my God! You've been hanging out with Laird Michael and you didn't even know it?"

"We weren't really hanging out," Tawnyetta said.

"He is gorgeous." Bridget peered through the crowd to watch as Michael and Bea began to dance. "Seeing him in that kilt!" Bridget pretended she was about to faint and fanned herself with her hand. "And," she whispered as she leaned closer to Tawnyetta, "We know what's under it!"

Bridget laughed and Tawnyetta did too, but Bridget's tone rang humorless in her ears. Tawnyetta felt so stupid. All this time she had been basically sneaking around behind her best friend's back while pretending to look for Laird Michael with her. Of course she hadn't been pretending. And she hadn't known she was sneaking around with Laird Michael himself. But still. She felt strange.

"Bridge," Tawnyetta began. She wanted to ask her how she felt about the situation. She wanted to clear the air regarding this unexpected man in their midst. If receiving the attentions of Laird Michael was going to put a rift between them, she didn't want to encourage him.

"There you are!" A familiar voice rang clear and strong through the crowd behind them. Tawnyetta and Bridget turned to see who it was.

Sofia! She stood with her arms out and up in the air, as if awaiting a group hug. Decked out in a splendid yellow ball gown that hugged her ample curves and made her dark skin and long, black locks look even more exotic than normal, Sofia's presence was astonishing. For a moment Tawnyetta thought she was seeing things, but then Bridget reacted.

"Fifi!" Bridget ran to Sofia, taking tiny little high heels steps. There was another squeal from just behind Sofia and Angie appeared. Her red hair cascading down a deep lavender dress with a fairy like tulle skirt. She waved excitedly at them both.

"What?" Tawnyetta stepped forward just in time to see Thomas in a tuxedo escorting Luna who wore a cream colored floor length dress reminiscent of the 1940's.

Angie came to Tawnyetta and gave her a big hug before holding her out at arm's length. "We're here!" she exclaimed. Then she looked Tawnyetta up and down appreciatively. "You look exquisite, Tawnyetta. Have you fallen in love or something?"

The friends all gathered in a circle in the middle of the ballroom.

"We look like an Easter basket with one chocolate and one white chocolate Easter bunny in it," Bridget said with a laugh, nodding towards Thomas in his black and Luna in her cream tones. They all agreed, except Thomas.

"I don't know if I like being compared to a bunny," he said.

Bridget laughed again. "Okay then, how about you're a black jelly bean!"

Thomas scoffed in mock disgust. "That's not much better."

"What are you guys doing here?" Tawnyetta asked.

"We wanted to join the fun," Thomas responded.

"It sounded like you two were having such a good time, we thought 'why not?'" Sofia answered. The others erupted into chatter about their surprise. All except Sofia. She leaned in to talk into Tawnyetta's ear. "We also thought you might like reinforcements to support Bridge in her time of need."

Tawnyetta smiled. "That's very kind."

Sofia looked around the ballroom and shrugged. "It's our pleasure, truly. I mean, we're at a ball!" This made Tawnyetta laugh. Sofia's expression shifted to concern. "Really, though, how has it been? Have you found time to have any fun yourself? Or have you been only taking care of Bridget?"

A stab of guilt penetrated Tawnyetta's chest. She felt bad for having forgotten so completely why she was on this trip to begin with and allowed Shau– *Laird Michael*–to be such a distraction.

She dipped her head in a quirky nod. "Oh, you know, a little bit of both."

"Well, you're not on your own any longer," Sofia took Tawnyetta's hand in hers and squeezed it warmly.

With a fleeting glance toward the dance floor where Michael and Bea could be seen swirling through the crowd, Tawnyetta determined to stick close to her friends, especially Bridget, for the rest of the evening. It was the reason she was here after all, and the least she could do for her best friend.

Chapter Fifteen

"It's enchanting!" Angie declared as she slowly twirled through their bedroom. Her arms flowed loosely at her sides as she pirouetted delicately across the open floor. Her wispy blue sundress fluttered. "Like Rapunzel!"

"You're far enough up here to be Rapunzel, that's for sure," Sofia agreed. She was perched on the side of the king size bed admiring the arched beams in the ceiling and the other architectural features of the room.

"We're in the keep," Tawnyetta informed them.

"The what?" Bridget asked, lifting her head from where she was rummaging through her suitcase.

"Oh yeah, the keep." Thomas nodded as if remembering. He was leaning against the stone fireplace. "That's where they would all hide during wartime. It's impenetrable."

"Yes, it's where all the most important things were kept so they couldn't be stolen," Tawnyetta explained from the chair near the windows overlooking the formal garden.

Luna sat in the other chair opposite Tawnyetta. She let her gaze wander around the room, taking in the space. "I suppose it's symbolic that Rapunzel was being held in the keep," Luna mused.

"So she was their most precious possession?" Sofia asked, a ring of annoyance in her voice at the fact that anyone ever treated women like possessions.

"Kind of like that, but slightly more romantic." Luna smiled at her cousin.

Tawnyetta watched the chaos that was Bridget getting ready for the day. They had planned a group outing to go into Eldin for lunch. Everyone was ready except for Bridget. She had insisted on repacking her purse and trying on different pairs of shoes to determine which looked best with her shorts and which would be the most comfortable. The day was overcast which meant it could rain. This made her decision making process even more complex.

"Of course the woman is the most precious possession," Bridget said.

Sofia arched an eyebrow at her. "Possession? The women were owned. That's not very romantic."

"Maybe you should focus on the word precious instead of possession," Thomas suggested.

Tawnyetta stood up and stretched her shoulders. She had kinks in her muscles and hadn't had time to do any exercising of any real kind in the last couple days. After all of the dancing last night she felt stiff. Waltzes, being mostly classical music, were extremely long. After dancing the first four with Michael, then one with Thomas, and once with each of the three Prescott men, there had been several more gentlemen who asked her to waltz. So many, in fact, that she successfully avoided Michael for the remainder of the night. Though this was a triumph in a way, it made her a little melancholy. She wanted to steer clear of him. She didn't want to get in the way of Bridget's fascination with the Laird of Claymore Castle. She closed her eyes and considered the fact that she'd been slowly getting to know the very man she'd been trying to help Bridget meet.

"Are you all right?" Luna asked.

Tawnyetta opened her eyes and looked down at Luna who was watching her the way that Luna watched everything, quietly and thoughtfully.

"I'm fine," Tawnyetta answered. "I guess I'm just a little sore."

"How long does it take to get to Eldin? Luna asked, eyeing Bridget who had taken several new shoe choices out of her suitcase and was trying them on.

"Maybe an hour?" Tawnyetta answered.

"And we'll all be squished in a car?" Luna clarified.

Tawnyetta nodded with reservation. There was only the one car for them to use and six of them total. Not including Allen who needed to drive them.

Sofia, Thomas, and Bridget were happily bickering about the difference between love and obsession, being precious to someone as opposed to being their possession, and how that translated into modern day romantic relationships. Tawnyetta sighed internally. She knew this was going to extend the amount of time it took Bridget to get ready. Wishing she could get outside and stretch her legs, she turned to look out the window.

That's when she saw him.

Michael, wearing his humble gardener clothes, was pushing his tools in a wheelbarrow up to the fountain. The moment she saw him, Tawnyetta's stomach trembled. She chastised herself quietly for reacting, but did not look away.

He lifted tools out of the wheelbarrow and placed them on the side of the fountain. She watched as he reached up with a wrench and twisted something so that he could remove the heavy top piece off of the fountain. As he set the piece carefully down on the ground, his muscles strained a little bit at the effort, and she thought about those same strong arms wrapped around her on the dance floor.

The sensations rushed back to her in an instant. The sound of the music, the way it seemed they were floating across the dance floor in perfect unison. His scent, spicy and fresh. His hand on her waist, holding her as close as possible without breaking form. His voice, deep and gentle. The way he chuckled as he teased her while they danced. The twinkle in his eyes.

She wanted him to hold her again, to look down at her with amusement in his eyes and try to get her to tell him what was on her mind.

Suddenly, Michael straightened up from his work on the fountain and turned toward the window. He looked straight up at her as she watched him.

She sucked in her breath, her heart skipping a beat. Could he see her? She was sure he could. She was sure he was looking directly at her.

She should step away from the window and not be so obvious. She should turn and join the conversation with her friends and put him out of her mind. But Tawnyetta found that she couldn't move. Her feet were stuck to the floor, her eyes were locked on Michael in the garden below.

"Tawny?" Luna's voice, soft and concerned came to her. "Are you all right?"

She forced herself to take a step back even though Michael still gazed up at her from the ground. "I'm fine," she said.

"Maybe you need some fresh air? Or," Luna looked at her meaningfully. "Maybe you should take some time for yourself. You've been here for Bridget all week. I'm sure there's time for you to take a walk or something before we're ready to go."

"Yes," Tawnyetta nodded. She couldn't form words. Her heart had started pounding, forcing blood quickly through her veins, making her light headed. "I would like to take a walk."

She needed to be alone, she knew that much. To avoid Michael in the formal garden, she slipped out one of the side entrances of the castle. This placed her right where the path opened up onto the wooded area, which offered a welcome retreat from the more landscaped sections of the estate.

The path leading into the woods was crude. Her feet crunched on it as she walked. The pebbles and debris were undisturbed, showing that it wasn't followed very often. That was fine with her.

Tawnyetta strode quickly along the path through the woods, taking deep breaths of cool morning air. The sun had not yet made an appearance today and she could see patches of the overcast sky through the tops of the trees. Filling the sky above her with their deep green branches, the trees smelled lush and wet. It was like another world inside these woods, like she was miles away from everybody and everything.

As Tawnyetta walked she tried to work out why she couldn't get a grip on her feelings for Michael. He was handsome and everything, but he was just some person flitting through her world. He had only been in her life for one week. Not long enough to mean anything. Besides, she would be going home in one more week, to the other side of the world almost.

That thought increased her melancholy.

"Stupid," she mumbled under her breath. Meeting some man, even a very good looking, charming man who owned a castle, was no reason for her to go off the deep end and feel so incapable and silly. None of this was necessary. She could enjoy her vacation without getting all worked up over some guy. She was in Scotland on vacation, living in a castle for heaven's sake, she needed to get a grip.

Suddenly the forest opened up into a clearing. The trees

thinned to nothing and the path led into thick, green grasses, where plants with pointing purple flowers grew in patches. Was this the famous heather of the Highlands? As she looked down the path she could see that it rose up into a grass covered hill. And after that hill there was another, and hill upon hill beyond.

The beauty enticed her. A cool breeze brushed against her cheeks, carrying the scent of the hills, calling her to explore.

What she needed was to work off some of this frustration, get some endorphins going in her brain, build up a good exercise induced sweat. She glanced behind her at the path that led back to the castle. She turned back toward the hills and took another deep breath of the clean, cool breeze. She decided she would just run up to the top of the first one and look around. It shouldn't take too long.

Ten minutes later she was halfway up the first hill. It was higher than she'd originally thought–and wilder, too. The landscape wasn't smooth or manicured, but full of dips and craggy rocks that jutted up unexpectedly. Though this made it more of a challenge to climb, there was a rough path for her to follow and it felt good to push herself a little and release some tension.

A bubbling, cheerful sound caught her attention and Tawnyetta stepped off the path to look for the source. She was rewarded a few feet away when she came across a stream tumbling happily through the thick green grass and purple heather.

Pausing for a moment, Tawnyetta looked up the hill where the stream came from and followed it with her eyes as it bubbled past her feet and down the hill back toward the castle. She could see the very top of the keep from this position, but not much else due to the woodlands below. She wondered briefly if Bridget was still trying on shoes, then she looked toward the peak of the hill. If she could make it all the way to the top, she should have a good view of the castle and all of its surroundings.

Following the stream instead of the path was a little more cumbersome, but just as satisfying. The air was still cool, in fact it seemed a little cooler now that she was high above the woodlands. The overcast sky blocked the warming rays of the sun ensuring she wouldn't get too worn out. The fresh air and quiet sounds of nature were all she needed right now. Birds chirped nearby and the water in the stream splashed and gurgled pleasantly.

Almost at the top she came over a low rise where the landscape dipped down in the shape of a large oval before turning into the final slope that led to the peak. The large oval space was almost concave, like it may have originally been a lake that etched out this shape in the land before drying up and allowing grass to take over. The stream led directly through the middle of the oval and, to her delight, Tawnyetta saw an ancient stone bridge that crossed the stream at the lowest point in the dip.

The bridge looked wide enough for a compact car to cross, though there were no roads in sight leading to it from either side. It stretched much wider and higher than necessary to cross the small stream. This led Tawnyetta to believe it had been built when the stream was the size of a river, perhaps hundreds of years ago. The stone was loose and crumbling in places, yet solid in others. She carefully walked over the top of it to see how sturdy it was and came to the conclusion that it was probably considered a ruin more than an actual bridge. Still, it was lovely and an enchanting feature in the landscape.

The clouds hung lower and looked thicker from her new vantage point nearly at the top of the hill. The soft, cool breeze she'd felt earlier came in shorter, stronger gusts. She realized that it might be getting ready to rain and she should probably finish her walk and get back to the castle.

Determined to make it all the way to the top, she trudged up the last steep slope of the hill using clumps of grass to hold and steady herself on the most precarious sections. The climb along the stream was so difficult she had to abandon it and just head toward the top of the hill. Upon reaching the pinnacle she turned to see the view and was instantly triumphant. From where she stood she could look down the slope across the woodlands and see Claymore Castle with all of its surrounding estate.

Tawnyetta took in a deep breath and was struck at how truly beautiful the great stone castle was in the vista. She could even see some of the farms and pastures in the countryside beyond the castle. Like a picture postcard of beautiful places to visit in Scotland, Claymore Castle and all that surrounded it was a sight to behold.

Cold, wet gusts of wind buffeted her with more vigor. The tails of her blue, cotton shirt flapped madly as her hair was tossed into a frenzy. She was happy for the wind. It refreshed her after her long climb. She took in another deep breath. How many people had stood in this place, in these hills, and looked down at the castle during the years since it had been built? The thought gave her goose bumps.

A low rumble sounded in the heavy cloud cover. Tawnyetta turned to look at the wild hills that lifted higher behind her. These beautiful, ancient peaks were still left to be explored and a piece of her didn't want to go back. However, her years of hiking in the Rocky Mountains gave her enough experience to know she shouldn't lose sight of the castle. Besides, if a thunderstorm was on its way staying on top of a hill wasn't the smartest idea.

When she turned around to head back from whence she'd came and gasped out loud at what she saw. Which was to say, nothing. Absolutely nothing–except fog.

The thick grey clouds that had been hanging in the sky

had sunk down over her and covered the top of the hill rapidly. She was disoriented for a few moments as she realized what had happened. Turning around again, she found fog blocking the view of the higher hills she had just been admiring. It had surrounded her on all sides in a matter of seconds. She needed to climb down. But which way had she come from? All she could see now was thick, white fog. No castle or broken down bridge were in sight. There was nothing to guide her way.

Tawnyetta felt panic rise in her stomach. She fought the urge to turn in a circle searching for a sign of the castle in the distance. That would make it impossible for her to determine which way was the correct way down.

"Calm down," she said out loud. The sound of her voice in the fog was eerie and she pressed her lips together to keep from speaking out loud again.

She looked at her feet and the ground stretching out about five feet around her in each direction. That's as far as she could see, but all she needed was to look for signs of her climbing up. She hadn't been too careful, surely she had left behind a footprint or some trampled foliage. From there she would just move downward, hopefully encountering the stream or the path or the bridge so she would know what direction to go to get back to the castle.

She found a depression in the earth that could only be a shoe print from her tennis shoes and breathed a sigh of relief. Using that as her guide she walked purposefully, if almost blind, into the low hanging fog.

Chapter Sixteen

Making her way down a steep slope through fog as thick as pea soup was difficult enough, but just as she started to feel she was making headway the misty feeling of fog against her skin turned to chilling rain drops.

She cursed under her breath. Rain. Great.

Rain would make everything harder and more uncomfortable. With the wind picking up it would be cold. It was already slow going since her visibility was almost nil. Scooting down the hill on her rump to avoid falling forward, Tawnyetta had to lean back and hang on to clumps of grass as she slid her feet sideways in careful steps.

More than once she lost her grip on one of the clumps of grass and had to scramble to find another one. Her little morning jaunt was turning into a nightmare. Tawnyetta shook off the negative thinking. No amount of worrying or complaining was going to get her down this hill any faster. She focused on carefully descending the rough landscape as the wind gusts picked up, bringing with them stinging rain.

She was surprised at the ferocious suddenness of the

storm. She was also seriously disappointed in her planning and the fact that she had not taken into account the fact that she would have to move much slower while going down than she did on the way up. As she maneuvered, the rain grew heavier. The wind whipped and pummeled icy cold drops against her body, like someone spraying her with a garden hose. Within a very short time she was soaking wet and cold. Very cold.

The ground beneath her felt spongy. Trickles of water from the rain crept down the hill and around the clumps of grass she was using to stabilize her descent, turning what had been solid ground into slippery mud. Tawnyetta decided she would aim for the bridge and take cover there until the rain stopped. That is, if she was heading toward the bridge.

A smack of lightning crackled through the air and she let out a small cry of surprise. Startled, she was thrown off balance and grabbed for a nearby clump of grass, but missed. The mud slipped underneath the rubber soles of her tennis shoes. They weren't built for climbing. Before she knew what was happening Tawnyetta was falling down the slope through the fog, unable to see where she was going. She cried out again, flailing desperately to grab hold of the grasses that were now moving past too quickly to grip. At the bottom of the slope she landed hard and sideways and felt a pop in her ankle.

Pain shot up her left calf into her knee. She cried out for the third time then crumpled and sat down hard in the mud favoring her left ankle. The rain was coming in sheets, soaking her to the bone. Water ran down her face and into her eyes, blinding her. Lightning flashed across the sky and she knew, broken ankle or not, she had to find cover.

Afraid to put pressure on her foot, Tawnyetta crawled in the direction she hoped the bridge lay. Wincing at the pain in her ankle as well as the rocks and pebbles that dug into her knees as she crawled, Tawnyetta blindly felt for any sign that she was getting close to the bridge. In a few minutes, which felt like hours, she found the stream.

She could have cried with relief. If her memory served her right the bridge would be about 30 or 40 feet downstream from where she was at the base of the steepest slope.

By the time her hands finally felt the crunching ancient stone under them, she was covered with mud. Rainwater ran off of her in buckets and her shorts and shirt were so wet they stretched out and hung off her body as if they were three sizes too big.

Gratefully, she crawled under the bridge. Sharp stones surrounded it and dug painfully into her palms and knees, but at least she was out of the rain. She scooted to one side of the bridge and leaned against the solid stone, catching her breath.

Her ankle throbbed. She pushed her soaking wet hair out of her eyes, smudging mud from her hands along the side of her face and into her hair. She brushed her kneecaps and palms where small stones had pressed into them and stuck. As they tumbled to the ground they left little pockmarks in her skin. When that was done, Tawnyetta braced herself and took a look at her ankle.

It was already swollen, puffed up and angry, but it was not sticking out sideways or anything horrible. Gritting her teeth, she focused on moving her toes. Success! This was a good sign. She moved her foot up and down and side to side an inch each way to make sure it wasn't broken. It wasn't, which was also good. But it might be sprained from the look of the swelling.

The rain still came down fast and hard. Gusts of wind blew under the bridge, spattering her every now and then with droplets. She started to shiver and wondered how long this rain could possibly go on. In the short time she'd been in the Highlands, it seemed the rain lasted a while once it settled in. This realization alarmed her, but what alarmed her more was the fact that nobody knew she was up here.

"This could be a very long day," she said to herself. Another bout of shivers hit her and she rubbed her arms with her hands to try and warm up. Her fingers felt like icicles against her skin.

Tawnyetta grew up hiking in the Rocky Mountains and was aware of the dangers of hiking alone. She had broken every rule today. She'd hiked up the hill wholly unprepared, carrying no supply of water or any kind of jacket to protect against the elements. She had even left her cell phone in her purse at the castle, though she doubted there was a signal out here. Still, it would have been wise to bring it with just in case. All of these beginner outdoorsman bumbles paled in comparison to her most foolish mistake–not telling anyone where she was going.

"Stupid," she chastised herself out loud while peering at the heavy rain pouring down on both sides of the bridge.

Waterfalls had formed from the rain pouring off the stone, adding to the tumbling stream. She hadn't taken these hills seriously. Compared to the 14,000 foot mountains she'd tackled back home, these hills had looked so inviting and, well, small. Big mistake.

Another crack of thunder interrupted her thoughts. It was difficult to see through sheets of rain and she had not noticed any flash of lightning, but that clap of thunder was much closer than the others had been. The pain in her ankle deepened and cold crept into her bones. Miserable, stuck, and injured she watched the stream roiling with all of the extra rainwater and realized there was one more thing she could add to her list of problems–flash floods.

Flash floods came fast and furious during sudden downpours. The rain pummeling the top of the hill would naturally flow through this low area. Her position under this bridge was a terrible place to be if the water rose. A sense of dread filled her as she thought of this decidedly real possibility.

Trying to remain calm, she debated which danger was the

least in this situation; a flash flood under the bridge, or being hit by lightning, or falling down some uneven spot in the land as she tried to maneuver with a bum ankle. Before she could decide Tawnyetta heard something shift on the stones overhead. At first she thought it was only the natural movement of loose stones under this heavy rain. But the scraping and clumping that followed was definitely being made by something else. Perhaps an animal. Or a human.

Immediately her senses went on high alert. She didn't know which she would rather have, a wild animal of some kind sniffing around or an unknown man or group of men who found her huddled and injured. She was vulnerable and unable to stand or run away. Were there bears in the Highlands? Or maybe wild boars? Or were they warthogs? Her mind flew back to meeting Clark on the plane and all of his stories about the strongmen of the Highlands. His stories had been full of excessively masculine, wild, and uncontrollable beast-like men. Surely they wouldn't be out in this kind of weather.

Another scraping sounded.

Tawnyetta looked around for some kind of weapon and found a rock the size of a large orange. She hoisted it and made sure she had a good grip. If it was a bear, should she hit it on the nose or remain still? What should she do if it was a wild boar? Or a Highlander man?

The scraping and clumping grew louder as whatever it was moved along the edge, then silence. She held her breath. The sheet of water pouring over the sides of the bridge obscured her vision so badly it was impossible to know what was out there.

Suddenly a shadow interrupted the glassy sheen of the water.

"Who's there?" She tried to sound tough and angry.

A boot stuck through the water, then a leg, and a body

quickly followed. It was as if the water was giving birth to a full-grown man who had to crouch after entering the world because clearance was low under the bridge. It all happened so fast she went into action without thinking, raising the rock up over her head and shouting out something unintelligible.

The man looked up through dripping hair and her fear collapsed. Michael.

Looking like he'd just climbed out of a swimming pool fully dressed, he broke into a surprised smile. The kind of open mouthed glee that happens when children play hide and seek and finally come across the person they've been seeking.

"Here you are!" he said.

She was still too surprised to answer. Here she was expecting a bear or a warthog or the wild Highland Scottish men ready to manhandle her under the bridge. Instead it was Michael. A wild Highlander in his own right, she supposed, but definitely not as frightening as a warthog.

He was soaking wet. The work clothes she'd seen him in this morning hung like so many flopping rags from his body. But still, he was here. She was saved.

Without looking for a response from her, Michael glanced quickly at the stream that was rushing faster and higher than it had been only a minute ago.

He looked back at her, his face a mix of stern worry. "We can't stay here. The water's rising." Still crouching he took a few steps toward her and offered his hand. "Let's go."

"My ankle," she said miserably, pointing at her left leg. "I can't."

His eyes traveled down her body and rested on the fat bulge that used to be her ankle.

"Damn," he said under his breath. Then he lifted his eyes, pools of dark blue concern, back to hers. "Can you walk at all, lass?"

Lass. The word melted her chilly core. Even in these circumstances he charmed her.

"I don't think it's broken," she said. "But I can't walk on it very well."

Michael looked at the stream, then back at her, then back at the stream. He pressed his lips together and made a decision. Without warning he dropped to his knees and pushed one arm around the small of her back and the other arm under her knees, pulling her towards his chest.

"Can you grab my neck?" he asked, his body warm against hers.

She did the best she could to wrap her arms around his neck though her muscles were stiff with cold. Without another word, Michael hoisted her off the ground and stood halfway up, hunched over to avoid hitting his head.

She started to protest, but was quickly quieted by the sheer effort of his body. His muscles strained around her, yet never held her too tight. All she could do was obediently keep her arms around his neck so he wouldn't have to worry about her falling. She let him carry her through the waterfall and it felt like someone tossing a bucket of cold water over them. Once outside they were immediately drenched again with torrential rains.

"Hold on," he shouted over the monsoon. She buried her face into the nape of his neck where it was warm and semi-protected from the water. Gripping her freezing fingers as best she could behind his neck, Tawnyetta held on as he ran with her in his arms. She had no idea where they were going.

Everything was a blur of sensations. The strength of his arms holding her aloft, the warmth of his chest, the sound of his heavy breathing, the ice cold rain hitting her back and legs, drenching her hair so that rivulets ran down her scalp while her face stayed protected, buried into Michael. She couldn't use her hands to wipe the rain away from her eyes and she knew he couldn't use his either. How was he seeing where they were going? Did he have any idea where they were?

Michael stumbled a few times, but kept her firmly in his arms as he steadied himself. His running slowed into a fast trudging. They were moving uphill. His breathing came harder and harder. She could feel his heartbeat against her cheek. She was about to tell him that she could try and walk when the rain gave way and he stopped.

She hesitated and thought about pulling her head back to see where they were. But then she felt his body lift then lunge. He grunted with effort. There was a loud crash of wood and she whimpered into his neck.

"It's all right, lass," he said calmly, though he was out of breath. His voice was easier to hear. The sound of the storm had lessened. Raindrops no longer stung her back.

She lifted her eyes from his neck just as he bent over and placed her carefully down on a seat. She tried her best to wipe the water out of her eyes. They were inside a small shack of some kind. It looked old, made of stone with a peaked roof held up by rough hewn beams. The wooden door hung crookedly on its hinges, having just been kicked in. Pieces of splintered wood lay shattered on the floor. Outside the rain still poured.

Tawnyetta shivered uncontrollably. Michael pulled his denim work shirt off and let it fall sloppily to the floor. Underneath he had a lighter white shirt that was so wet it stuck to his skin, making the material almost see through. Tawnyetta only had a few moments to notice his physique underneath the thin film of cloth before he pulled the sticky wet shirt up and over his head and stood before her bare chested.

She had a sudden flash of watching his thickly muscled back and buttocks dancing down the hallway as she and Bridget spied from behind the door. This time she had a front row seat and noticed that he had a tattoo on the left side of his chest over his heart. A circle with some kind of Celtic symbol inside. She stared at the tattoo.

Michael stopped undressing and turned his attention to her, his expression humorless. With zero tact and even less grace, he said, "Get with it, lass. You're fair drookit. Take off your clothes."

Chapter Seventeen

"Wh-what?? Tawnyetta stuttered, partly from being cold, but mostly from shock.

Michael gestured to his soaking wet pants. "We have to get out of these wet clothes."

"I'm not–I'm not–,"she tried to speak, but was overcome with another wave of shivers.

"This is not the time to be modest, lass," Michael said.

She couldn't speak. Instead, she shook her head meekly.

"Here," Michael said as he produced a blanket out of nowhere and held it out to her. "You can cover up with this." His brow wrinkled as he watched her body trembling. "I'll not have you catch your death." He crouched down in front of her, placing the blanket over her knees. He reached up to the top button of her shirt and paused, a silent request for permission. "I promise not to look," he said.

She tried to work with him in removing her shirt, but her fingers weren't cooperating. So cold. She was so cold. Tremors moved through her and she gave up, letting Michael unbutton each button.

True to his word when it was time to pull her shirt off he

closed his eyes and did everything by touch. His hands found her shoulders and he pulled the sopping wet shirt off, throwing it on the floor next to his. Then he felt for the blanket and pulled it up and over her shoulders.

Still unable to control her fingers, Tawnyetta admitted, "I–I can't–I can't undo my bra."

Eyes still closed, a ghost of a smile flickered across Michael's face. He reached around her waist, careful not to touch her much. The tips of his fingers barely grazed her skin, yet even this caused another bout of shivers. When he had reached completely behind her, he ran a finger up her spine to find the clasp then undid her bra expertly. He pulled the satin shoulder straps down so she could wriggle out of it. Then he grabbed the edges of the blanket and pulled it tightly around her. He did not open his eyes until he was sure she was covered. When he did open them they were dark, like a storm at sea, and so close to her own that her heart twisted in her chest.

Black hair still dripping, and eyes twinkling with a hint of amusement, his presence made her head spin. His shoulders were wide and strong, his biceps rounded, his arms flexed as he held her blanket closed over her naked breasts.

"Better?" he asked.

She nodded. It was better. Her skin was still freezing and covered in goose bumps, but the shivering had died down as soon as Michael took off her wet clothes. And the blanket must be the warmest, softest blanket she'd ever felt in her life.

She managed a quivering smile. He smiled back, and when he did his eyes shone and crinkled at the edges. Her heart twisted again.

"Can you manage your shorts?" he asked.

She nodded.

Michael stood and snatched up another blanket from a small cupboard Tawnyetta had not noticed when they entered the room. He wrapped his blanket around his shoulders so that it hung down to his knees.

Then he looked at her and winked. "No peeking," he teased.

Before she knew it he had slipped his pants off and added them to the pile of sopping wet clothes on the floor. If Tawnyetta could have laughed, she would have, but she was shaking from the inside out, which prevented it. Still, she managed to stand up.

"Can you stand all right?" He eyed her ankle.

It was still aching, but she found that she could put weight on it without falling over. She nodded. Then, following his lead, she let the ends of her blanket fall. She was shorter, so her blanket reached all the way down to the floor and covered her whole body. Her fingers had already begun to thaw. Putting her back to him she used both hands to unbutton her shorts.

While she did this Michael kept busy at a tiny wood stove that was positioned in the corner of the room. He purposefully averted his gaze from her as she undressed, grabbing wood and paper and kindling from a wood box and filling the stove.

Her blanket gaped open in front as she worked the zipper on her shorts. When she bent over to push them down her legs it gaped even further, but she wasn't facing Michael so she didn't think it would matter. It was as she struggled to push her wet, unyielding shorts past her knees that she felt the blanket slip.

"Oh!" She yelped as it dropped with a soft plop at her feet, leaving her standing in her undies only, her wet shorts wrapped around her ankles like shackles.

At the sound of her distress Michael stood and turned quickly. Seeing her almost completely naked backside, he turned away from her even more quickly and faced the wall.

He cleared his throat. "Are you okay?"

Tawnyetta snatched the blanket up off the floor, her chilled fingers fumbling with the soft folds. "Yes, I'm fine." But she wasn't fine. She was mortified, and freezing.

There was an awkward pause as she adjusted the blanket so it was once again covering her whole body.

He cleared his throat again. "Do you need any help?"

She couldn't tell if he was sincere or being flirtatious. The reality of the fact that she was basically naked in a shack with a handsome Scottish Laird, who was also basically naked, sent her emotions all over the place. She was nervous and embarrassed, that was for sure, but she was also more than a little thrilled at their situation. She wondered if he was, too.

"I'm fine," she told him.

When she was completely covered and safely clutching the front of the blanket closed in front of her, she turned back toward him and was amused to find that he was still standing stiffly, staring at the blank wall. Cloaked in his blanket, his well formed calves sticking out from underneath, he looked like he'd been sent to the corner. She suppressed the urge to chuckle.

"I'm decent," she said, releasing him from his stance.

In short order they were sitting next to each in front of a cheerful fire in the wood stove. Michael had moved a bench directly in front of the stove and positioned Tawnyetta so that she received most of the heat that poured out of the front. There was just enough room on the bench for both of them to sit with their shoulders and arms touching. The crackling fire did more than warm her body. It helped her forget the relentless sound of pounding rain on the roof, not to mention their narrow escape from a flash flood.

"What is this place?" she asked.

"This is a bothy. They were built all through the hills to offer travelers and hunters shelter when they need it."

Tawnyetta let her eyes roam around the small, square building. It was equipped with three rickety old wooden benches and one twin size iron cot that held only the exposed bed springs, no mattress or bedding of any kind. In one corner of the room there were upper and lower cabinets along with a steel sink that looked more like an old bucket with a hand pump sticking out of one side. Besides that limited indoor plumbing, there were no lights and no electricity. But the fire crackling spunkily in the wood stove gave the room not only light, but a warm, comforting glow.

"So anybody can use it?"

"Yes, they're kept unlocked."

She glanced at the splintered wood from the door, which Michael had pushed back shut. "So it wasn't locked?" she asked.

"It was stuck...and I had my hands full," he answered.

"Thank you so much for coming to get me," Tawnyetta said. She looked sideways at Michael who had turned his attention back to the crackling, popping flames. Tawnyetta took a deep breath and admitted to him, "I wasn't prepared for the storm."

He nodded. "When the others said you were nowhere to be found and you may have gone on a walk, I remembered seeing you head into the woods. The Highlands are known for the wild weather that can turn on a dime." Not an ounce of regret or scolding in his tone.

"How did you know I came all the way up the hill?"

"I didn't know for certain. But the hills have a way of calling a person into them, so I thought I'd better check."

An interesting way of putting it, she thought. She had felt like the hills were calling her to climb higher and higher. Telling her that if she got to the top she could turn around and see the castle and the whole world beyond. It had been absolutely beautiful until the clouds came in. Tawnyetta looked down and pushed her toe through a layer of dust on the stone floor. This place had not been used in a while.

Michael looked at her and smiled. "I hope you don't feel foolish for getting caught in the rain. Those sudden storms could take anyone by surprise. Especially a wee American lass." He delivered the last comment with a grin.

She grinned back. "How often do travelers use this place?"

"Not often from the look of it," he answered. "It's been a while since I've been up here myself." His eyes wandered around the room and he appeared to be lost in thought.

"So, you used to come here?"

"Ach, yes." He didn't look at her when he spoke. "My brother and I used to come up here all the time when we were kids."

A twinge of sadness in his voice plucked at her heart. They fell silent and Tawnyetta watched him out of the corner of her eye as she pretended to gaze at the flames in the wood stove. He, too, watched the fire, but his thoughts were obviously far away. They stayed that way for a while until Michael took in a deep breath and came back to the present.

"In fact..." He stood up and Tawnyetta, newly reminded that he was not wearing any pants, averted her eyes. Michael went to the cupboard above the sink. "If I remember right." He opened the cupboard and rummaged around for a moment before exclaiming, "Here we are!" He held up a green and black tin to show her.

"What's that?"

"Tea!"

Now on a roll, Michael pulled a teapot out of the cupboard and blew the dust off the top of it. Using a corner of his blanket he wiped it clean then placed it in the old sink as he started pumping the hand pump.

He was making tea. The idea of it made her shiver. Hot tea would be wonderful right now.

Water spurted and gurgled out of the old pipe and Tawnyetta was afraid to look at it, thinking it would be a sickly brown color. Michael didn't seem fazed. He let the water run for a minute then rinsed and filled the tea kettle and placed it on top of the wood stove.

"Can I help?" She felt a little useless just watching him.

"Aye, you can put some more wood in the stove if you like."

Tawnyetta got busy stoking the fire, glad she didn't have to leave its warm glow. Meanwhile, Michael rinsed out two bent tin cups in the sink. Then he twisted off the top of the green and black tin and took a whiff of the contents.

"Still good," he said, pleased.

Soon steam pulsed out of the little spout on the kettle. Using the corner of his blanket again, this time as an oven mitt, Michael pulled the lid off. He tilted the open tin and poured some loose tea leaves directly into the bubbling water and replaced the lid.

His homey activities made Tawnyetta relax. The storm that pounded this little bothy didn't seem as terrible when they were playing house.

As they waited for the kettle to boil they spread their sopping wet clothes over the bare iron springs of the cot. Michael carefully lined up the seams of his shirt and slacks before laying them flat. It seemed the Laird of Claymore Castle was adept at doing laundry as well.

"You're kind of domestic for being royalty," she observed.

His eyes twinkled. "I'm not really royalty, not exactly. Besides, I am more of a replacement Laird."

"Oh, right," she said thoughtfully, "Your brother was Laird before you, wasn't he?"

A shadow flickered across his face and she couldn't believe she had said something so insensitive. She had two older brothers, much older. She'd been a surprise to her parent's retirement plans. Still, if anything ever happened to one of her brothers she would be devastated.

"I'm sorry, I didn't mean to ask you such a personal question," she said.

Michael looked down at his nearly nude body encased in a blanket then indicated her similar attire with a quick nod of his head. "I don't know if we could get much more personal than this if we tried."

Before she could stifle it, a giggle escaped Tawnyetta's lips. Michael grinned mischievously.

He swept his arm gallantly toward the bench. "Have a seat m'lady and I shall pour the tea."

They nestled comfortably on the old wooden bench, cupping hot tin cups full of steaming tea in their hands. Maybe it was her imagination, but it seemed like the rain had calmed some and it was now landing more softly on the roof.

"Do you have any siblings?" he asked.

"Two brothers, Kevin and Lonny," she answered. "Kevin is a salesman for a software company and Lonny owns a ski lodge in the mountains near Breckenridge. They were already in college before I was out of elementary school, but they're great guys. And I love their wives. They're more like my aunts than my sister-in-laws though," she explained.

Michael grunted his understanding as he took a sip of his tea. There was a lull in the conversation as he considered the steam rising from his cup. He didn't look up when he started talking.

"Greg and I were two years apart," he told her. "We grew up right alongside each other. Very competitive...in a good way for brothers I suppose."

"What were you competitive about?"

"Ach, well, just about everything really. Sports, grades...height!" He chuckled at that. He looked sideways at Tawnyetta and added, "Bonnie lasses."

She lifted her eyebrows. "Oh, really? Were you ever in love with the same girl?"

"I don't think either of us were ever truly in love growing up. But we did like to try and outdo one another by impressing the bonnie ones."

She wondered what that must have been like for whichever lucky girl the two young lords were competing over. Given genetics, Greg had probably been equally as impressive as Michael. It must have been quite an experience for a young lady to have them both vying for her attention.

Michael had a thought and craned his neck trying to look into the far corner of the room. "In fact..." he said, almost to himself, as he stood and went to the corner. He crouched down and scratched at an open space about the width of his finger between two stones in the wall. He was able to work his finger into the space and pull out one of the stones. It fell with a thud to the floor and Michael peered into the hole that it left. "I can't believe it."

"What is it?" Tawnyetta asked.

He reached into the hole and retrieved something then stood and turned to present it to her with a flourish. In his hand he held a fat, round bottle of amber liquid. She couldn't read the label, but knew that it definitely was liquor.

Michael brushed the rock dust off of the label and laughed a little as he read it out loud to her, "Aberlour, Highland Single Malt Scotch Whiskey."

"Why in heaven's name was it in the wall?"

Chapter Eighteen

Michael held up the bottle of whiskey with an expression of joy on his face similar to one a child might have if they actually won a toy out of a claw machine. Pure unadulterated happiness.

Tawnyetta was still full of questions. "How did you know that was in the wall?"

Michael inspected the bottle as he sat down next to her again. "My brother hid this up here when I was 16-years old."

"16?" She was surprised. Hard liquor for a 16-year-old?

Michael nodded thoughtfully, his eyes still on the bottle. "Greg took to drinking earlier than most." It wasn't a judgment or a statement of approval, he seemed to be lost in memories. Tawnyetta got the feeling they weren't necessarily good memories either.

"Did your parents know?"

He shook his head once. "No, they were lost in their own vices. And when you have several full bars scattered throughout a castle, it's an easy task to get your hands on liquor when you're a teenager."

Tawnyetta looked at the bottle in his hands and back at him. "But you didn't hide this bottle?"

"No," he said the word like it was a sigh, like he was admitting something not only to her, but also to himself. "Greg knew that I was bringing a lass up here. And he told me he'd hide this for me in our hiding place..." his voice trailed off.

"So you could get her drunk?" Tawnyetta was surprised again, not to mention offended.

"No, no, nothing like that. Well, at least I wasn't thinking of anything like that." He looked at her sincerely and she believed him. "I think on one hand Greg thought I needed to loosen up, I was always nervous around the lasses," he admitted. He hefted the bottle up and down a few times, feeling the weight of it. "And on the other hand I think he wanted to get me into trouble. Then he could show up like a knight on a white horse and save the day. Ride off with the pretty maid."

"The brotherly competition thing?"

He nodded.

"So what happened?"

"Neither," he answered. He thought for a moment. "If I remember correctly I froze like a deer in headlights and never even dug the bottle out. Greg showed up, unannounced, but he was completely blootered and that didn't go over well either."

"Blootered?"

"Drunk."

"Oh," Tawnyetta said. She made a 'yeesh' face. "That sounds awful."

Michael nodded. "Aye, it was."

"What did the girl do?"

"Well, she yelled at both of us, rightfully so. And then she made me take her home."

"She wasn't impressed?"

"Decidedly unimpressed," he admitted. He let his gaze

wander around the room, remembering. "She wasn't really impressed with the bothy either. I think she was expecting to be wined and dined by the son of a Laird. Not stuck in an old shack with an awkward teenager."

She chuckled at his self-deprecating remark. "A little stone shack and a bottle of whiskey hidden in the wall wasn't her dream date?"

"I don't think so." He unscrewed the cap and tilted the bottle towards her. "Would you like a wee bit in your tea m'lady? It will warm you up from the inside out."

Tawnyetta considered it for a moment before she shrugged, "Why not?"

The whiskey did warm her up. The amber liquid burned a little going down, but it sent a warm tingling sensation through Tawnyetta's blood and she noticed Michael relaxing a little, too. Soon they were sharing completely embarrassing stories of their youth.

Tawnyetta had plenty of horrible dating stories from her teenage years. She told him about homecoming her junior year when she refused to admit that she had the flu because she didn't want to stay home. Instead she threw up in the middle of the dance floor, all over her new dress and her date.

"No!" Michael laughed, lifting his palm towards her as if to ward off the very thought of it.

"Yes!" Tawnyetta giggled, taking another sip.

He told her how he and his brother had snuck out of the castle when they were kids and ran away to the village. How Dougie had found them when he drove through Eldin on his tractor, hauling a trailer full of manure to lay across the spring fields. How he had made them sit on top of the pile of manure the whole ride home.

"By the time he marched us back in to see our parents and let our father deal with us, we stunk to high heaven," he admitted, the memory obviously amusing him.

Tawnyetta smiled, her thoughts drifting to the elderly little man she'd met in the garden and how fondly he had spoken of Michael. "Dougie certainly thinks a lot of you," she said.

"I suppose now he does," Michael laughed. "When we were kids he was always on top of us. Trying to control two unruly boys." He fell silent for a few moments, thinking. When he spoke again he was still looking down into his cup. "Of course my parents would only let Dougie go so far in teaching us lessons. That's probably where Greg got into trouble. We never had consistent discipline."

"Your parents weren't tough on you?"

"No," he answered. "They left us to the nanny and the servants for the most part. We were terrors to have around, of that I am certain."

She looked him up and down as he sat next to her lost in reverie. His blanket had slipped a little low as they talked, revealing round, muscled biceps and shoulders. He had stretched his legs out in front of him toward the warming fire in the stove. He exuded confidence, intelligence, and strength, even wrapped in a blanket warming by a fire. In fact, he had captured her attention so completely that she had all but forgotten about the storm outside and their predicament.

"You seem to have turned out all right," she said.

There was a hint of reddening on his cheeks as he looked at her. Then he lifted one shoulder and let it fall in a half shrug to brush off the compliment.

"I left when I was eighteen. Wanted to make a life of my own, away from the castle and the lairdship...and my family."

"Where did you go?"

"I worked for a few years doing general construction and landscaping. I didn't know what I wanted to do. But then I decided to go to university in Edinburgh."

"What did you study?"

"History, my father insisted." He gave her a sheepish look. "And social work."

Tawnyetta was surprised. "Really? You wanted to be a social worker?" She tried to imagine him helping the needy. Sitting in this humble shack, making her tea, she could see it. Though she imagined it was a far cry from being a Laird.

"I thought, perhaps, I could use my family name to help people," he continued. "Maybe start a foundation for wee little ones growing up in poverty." He paused, waiting for a response.

She pushed out her jaw and nodded thoughtfully, indicating his thought process sounded reasonable. "I can see you as a helper," she offered.

Giving her a nod of thanks, he half-shrugged again. "It didn't work out that way."

"Because you had to come back here?"

He nodded and looked back into the flickering fire. "Not much social work going on at the castle." An air of melancholy rose around him, but then he switched his attention to her. "What about you?"

"Me?"

He nodded, pushing his shoulder gently against hers as encouragement. "Where are you from in the United States? Did you go to university?"

"I did. I'm from Colorado?" Her voice rose at the end of her statement, making it a question. She wasn't sure he would know about Colorado.

He wrinkled his brow, searching for information in his mind, then asked, "Mountains?"

"Yes, the Rocky Mountains."

"I've heard about skiing in Colorado."

"Yes, we do a lot of that."

"And what did you study at university?"

"Industrial Design," she answered, expecting him to be ignorant on the topic.

"Doesn't that have something to do with teaching?"

She lifted her eyebrows at his knowledge. "Yes, it does. Basically I help professors design online courses for their classes."

"Sounds very smart," he said. Tawnyetta shifted her body a little under his gaze, but he didn't look away. He considered her for a moment before asking, "And you joined your friend on her honeymoon because her wedding came to an abrupt halt?"

"Yes," she answered with a small, forlorn sigh. "Unfortunately Bridget has had a rough time lately."

"I'm sorry to hear that."

They sat in silence for a few moments, sipping their spiked tea, warm and comfortable by the fire.

"So you're a helper, too," he said. It was a statement more than a question. When she looked at him his eyes were twinkling. Tawnyetta felt invisible fingers flicking her heart and making it flutter.

She grinned. "Maybe."

For a while they didn't say anything at all, just sat comfortably together and finished their tea. The drumming of the rain on the roof combined with the crackling of the fire to make a particularly pleasant sound. Tawnyetta was warmer now, almost completely dry and wrapped inside her blanket. Michael's body put off its own warmth and it took everything in her to keep from snuggling up against him. She wouldn't mind feeling his arm around her, but that wouldn't be exactly proper, especially considered their state of undress. Still, it was a nice thought.

"It's hard to help people," Michael said, interrupting the pleasant silence.

Tawnyetta wrinkled her brow. "What do you mean?"

Michael started to speak, but had to stop to clear his throat before continuing. "Sometimes I think I could have done more...should have done more."

She looked at him, but he kept his eyes trained on the fire. Something in his tone told her he was trying to convey something important. Intimate.

"Should have done more about what?" She asked, keeping her voice calm and soft.

He glanced at her then back to the fire. She could see his jaw flex as he found the words.

"I should have done more about Greg's drinking. I knew he drank too much." He dropped his gaze into his lap as his shoulders slumped slightly forward. The teacup looked so small in his large hands. He held it gingerly as if it was a fine porcelain cup or a baby bird. "Maybe if I'd said something, or done something, there wouldn't have been an accident."

Tawnyetta's heart filled with sorrow. He looked so sad, so lost. Instinctively she reached out and placed her hand on his forearm.

"You can't blame yourself for something like that," she said.

He turned his head away from her, sniffing loudly and clearing his throat again. When he had regained control, Michael turned back and looked into her eyes with a kind of fascinated confusion.

"It's not your fault," she said with determination.

"How can you know?"

Fair question. How could she know? Why did she feel with such certainty that Michael should not blame himself so harshly? She started to answer, but hesitated. She didn't know how, but she was sure that this kind, strong man would not have purposefully harmed his brother.

"I just know," she said, setting her jaw.

He watched her steadily without answering and she held

his gaze, captured in the moment. She wished she could say something more, explain what she felt, but she had no words. She was gripped by his intensity and overwhelmed at this strapping man who had swooped her up in his arms and carried her through the storm without a second thought. Her hand tingled where it still touched his arm, but she didn't move. Couldn't move.

He looked into her, searching for an answer. Loneliness washed across the planes of his face, making her heart feel like glass that was in danger of being shattered in an instant. Then another expression took over, something more carnal. Yearning.

Her heart skipped a beat.

Tawnyetta lifted her other hand, the one that wasn't tethered to his arm, and brushed the back of her fingers across his cheek. She touched him along the line of his beard so that she could feel both the smooth heat of his skin and his soft whiskers.

A jolt of attraction shot through her fingers, through her arm and into her chest before wrapping around her heart and traveling quickly, like liquid, down towards her stomach and below. His eyes sparked. She sucked in her breath. Want, desire, passion, all danced in his eyes as they left hers and traced along her cheek before finally landing on her lips. She felt a tug on her mouth as if he was willing her lips to come to his.

Bang! Bang! Bang!

The sound of knocking jolted them both and they jerked away from each other.

"Laird MacBrody!" A man's voice called out as the door flung open.

Tawnyetta fumbled for her blanket, pulling it more tightly around her naked body. Michael stood. A young man, skinny and pale, with a shock of red hair that was sopping wet and sticking out in all directions stood in the doorway.

"Shaun," Michael said.

So this was the real Shaun. Tawnyetta peered around Michael to get a look. Michael checked over his shoulder to make sure she was decent before stepping toward Shaun and others who stood behind him on the small porch. For a second, she read regret in Michael's eyes as he looked at her one last time, then it was gone and he was on to business.

Saved from their troubles, the moment was over.

Chapter Nineteen

With great competence the real Shaun and his companions escorted Tawnyetta and Laird MacBrody down from the hills. The heavy storm had lifted and they no longer moved through pouring rain.

Though thin and pale, Shaun had a deep commanding voice that belied his frail appearance. He moved gracefully between leading the rescue party and following the Laird's wishes of taking special care of Tawnyetta. Shaun treated her as if she was a fine lady being rescued in a fairy tale. She liked him. He hadn't gaped at her and Michael when he walked in on them wearing only blankets and leaning in for a kiss. His eyes had only skimmed over the open bottle of whiskey and quickly averted from her undressed state when Michael stood to block his view. She was thankful he had come with the others to rescue them, if a little put out by their timing.

Soon they arrived in their mostly dry and wrinkled clothes at the castle steps. Tawnyetta was limping and supported by Shaun on one side and Laird MacBrody on the other.

"We found them," Shaun's booming voice called out as

they approached the grand steps leading to the main entrance. Staff, guests, and friends spilled out to greet them. Anne made a beeline to Shaun's side while the rest of the staff bustled to assist Michael.

He brushed their attention aside, directing instead, "Make sure Miss Campbell is looked after."

But there was no need for that, for Tawnyetta was surrounded by all five of her friends who hustled her immediately into the kitchen to be hovered over by the cook.

Thomas, his hair still damp from searching for her in the rain, scolded her lightly, "Next time, please tell us exactly where you're going. There's no such thing as reliable cell service here."

"Leave her be," Angie instructed him. She smiled sweetly at Tawnyetta, her deep red ringlets in wild disarray as she placed a cup of hot raspberry tea in front of her. "All's well that ends well."

Sofia's brow was puckered in what seemed to be permanent concern. "You're lucky you didn't fall off a cliff or something."

"Not only that, they said there was some flooding," Thomas added.

Tawnyetta wrapped her hands around the steaming tea and let the warmth permeate her fingers. The memory of watching the rising water while huddled under the bridge came back to her, sending a shiver through her body. How close had she been to getting swept down the Highland hills in a flash flood?

"How does your ankle feel?" Luna asked.

"It still hurts, but I think it's going to be fine. It's not broken," she answered.

Bridget swept into the room with an armload of clothes. "I brought you something warm and dry," she said, a little breathless.

Tawnyetta glanced around the large kitchen, confused at where to change in this public space.

"Not here, Tawny," Bridget chided her gently. Then with more excitement, "The Laird doesn't want you climbing all the stairs to our room, so he's assigned you a different room on this floor. At least until you get that ankle looked at."

Something in Bridget's expression made Tawnyetta cringe.

Before long she was settled into her own king size bed in the largest bedroom she had ever seen. Apparently it was the grandest single room in the castle. This bedroom had only one wall made of stone, the outside wall, which was graced with the same floor-to-ceiling cathedral style windows that were in the ballroom. The other walls were the near black, wood common throughout the castle. This would normally make a room appear small, but with the grand height and the massive square footage of this bedroom it did nothing to minimize its magnificence.

"They call this the Queen's room," Bridget informed her as she shook out some of the clothes she had brought down and hung them in the wardrobe. "You should see the view of the garden, it's absolutely gorgeous," she continued.

Tawnyetta had not seen the view. In fact, Tawnyetta had not been allowed to stand up and move from the bed since Shaun and Thomas had helped her in.

"Laird MacBrody's orders," the doctor had told her when he paid her a call just moments after she was settled into the massive bed.

"It's just a twisted ankle," Tawnyetta had argued. "I can put weight on it and everything."

The doctor tsk-tsked and shook his head, peering at her over thick bifocals. "Laird MacBrody and I believe you should stay off your ankle until morning." Tawnyetta let out a frustrated sigh. The doctor, who had wild gray hair that dropped over his bulging forehead gave her a sharp look and lifted his brow in warning. "Unless you want to take a ride to hospital for an x-ray instead?"

"Fine," Tawnyetta agreed, though not happily.

Everyone went to an early dinner since they had skipped lunch searching for Tawnyetta and Laird MacBrody. Bridget stayed back with her friend, curious about the circumstances she'd been discovered in with the handsome Laird.

"He carried you?" Bridget asked in disbelief after Tawnyetta recounted the story for the third time that day. Bridget, especially, found the details of her rescue fascinating.

"Yes," she admitted. Though the more everyone around her fussed about it, the more she felt that they were all overreacting. "But it wasn't that far," she added. "I mean, it felt like a long way from the bridge to the bothy when he was carrying me, but when we came back down it was only about 50 yards, maybe less."

"Still, Bridget said. "That's pretty impressive."

Tawnyetta readjusted her leg where it had been propped up on a stack of pillows. She didn't want to talk about the incident anymore. The whole thing had been blown way out of proportion. Besides, she didn't like everyone making such a big deal out of her mistake.

Bridget, on the other hand, could not seem to let it go. She sat down on the edge of the bed and threw her legs up next to Tawnyetta's propped leg, leaning her head back against the headboard. She took a piece of shortbread off of the silver tea tray that Anne had left earlier and nibbled on it, staring meaningfully at Tawnyetta.

Finally, Tawnyetta couldn't take it anymore. "What?"

"I'm just curious."

"Curious about what?" Tawnyetta could barely disguise her annoyance.

"Exactly how naked were you both? And exactly how did you pass the time?" Bridget giggled.

Before Tawnyetta could finish rolling her eyes there was a knock on the door.

"Miss Campbell?" A man's voice came through the door. A voice Tawnyetta recognized and at the sound of it her heartbeat sped up.

Bridget's eyes flew open. "Is that him?" she whispered.

Tawnyetta tried to act nonchalant. "I don't know, will you answer it for me?"

Bridget got up and smoothed her hair. She hurriedly arranged Tawnyetta's covers as attractively as possible while still allowing her ankle to remain up on the pillows. "I'll be right there," she called out to their visitor. Tawnyetta could tell she was thrilled at the prospect of Michael coming to see them and that realization dulled her own excitement. She swallowed hard and focused on staying calm and cool. All plans went out the window when she saw him step into the room.

He too had changed into dry clothes and his hair was no longer damp. But there was an air of the hills with him still. She could sense it on him. It tickled along the top of her skin and as he looked her over assessing her condition she felt as if the cool wet breeze of the Highlands was moving up and down her body. Her heart started beating wildly the moment he caught her eye. He said something, but she couldn't hear him over the sound of her own blood rushing through her veins. All other noise had disappeared. Amidst Bridget's twittering chatter, Michael made his way to the foot of Tawnyetta's bed.

She blinked. "I'm sorry, I didn't catch that."

His eyes twinkled at her and the position he took at the end of her bed somehow felt even more intimate than if he had been standing right beside her.

"I asked how you are feeling," he repeated.

"Fine," she said. She followed his gaze as it moved to her

ankle. "My ankle is fine. I think I must have just twisted it," she insisted.

"Did the doctor instruct you to stay in bed till morning?"

"He did." She bristled a little bit. First at the insinuation that she wouldn't listen to the doctor. Second at the knowledge that he had co-conspired with the doctor and knew exactly what instructions she had received.

A myriad of thoughts raced through Tawnyetta's mind. Dancing with Michael at the ball. Sneaking around with Bridget and seeing him in his birthday suit...the first time. The moment he lifted her up and carried her out from under the bridge. And, finally, the instant before they were discovered in the bothy when she knew he was about to kiss her. Her cheeks reddened at the memory. The way he was gazing at her from the end of the bed made her feel lightheaded. That stolen moment hung between them still. She could feel it and she was certain he could feel it too.

Bridget ran her fingers along the duvet cover the way she did when she was flirting. She was saying something to Michael, but Tawnyetta was again distracted and did not hear it. She didn't hear his response either, though she could see him smile charmingly at Bridget. Tawnyetta was overwhelmed, conflicted. She must be tired, more tired than she had realized. Her ankle did still hurt and exhaustion might be setting in from her ordeal.

"I'm tired," she blurted out.

Both Bridget and Michael looked at her with curiosity.

"I'll leave you to rest then," Michael said. He smiled at her and his hand reached toward her instinctively, though he pulled it back without touching her or even the covers on the bed. He had wanted to touch her. And she him.

As Bridget closed the door after him, Tawnyetta's stomach sank. Her best friend whirled around, her face bright and excited, happy at the prospect of such an attractive, eligible man in their midst. Tawnyetta didn't have the energy to deal with it right now. She feigned exhaustion. Convinced that her friend needed to sleep, Bridget left soon after.

Tawnyetta drifted into a fitful sleep. She didn't have to think about how her feelings for Michael were betraying her best friend any more that night. But she couldn't ignore it forever. In fact, the whole situation reared its ugly head the next morning at breakfast.

Chapter Twenty

As the sun rose the next morning, Tawnyetta was officially released from her bed. She joined the others for breakfast. Bridget, Sofia, Angie, Luna, and Thomas were there. As were the entire Prescott clan, including Bea, who was dying to find out about Tawnyetta being found naked and alone with Laird MacBrody.

"I'll tell you later," Tawnyetta promised in a low voice.

She didn't really want to rehash everything that had happened with Michael right now. Besides, she was starving.

The large group of guests were enjoying a buffet style meal in the dining room. Though she had been cleared to walk on her bad leg, she was under strict instructions to take it easy. For that reason Thomas insisted on filling her plate for her. Tawnyetta did not hold back.

"Give me at least one of everything," she instructed him.

"Roger that," Thomas responded as he dutifully loaded her plate.

Mouth watering, Tawnyetta watched him from the other side of the table. Her stomach growled as he approached a platter piled with link sausages, or 'bangers' as they called them here. She had grown used to the heavy, greasy breakfasts at the castle and could almost taste the delicious sausage. She tried to catch Thomas' eye but he was busy maneuvering through the others at the buffet who were all talking and laughing and generally making a great deal of noise.

Worried he was going to skip the sausages, she shouted at him over the din of breakfast chatter, "Thomas, give me a load of bangers."

A hush fell over the busy room while she was still forming the 's' sound in 'bangers'. Tawnyetta froze. All eyes turned to her. Then she realized they weren't looking at her, they were looking past her into the hallway. She was seated with her back to the door and had to turn slowly in her chair to see the object of everyone's rapt attention.

Michael.

He stood in the doorway looking bright eyed and rested. Though this was his castle and he was by all rights the Laird of it, he greeted them with a shy smile.

"Good morning," he said. His deep voice cracked a little as he spoke, like a nervous teenager. A tall, dark and handsome Scotsman who was also humble and a little uncertain about joining their lively breakfast could make any woman's heart flutter. And Tawnyetta's fluttered like mad. "Do you mind if I join you?" he asked.

The sight of Laird MacBrody at breakfast was wholly unusual. They had all grown accustomed to dining without his presence. Now that he was standing here, even the Prescotts hesitated. No doubt they were flipping through all of the polite protocol they stored in their brains to find the correct way to proceed. Thank goodness, because Tawnyetta and her American counter parts had no earthly idea what to do or say.

"Laird MacBrody," Mrs. Prescott's smooth voice broke the silence. "What an honor to have your grace dine with us."

Michael shifted his weight from one hip to the other, still uncomfortable. With a half-smile stuck to his lips he swept his gaze around the room, making eye contact with each of them for a split second before moving to the next. His eyes landed on Tawnyetta last, where they softened and stayed.

"I hope you are well this morning?" he inquired.

Singling her out in the crowd caused all the others to look at her and she could only guess what they were thinking. Why was he here? What will she say? What happened between the two of them in the bothy?

She nodded mutely.

"Good," Michael said, the word resonating through her body like a rumble of thunder. He remembered to look up at the rest of the group and his smile broadened as he stepped into the room.

Thomas returned to his seat on Tawnyetta's left, gently placing her breakfast in front of her, a plate piled high with every item from the buffet plus the mountain of sausages she had requested. Tawnyetta grimaced. Luna was already seated on her right, which left no place for Michael to possibly join her. Part of her was relieved. His presence put her aflutter and she wasn't sure she could eat at all, plus the pile of sausages wasn't exactly the sexiest way to present herself.

To her chagrin, Michael found a spare seat directly across from her at the table. As he sat down, Anne and another server started toward him to find out what he wanted no doubt. With a quick shake of his head he indicated to them that he didn't want any special treatment and they returned to their posts at the buffet table.

The room was silent except for some clinking of silverware and serving dishes. Everyone seemed to be waiting to see what was going to happen. Tawnyetta sank back into her chair and stared at her coffee cup, wishing the floor would open and swallow her up. After a few moments she had to look at him, unable to contain her curiosity.

He was grinning at her, his damnable deep blue eyes twinkling and making her breath catch in her throat. She felt her cheeks flush under his attention and could sense Luna noticing their exchange.

Michael dropped his gaze to the pile of sausages on her plate and looked back up at her. His eyes danced with the humor of it all and he opened his mouth to say something.

"Do you mind if we join you, my Laird?" Bea butted in. She and Bridget had materialized on either side of Michael. Bridget was already pulling the chair to his right away from the table to sit down.

Michael stood quickly to pull their chairs out for them. "It would be my pleasure."

"Thank you," Bridget said. Her smile beamed brightly. "I'm dying to know every detail of how you saved our dear friend, Tawnyetta, yesterday."

Thomas' brow screwed into a scowl and he leaned into Tawnyetta, whispering. "Why is she talking like she's in Pride and Prejudice?"

"Look around," Tawnyetta whispered back.

Thomas eyed the huge room, the fine furnishings, the expensive china, and the servants hovering nearby. He shrugged and murmured quietly, "It's not bad for a relic. I could build something better."

She had no doubt that he could. Thomas was a builder, a talented carpenter since they were young. Still, he was pouting. "You're pouting," she told him.

Thomas continued to scowl as he took a huge bite of fried egg and watched the antics on the other side of the table.

"Do tell us everything, Laird MacBrody," Bea was encouraging Michael as Bridget nodded emphatically.

Michael arched his eyebrows at Tawnyetta. She shrugged,

not sure how to explain their time in the bothy to the others. It had been completely innocent, even though they had been wrapped only in blankets. But they had also shared an intimacy that she still hadn't wrapped her mind around. At least *she* had felt that intimacy. At this moment, she wasn't sure if he had or not. She also didn't know if he was going to share all of the details with the whole world right here at the breakfast table.

Michael cleared his throat, buying time. He looked to Bridget then Bea, then back to Tawnyetta, saying, "It was an honor to get to know your dear friend."

Thomas scoffed into his coffee cup at the use of the antiquated language. Bridget shot him a reproachful look.

"She was very brave," Michael added, holding Tawnyetta's gaze. Warmth ran over her shoulders and down her spine, as if someone were pouring honey that had been sitting in a sunny windowsill down her back.

Bridget was not satisfied with his answer. Tawnyetta could read it on her face. She was about to push for more information from Michael when Mr. Prescott spoke up from the coffee carafe.

"I say, Laird MacBrody, will you be at the Games tomorrow?"

Michael turned his attention toward the older man. "Yes, I will."

"Games?" Thomas perked up a little.

"The Highland Games," Mr. Prescott explained. "Great tradition. We're supposed to have good weather for it, too."

"Yes, we are," Michael added. He spoke to Thomas hopefully, "Would you like to join our team?" And to the Prescott men, though with a little less enthusiasm, he said, "You're all welcome."

"I can be on your team?" Thomas warmed quickly to the idea.

Michael nodded.

"But you don't even know what they play," Bridget said to Thomas. He glared at her.

"Are they traditional Highland Games?" Sofia asked.

"Yes," Michael answered. "Most of them have fairly simple rules. They're more about strength and stamina."

"We can all come and watch?" Luna asked.

Michael smiled at her and nodded then shifted his eyes quickly to Tawnyetta. "I was hoping that you would."

"Won't that be interesting," Bridget exclaimed, touching Michael's forearm as she did.

Thomas noticed the touch and gave Tawnyetta a look. "It will definitely be interesting," he said to her in a low voice with more than a hint of sarcasm.

Tawnyetta stabbed the top sausage off of her pile and bit into it. May as well eat up, she would need all of her strength to get through this week.

Chapter Twenty-One

The day of the Games dawned and the castle was abuzz with excitement. Preparations for getting guests, staff, and Laird Michael to the grounds on time overrode all of the normal formality of their mornings. Tawnyetta couldn't help but get caught up in the mood. She agreed to go with Angie to the Secret Garden to gather flowers to braid through Angie's red ringlets. They ran into Anne and Erin at the back entrance to the castle upon their return.

"Can we help you with that?" Tawnyetta asked the two maids who were struggling with a huge cooler.

"No, thank you," Anne answered politely, though they were obviously straining under the weight.

"Don't be silly," Angie said. She tucked her small bouquet of pink and white flowers into the pocket of her sundress and went to Erin's side to help lift.

Tawnyetta went to Anne's side and grabbed the handle next to the maid's hand. She was surprised at the weight. "What's in this thing?"

"Ale and Irn Bru," Erin answered, slightly out of breath.

"Iron Brew?" Tawnyetta asked, for that's how the maid pronounced it. "No wonder this is so heavy!"

"You've not heard of Irn Bru?" Anne was surprised. The two Americans shook their heads. "You're in for a treat, then," Anne informed them.

The four of them managed to get the cooler down the steps and were approaching the truck carrying supplies when Michael and Thomas appeared beside them.

Both men wore kilts. Tawnyetta's stomach did a flip-flop. The kilt again. Michael's was the same black and grey tartan he had worn at the ball, though this one looked like it wasn't brand new. Thomas' was green and black.

"Thomas!" Angie was delighted with his new look.

His cheeks reddened. "They let me borrow a kilt. I guess it's tradition."

"Ladies, let us get this," Michael said.

He was at Tawnyetta's elbow and the sound of his voice was so close it gave her goose bumps. She tried to avoid looking back over her shoulder at him so nobody could tell that his kilt and billowy white cotton shirt was making her weak in the knees.

The women placed the cooler gently on the ground, thankful to be free of their burden. Before Tawnyetta could let go of the handle, Michael's hand ran over hers where he was taking hold of the cooler. Their bodies touched, her backside to his front, sending ripples of excitement across her skin.

Hosted by the town of Eldin, the Games were held on a neatly manicured grassy meadow less than a mile from the city limits. There was a dirt parking lot with no lines to guide drivers, one small building that provided running water and restrooms, and very little else in the way of parks and recreation maintenance. It reminded Tawnyetta of small town fairgrounds she'd been to in the more rural areas of Colorado when she was a child. With the gorgeous blue skies, tame puffy clouds, and deep green hills rising around them, it was sure to be a beautiful day.

Tawnyetta found the events fell somewhere between a county fair and a high school track meet. There was the 5K run and other track competitions like the shot put throw. Or at least that's what they called it in the states. Here in Scotland large men heaved heavy stones across the field and called it the Stone Put. Or they whipped them around in frantic circles on the end of a steel wire before throwing them. That event was called the Hammer Toss.

There were also Celtic dancers made up of groups of girls and young women. They were accompanied by bagpipes and heavy drums as they danced under a portable tent that had been set up for them. Other smaller tented booths served food and drink. A few held locals selling their Artisan crafts. Eldin's mayor was present and led the parade first thing in the morning into the fairgrounds. Michael had accompanied the mayor and was given the place of honor directly in front of the group of bagpipe players in the small parade. Being the Laird of Claymore Castle, it would seem, had its perks.

Most impressive, however, were the games of strength. Tall, thickly muscled, kilted Highland men competed in various feats of lifting, pulling, and tossing of different heavy objects. They pitted their strength against one another in an intense game of Tug of War. And, of course, there was the Caber Toss, the competition where each man lifted what looked like a telephone pole straight into the air and heaved it forward attempting to make it flip longways on its end. It was nothing if not a way for men to show off superior upper body strength.

Tawnyetta wore a mid-calf pair of spandex running shorts, a purple Colorado Rockies baseball T-shirt, and a black hoodie, which she tied around her waist. She had convinced Luna to join her in the 5K run that was part of the Games. She made sure to wrap her ankle and promised she would go no faster than a slow jog to get Luna to agree. The run was set up for the participants to loop around and around the edge of the fairgrounds until their three plus miles was complete. From this makeshift track they could watch most of what was going on, especially if they were jogging at a slower pace.

"I can't believe Thomas is wearing a kilt," Luna giggled when they caught a glimpse of him through the crowd preparing for the Tug of War.

"I know," Tawnyetta agreed. "He looks good in it, though. Kilts make men look good."

Luna gave her a sideways look as they rounded a curve. "Yes, I've noticed you noticing."

Tawnyetta laughed at the idea. "Noticing Thomas? I don't think so."

"I wasn't talking about Thomas," Luna said slyly.

Just then the Tug of War began and they slowed down a little more to peer through the crowd and watch. In this setting Tawnyetta could see where the name Tug of War came from. There was something medieval about these brutish men gripping a thick heavy rope and pulling against each other with all of their strength. It put her in mind of ancient wars that were fought using hand-to-hand battle instead of with computers or airplanes like they were nowadays.

Thomas was part of the castle team. It was fun to watch him pull with all of his might, grunting and sweating with his teammates. Sometimes Tawnyetta thought he spent too much time with her and the other four girls and didn't have enough male bonding. She was glad to see him enjoying himself in such a masculine contest.

It was, she had to admit, also fun to watch Michael.

He had started the day with a wool jacket worn over his white shirt during the parade. But after the chilly morning air dissipated and the formality of the parade ended Michael had taken off the jacket, revealing his impressive physique. As he dug in with the other men his legs were taunt, his strong hands gripped the thick rope, his powerful torso was easily seen under the light cotton cloth of his shirt, his roped muscles strained and, eventually, helped win against the fierce competitors. The whole scene was decidedly virile.

Tawnyetta's steps slowed significantly as she caught glimpses of him celebrating the big win with raised fists and shouts of encouragement to his team. Good manners were out the window as he and his mates formed a tight circle and chanted something she couldn't quite make out. Like all sports teams celebrating big wins, there were plenty of deep voices, sweaty bodies, back slapping and guffaws of laughter. Her view was interrupted by a young family with several children, one of which rode on her father's shoulders. She only saw pieces of the scene as the celebratory circle broke apart and the men started shaking the losing team's hands in a show of good sportsmanship.

"He sure is excited," Luna said.

Tawnyetta nodded, her eyes still searching for Michael through the crowd. "It's probably a matter of pride for the castle to win at something like this." There was a pause and Tawnyetta sensed Luna looking at her. She tore her eyes away from the Tug of War victors and looked at her friend. "What?"

"I was talking about Thomas," Luna said, amusement lifting the corners of her mouth.

"Right." Tawnyetta flounced her short hair as much as it would flounce and turned back to look at Thomas, pretending she'd been watching him the whole time. She found him almost immediately, standing next to Michael as they both looked intently in the opposite direction of where she and Luna stood.

Unlike her and Luna running in the race, and Thomas taking part in all of the man games, their other three friends had chosen not to work up a sweat at the Games. Angie was fascinated with the arts and crafts available at the tents and enthralled with the Celtic dancing. Bridget and Sofia were happy to wander the grounds and observe all of the activities as spectators. Tawnyetta hadn't seen Bridget and Sofia since the race had started.

Until now.

As she looked to where Thomas and Michael were gazing with such interest, Tawnyetta saw them. Sofia, looking exotic and sensual in a tangerine sundress, was stunning. But it was Bridget who was the picture of lush femininity today.

In a dress Tawnyetta knew came directly from her trousseau, Bridget commanded the attention of every man, and most women, in her immediate presence and across the field. Her hair was a cascade of golden curls tumbling down her back. Her perfect Pilates body was wrapped softly in a low cut white sundress that had a tiny pink polka dot print. Fine lace curled along every edge of the dress, giving it a dreamy quality. If that wasn't enough, on top of her head of glorious blonde tresses she wore a floppy white hat. The rim of the hat fell just across her brow, perfectly framing her wide, blue eyes and full pink, pouty lips.

At the sight of Bridget in all of her glory Tawnyetta's heart sank a little bit. Then she saw Michael nudge Thomas and nod towards Bridget. He made a comment to Thomas who responded with a nod of his own and a good-natured chuckle. Tawnyetta's heart slipped again and landed with a thump in her stomach. She felt queasy.

"Are you all right?" Luna asked. Tawnyetta had slowed to less than a walk. "You look a little green."

She gave Luna what she hoped was a reassuring smile and picked up her pace. "I'm fine."

But she wasn't fine. Not at all.

After they finished the race, coming in dead last, they

joined Bridget and the others. Tawnyetta fiercely wished she had planned ahead and brought a change of clothes. But she hadn't and was stuck trudging around in her sweaty running clothes next to the captivatingly exquisite Bridget.

"It's the Caber Toss!" Bridget exclaimed, placing her hand on the crown of her white hat as if the thrill of watching kilted men throwing tree trunks around would blow it right off of her head.

She wasn't wrong.

A whole line of vigorously masculine Highlanders waited to take their turn hoisting the Caber. Testosterone was heavy in the air and Tawnyetta couldn't pretend she wasn't interested. Besides, Thomas was trying his hand at it and she told herself that she would be a bad friend if she didn't watch.

Thomas and Michael stood just ahead, side-by-side in line with the other men. They were talking and laughing like old buddies and Tawnyetta felt another jolt of jealousy. She shook her head in disgust at this reaction. What was her problem? Nobody was allowed to speak to Michael except her? She hovered behind the others, simultaneously hoping Michael would turn her way and catch her eye and also not be able to see her in her dumpy running clothes.

"Mister!" Bridget called out Thomas' nickname, clapping her hands as he stepped up to take his turn. He turned to them and gave them a little wave.

"Go, Thomas!" Angie shouted.

Tawnyetta clapped heartily along with her girlfriends for their favorite buddy. She laser focused on watching Thomas struggle to pick up the Caber and balance it. She didn't want any of them to think she was more interested in Laird MacBrody than their very own Thomas.

"You can do it!" Tawnyetta called out to him when it looked like he was thinking about giving up.

"Getting the grip on it is the hardest part," a man's voice said just to her right.

The sound startled her and she twisted quickly to face Michael. The sun was behind him, surrounding his charmingly messy dark hair with a glowing halo. He seemed taller than normal or maybe his appearance was altered in her eyes because of the pheromones radiating from his powerful frame after all of his recent exertion.

"Yeah," she said, the sound a faint squeak in her throat. She couldn't say anything else because her mouth had gone completely dry.

Michael's eyes shone as they swept down her body, all the way to her feet then back up to her face. "Nice trainers," he said, rolling his 'r's' like only the Scottish can. Then he gave her a wink before jogging back to the line. All of his mates were shouting and waving at him to take his turn. He looked back at her once, catching her eye and holding it for a second with a mischievous twinkle.

It was his turn next at the Caber Toss and Tawnyetta could not tear her eyes away.

<h1 style="text-align:center">Chapter Twenty-Two</h1>

"It's like they're best friends now," Bridget declared. Her voice tinged with annoyance.

"Don't be snarky," Sofia scolded her mildly. "You should be glad Thomas has found a friend."

Tawnyetta listened to Bridget whine about the absence of Thomas and Michael from their morning adventure and was beginning to think she was mostly put out because there were no men around to fawn over her. The two men had got along wonderfully the day before at the Games and left early in the morning to go fishing in a nearby loch. They had skipped breakfast and had been away for hours, leaving the women to entertain themselves. It was wearing thin.

They had ran out of things to do before mid-morning and been roped into helping Angie collect more wildflowers. She was planning on drying all of them to make her own "Highland Potpourri" so they could "Always remember their trip to Scotland". The five of them made their way through the woodlands next to the castle collecting wood anemone with tender white petals. On the other side of the thick woods, they came upon clearer land that rolled and peaked in small hills.

Angie was in seventh heaven as these low hills were literally covered with heather and primrose.

Though Bridget was growing tired of their flower adventure, Tawnyetta was glad for the distraction. She hadn't slept well the night before with Michael and the Games still fresh in her mind.

"It is simply beautiful here," Luna exclaimed, inhaling the fragrance from the cut flowers she carried in her basket.

"I'm not being snarky you know," Bridget said, ignoring Luna's current comment and unable to let go of Sofia's earlier one. "I just think he should be spending time with us."

"Who?" Sofia teased. "Thomas or Laird MacBrody?"

Bridget's cheeks pinked prettily. Tawnyetta pretended to spy a new patch of flowers further away and walked quickly towards them. She didn't want to be part of this conversation anymore. Nor did she want anyone to suspect her feelings.

These feelings were so fresh and new she didn't know if they could withstand being out in the open yet. They were the reason she hadn't slept a wink the night before. She had stared at her ceiling all night thinking about him, wondering if he was thinking about her. All of the emotions of the day at the Games, jealousy, attraction, anxiety, excitement, had played through her mind on a loop. By morning she was groggy and exhausted, but she had figured it out. And her discovery had left her in a new quandary.

The truth she had been forced to admit to herself in the middle of the night was that she had fallen head over heels for Michael. The very thought of him sent her heart racing. Her senses tingled at the memory of their times together. His eyes, his scent, his voice. There was no question in her mind anymore regarding her feelings. The question that remained was how would she manage the rest of this vacation without revealing her secret to anyone?

As she neared the top of the slope Tawnyetta smelled the

unmistakable wet, dank scent of reeds. A soft splashing of waves sounded just over the top of the swell in the land. She walked right past the flowers she'd planned on picking and toward the sound until she came upon the edge of a lake, or loch rather, that had been hidden by the undulating landscape.

A bubble of excitement appeared in her stomach. Was this the loch where Michael and Thomas had gone fishing? Tawnyetta scanned the shoreline and didn't see anything but narrow rocky beaches. She took in the vastness of the body of water in front of her. The men could be anywhere. And she didn't even know if this was the same loch they had gone to, it could be a completely different one.

Still, the bubble of excitement grew.

"Tawnyetta?" Sofia called to her. She and Luna appeared at the top of the slope.

"Oh my," Luna released the words in one, long breath, her attention captured by the loch stretching out in front of them.

It was an amazing sight. Not wide and round like Tawnyetta would expect a lake to be, but long and narrow, and placed between higher, craggy hills on both sides. The loch looked like a canyon that had filled with water over time and now sat still and grey, shining like polished stone. More hills peaked on either side, higher and higher into the distance. Tawnyetta scrutinized the dark water lapping just below her feet and wondered how deep it was. It looked deep.

Bridget appeared behind them next. "Damned thistles," she muttered as she plucked spiny purple blooms from her linen shorts.

Angie had clambered up to the highest point nearby to look out over the loch. She gazed with delight at what she saw. "Now that 'tis a bonnie sight if I do say so myself," Angie said in a perfect Scottish accent. They all looked up at her in surprise. "I've been practicing," she explained. She gave them a joyful smile, which was magnified by her wild mane of red hair glinting in the sun. Her long, flowing skirt blew in the breeze, wrapping around her calves.

The shoreline Tawnyetta stood on had no beach. Instead, the ground sloped down and away from her feet to the edge of the loch. From there it simply dropped down several feet to the edge of the water, as if the loch was merely a huge pit dug out of the ground by a backhoe before being filled with water. On either side of where she stood the land rose higher, making the drop off more of a rough cliff overlooking the water. Where Angie stood the drop off was most extreme, at least twenty feet.

Tawnyetta lifted her flattened hand to her forehead, shading her eyes from the sun so she could see across the water better. No sign of any boats.

Suddenly interested, Bridget asked, "Do you think this is where they came to fish?"

Tawnyetta shrugged and was about to answer that she didn't see any signs of life on the loch when a sharp cry interrupted her. They all turned just in time to see Angie tumbling awkwardly from her perch and hitting the surface of the lake with an epic splash.

"Gigi!" Bridget cried.

But Angie couldn't hear her, because she had disappeared under the water.

Several thoughts flew through Tawnyetta's mind in that moment. She didn't know how deep or how cold the water was. Angie could have hurt herself falling or hit a rock under the surface of the water that knocked her unconscious. And, finally, was there such a thing as an undercurrent in a loch?

Not willing to wait to find out, and not wanting to waste any more time to see if Angie resurfaced unharmed, Tawnyetta leapt into action. In just a few seconds she pulled her shirt over her head and kicked off her shoes. Amid shouts of warning and concern from the others, wearing only her shorts and bra, Tawnyetta stepped to the edge of the loch and jumped in.

The water was cold, much colder than she had anticipated, and her chest clenched. Her lungs wanted to suck in air from the shock, but her mind knew better than to let them.

She was still plunging downward into the water that was no longer the shining grey it appeared from the shore. From inside the loch, the water was a charcoal black. Clear, not murky, but a weighty black that absorbed all of the rays of sun from the surface into an endless darkness. It was mesmerizing, surreal, like she was floating in outer space without a helmet surrounded by no atmosphere that held the warmth of the sun. Her hands and arms were visible, but they glowed a ghostly white in this eerie underwater visage.

Fear rushed through her. The loch seemed to be bottomless, without life and without soul. What if it was too dark to see Angie? What if she had already sunk beyond reach? Thoughts of the Loch Ness monster she'd read about as a child popped into her head.

No! She would not allow herself to panic.

Tawnyetta forced herself to focus and pointed her body in the direction she thought Angie had fallen. The cold had already sunk into her bones and kicking her feet was almost painful. But she had no choice. Angie was in trouble. So she swam as fast as she could.

In what seemed like forever, but could only have been a few moments, Tawnyetta spotted another ghostly white figure under the water. Her heart pumped loudly for a moment, then calmed. Her fear of running into a legendary underwater monster dropped away when she saw the cloud of red hair floating above the struggling figure.

By the time she reached Angie, Tawnyetta's lungs were starting to burn. She had no idea how deep they were, the way the loch absorbed sunshine made it difficult to gage. She was terrified of going for air and then not being able to find Angie again in the depths, so she kept swimming. When she was within a few feet of her, Angie's wide and frightened eyes focused on her. Tawnyetta remembered hearing how dangerous a drowning person can be, how they can grab hold of the person trying to save them and end up pulling them down as well. She didn't want them both to drown, but she had to take the chance. There was no way she was leaving Angie in this cold, dark place.

Tawnyetta looked hard into her friend's eyes and saw recognition, not panic. She reached out her hand and Angie took it firmly, but not so much that Tawnyetta couldn't swim. Then, dragging Angie behind her, Tawnyetta kicked like mad back toward the surface.

Lungs on fire, feeling like they might explode, Tawnyetta looked to the sparkles that she thought must be the sun glinting off the surface and pushed all thoughts of failure out of her mind. The water pressed against her from all sides, an oppressive force devouring both of them with its sheer size. The normal momentum she would feel moving upward in water was slowed considerably by Angie's additional pull. Letting go was not an option.

The sparkles grew wider, giving her hope. But then they started to blur. Her heart pounded in her chest sending shooting pains through her body. Her head felt drowsy. Tawnyetta had one terrifying thought–she was going to pass out.

She dared not look down at Angie and the depths below. Afraid of what she'd see. Afraid that was all she would ever see again.

Something large dropped into the water above. An unidentifiable form and a trail of white bubbles it brought with it from the world above. Then another object followed the first. Her vision narrowed so that it seemed she was looking through a telescope. Suddenly she was full of despair. The sparkles, the surface of the water, were quickly disappearing in tunnel vision.

She was cold. Angie's hand! Was she still holding Angie's hand? Something grabbed her roughly from behind, wrapping tightly under her arms and across her chest. She couldn't hold on to Angie anymore. She couldn't kick and fight away whatever underwater beast had taken hold of her. She couldn't think or scream or breathe. Even though her mind knew it was pointless, she opened her mouth to try. Cold, black water rushed in, filling the back of her throat. Everything went dark.

Chapter Twenty-Three

Tawnyetta awoke to voices. Some male, some female. Some shouting, some blubbering. One voice stood out. Deep, steady, close.

"Are you all right, lass?"

Her eyes fluttered open to see Michael, his hair dripping wet, his eyes full of worry.

"Tawny!" Bridget's face popped into view.

It registered in her brain that they were both looking down at her. She was flat on her back laying on something bumpy and hard. The ground.

Tawnyetta lifted her head suddenly, "Angie?"

"She's fine, everything's fine," Michael reassured her, reaching around the back of her head with his hand for support. "You should lay down for a wee bit longer, lass," he instructed as he lowered his hand, allowing her head to sink back to the earth.

Relief flooded through her body as her throat swelled hot with tears. This sent her into a coughing fit and Michael turned her to him and held steady so she was coughing into his bare chest. His skin was so warm and comforting that she didn't even think to wonder why he wasn't wearing a shirt. Or why droplets of water stuck to his skin. She had just come from the oppressive world underneath the surface of the loch. Everything was wet.

"You're all right, lass, everything's okay," Michael murmured to her as he brushed her cheek tenderly with his fingertips. He said it again, so softly that she realized he was comforting himself as much as he was comforting her. She looked up at him and was caught by the expression in his eyes. Fiercely blue, the worry subsiding, they gleamed with something else–anger. Surprised, Tawnyetta pulled away from him and tried to sit up.

"Thank goodness!" Sofia said. She and Luna sat on either side of Angie who was also flat on her back nearby, but alert.

"No wonder you couldn't swim," Thomas added. Shirtless as well, he was at Angie's feet untangling the mass of sopping wet cloth that had just recently been her beautiful skirt, but had turned deadly under water. The long, sweeping garment was twisted firmly around her calves and ankles and he cursed under his breath as he worked to get it loose.

Angie caught Tawnyetta's eye and Tawnyetta saw giant tears welling up in her big, brown eyes. "Tawnyetta..." Angie's bottom lip trembled.

Tawnyetta sat up, pushed away from Michael and scrambled quickly into Angie's outstretched arms just before they both burst into tears.

Michael sat back on his heels. He blew out a great breath of released frustration, his cheeks puffing out as he did. He ran both hands through his wet hair once then brought them back and covered his face. He let his hands slide his down his cheeks, pulling the skin under his eyes down as they did.

Bridget was hovering. Hopping nervously back and forth between Angie and Tawnyetta as they wept and Thomas as he worked on disentangling Angie's feet.

"This is awful! Oh my God, how did that even happen? Gigi you could have drowned! Tawny, you too!"

Her nervous chattering added to her incessant hovering and made Tawnyetta think of a neurotic humming bird. She giggled.

"Stop, Bridge," Tawnyetta said. "Before you hop yourself into the water." Laughter bubbled out of her at the image that formed in her mind. Angie's shoulders started shaking as she, too, giggled at the thought. Luna snorted, which tickled Sofia's funny bone, and then they were all laughing, including Thomas. All of them except Michael.

He had stood up and was pacing slowly between them and the water's edge. Tawnyetta laughed so hard her sides hurt and she couldn't catch her breath. For some reason this made it all even more crazy funny when she thought about not being able to breathe under the water.

Thomas had finished untangling Angie's skirt and noticed Michael's tension. He stood up and brushed off the debris that had stuck to his knees while on the ground. "It's all right now," he said to Michael. Tawnyetta noticed he was using the same soothing voice that Michael had used on her. Her laughter subsided and she wiped tears from her eyes.

Michael was shaking his head, then nodding it, then shaking it again. He tried to chuckle along with them, but it came out humorless.

"Thank you," Tawnyetta said to both of them. She had deduced that the reason they were shirtless and soaking wet was they had dove into the loch to save her and Angie. Her heart warmed to both of them. "Thank you for saving us."

Thomas' cheeks flushed under the sentiment, but Michael scoffed. They all turned their attention to him, surprised at his reaction.

"What were you doing out here?" He asked, his tone impatient.

"Picking flowers," Angie answered meekly.

He shook his head with disgust. He looked downward, averting his eyes to the ground just in front of them. His jaw clenched as he tried to control his tone, "You should not be playing in the hills where you do not know your way around."

"We weren't *playing*," Tawnyetta said haughtily. She disliked his use of the word, as if they were children needing scolding.

His eyes shot up and he glared at her for a second before he said, "These hills can be deadly. You of all people should know that."

Heat filled Tawnyetta's cheeks. He was acting like she was stupid. She was not stupid. She pushed herself off the ground and stood up, shoulders straight even if her knees were still a bit wobbly. She opened her mouth to respond.

"It's my fault," Angie interjected. "I slipped, I guess. I don't really know what happened. One moment I was standing up there," she swept her arm towards the place she'd fallen from. "And the next I was sinking in the water."

"Because the shore is unstable on this side of the loch." Michael gestured to encompass the entire area where they stood. "This water is ice cold." The muscles and veins in his neck strained with his anger as he jabbed his finger repeatedly at the loch behind him to emphasize his point. "Do you know how deep this loch is? Or that you can sink down so far into that black, freezing water that you go past the point of ever being found?"

Tawnyetta did know. She had felt it when they were underwater. The vastness of it. The way it had almost swallowed her, swallowed them both. Angie, still sitting on the ground flanked by Sofia and Luna, shivered.

Michael turned his pointing finger on all of the women. "You're not allowed to go anywhere on these grounds without me...or someone qualified to guide you."

Tawnyetta blinked. Anger rose inside of her pushing aside everything else. "Not *allowed*?" She was incensed at his tone. Her eyes narrowed and she spoke as evenly and coolly as possible. "You may be the Laird of this place, sir, but you are not in charge of me. Or any of us."

Michael's jaw clenched. He held her stare, his eyes flashing. After a long moment he fixed a hard gaze on each of them in turn before returning it to Tawnyetta. He stepped toward her so he was standing so close she could see every detail of the tattoo on his chest.

He leaned in and spoke to her, his voice as low and cold as hers had been. "I'll not be saving you a third time, lassie." Then he turned, snatched his shirt from where it lay on the ground nearby, and stalked away.

~

Dinner that night was a gloomy affair.

To Tawnyetta's surprise, Michael showed up to dine with the guests. Dressed formally, he looked stiff in a crisp white shirt and suit coat as he sat at the head of the long table in Stag Hall, dark and glowering. Tension was thick, but Tawnyetta refused to give him the slightest smile or nicety. She didn't care if he was offended. His behavior earlier had been horrible–after the part when he saved her life.

"Another narrow escape from tragedy, Miss Campbell?" Mrs. Prescott arched her left eyebrow as she asked. Bridget had just filled her and everyone else at the table in on their harrowing near drowning.

Tawnyetta didn't want to talk about it. She offered Mrs. Prescott a thin smile as she lifted a glass of red wine. "Narrow, but an escape nonetheless," she answered. She took a deep sip, flicking a look at Michael who was watching her evenly.

Tawnyetta looked away and swallowed hard, placing her glass back down on the table with great care.

"I say, you have a knack for getting into trouble, don't you?" Mr. Prescott said with a liquid chuckle. The other two Prescott men murmured in agreement.

Tawnyetta hated being the subject of the conversation, especially this conversation. Michael's eyes were burning into her and she was having a difficult time keeping her thoughts together.

"It wasn't anyone's fault," Sofia chimed in. "Tawnyetta jumped in to save Angie when she slipped. It was very brave."

"Well, I think we should plan to do something together tomorrow," Bea said. She had been stuck with her husband's family all day and was itching to spend time with the colorful Americans. "Something far from water and other dangers?" She smiled hopefully at Tawnyetta, who gave her a quick nod.

It would probably be best to steer clear of Michael. The blow up today was an indication that she had misunderstood his feelings for her, which made her question the feelings she'd thought she had for him. It was all a big mess. Maybe if they were part of a big group of people she could successfully avoid him.

"What do you say, Laird MacBrody?" Mrs. Prescott inquired.

Michael jerked a little at her question, surprised to be addressed. He cleared his throat. "Of course, what did you have in mind?" He turned his attention to Bea.

Thrilled to be taken seriously, Bea described what she had been thinking. A picnic in the hills. The same hills Tawnyetta and Michael had been stranded in.

"You can show us the bothy, too," Bea said excitedly to Tawnyetta.

It wasn't the best idea, but it was the only one on the table. She shrugged nonchalantly, as if what happened between her and Michael in that bothy meant nothing to her and she was happy to share the experience with everyone. She lifted her eyes to Michael and found him observing her reaction to the suggestion. Their eyes held for a moment, during which Tawnyetta attempted to convey a completely neutral attitude.

"That would be interesting. I'd love to see a real bothy," Bridget added her two cents.

Michael switched his attention from Tawnyetta to Bridget, then Bea, and smiled. He lifted his wine and announced, "A picnic it is."

Though she managed to keep a pleased expression for the rest of their dinner, Tawnyetta was determined not to enjoy one single moment of the next day.

<h1 style="text-align:center">Chapter Twenty-Four</h1>

For the third day in a row, a record since their arrival, the Highlands were sunny and bright. Still, Tawnyetta threw her favorite black knobby sweater on before leaving. She had learned a little something about the quick weather changes in the hills and she wanted to be prepared. A part of her wanted the picnic to be rained out. She secretly wished they would have two full days of grey clouds and drizzle to match her mood at the tail end of this Not a Honeymoon.

Falling for the gardener then finding out he was the Laird, then having him turn out not to be the person she thought he was, but in a completely different way, filled Tawnyetta with a sense of irony. She thought about it a lot as she climbed the hills behind the castle with the rest of the guests for the picnic. Lagging behind the others, she chose to keep to herself rather than get involved in any of the multiple conversations going on within the group.

Bridget had latched onto Michael from the moment he appeared, linking her arm in his and claiming him as her escort up the hill. Michael, Tawnyetta noticed, had not objected at all. They were joined by all of the Prescotts, of course, minus Bea. Bea had taken up the front with Sofia and the servants who were leading the way with supplies. Thomas walked with Angie and Luna, second to last in the group. Tawnyetta brought up the rear.

She was glad to be alone with her thoughts and was only intermittently annoyed by the sound of Bridget's laughter. There was no reason for her to be jealous of Michael's attentions toward Bridget. She had already decided that he wasn't her cup of tea, so to speak. What did she care if Bridget wanted to flirt mercilessly with him? It was none of her business.

"You all right?" Thomas had slowed his pace until she reached him so they could walk together.

Tawnyetta smiled at him and looked around at the glorious morning. "Yes, I'm fine."

Thomas cocked his head and gave her a knowing look. "That means you're not fine. I know that much about women."

This made her laugh. Thomas knew everything about all of them.

They walked together for a while in silence, enjoying the morning sun and the quiet camaraderie of old friends. Up ahead Michael said something that the Prescotts and Bridget found hilarious. Their laughter, the loudest of which was Bridget's, caught her and Thomas' attention. They both looked at the overly merry group then at each other.

"Could it really have been that funny?" Thomas asked her wryly.

Tawnyetta chuckled, then sighed. "Oh probably. We have to cut her some slack, she's had a rough few weeks."

Thomas nodded, though perhaps a little resentfully. It was a few moments before he, too, sighed and admitted, "I guess you're right." He nudged her arm so hard that she had to step sideways to keep her balance. "You're a good friend," he grinned.

She gave him a half-shrug, downplaying his comment. "I try," she grinned back at him.

His brow pinched together and he squinted at her in the bright sun. "You sure you're all right? You've been through some tough things in the past few days, too."

"I'm okay, really." Her eyes returned to the back of Michael's head.

Thomas followed them. It didn't take him long to connect the dots. "Oh, I see. You've got a thing for the Laird," he emphasized the word 'Laird' and nudged her again, more gently this time.

She shook her head 'no'. "It's not that at all," she lied. "It's the opposite, in fact. I'm not impressed with how he got mad yesterday. I think he has anger issues. Not my kind of guy." She pressed both of her palms forward as if stopping imaginary traffic.

He gave her a questioning look. "He wasn't mad."

Tawnyetta scoffed. "He wasn't? Did you see how he yelled at me? Treated us like we were children?"

"Well, yeah," Thomas nodded, though not like he agreed. "But he wasn't mad, Tawny."

"If he wasn't mad than what was all of the yelling about?"

"He was scared."

Tawnyetta stopped walking.

Thomas stopped too and looked at her earnestly. "Do you know how scary it was to hear all of the shouting and run to help? Then when we got there and they told us you and Angie were drowning?" He shook his head as if he'd like to remove the memory from his mind. "I was scared." He glanced up toward Michael. "I'm sure he was, too. Fear just comes out of guys as anger sometimes." He gave her his 'that's how it is' face.

"But you didn't get angry," she argued weakly.

"That's because I'm highly evolved." He puffed out his chest in jest, then let it fall. "And I've been hanging out with you girls forever."

Thomas' revelation stuck with her as they reached their destination, a beautiful flat spot on the hill halfway between the bridge she'd been stuck under during the storm and the bothy. The fact that Michael may have been afraid for her safety, and for Angie's, and acted out in anger after the crisis was over was a plausible suggestion. Tawnyetta hated to admit it, but she may have misread the entire situation. Not that Michael's behavior was excusable, but perhaps it was understandable given the circumstances.

At the picnic site Tawnyetta shared a red and green picnic blanket with Luna. The sky was bright blue with puffy white clouds and the view of the castle was stunning from this vantage point. As they munched on crackers with cold cuts and sliced cheese, Tawnyetta thought back to the moment Michael had stooped down and picked her up to carry her out from under the bridge. How he'd gotten her a blanket, started a fire, and made tea to keep her warm. All the while remaining a gentleman, even though they were both practically naked.

Glancing at Michael, who was seated on his own blanket with Bridget at his side, Tawnyetta was ashamed at how quickly she had come to judge him. How she'd forgotten his bravery and kindness so easily. He had saved her on this very hill, and saved her again when she and Angie were on the verge of drowning. Her heart twisted in her chest as she watched him laugh at something Bea said to him.

As if sensing her thoughts, he looked in her direction. Tawnyetta sucked in her breath when his eyes caught hers and held them. Laughter still danced on his face and his smile softened when she didn't look away. She did her best to smile back, though she felt foolish. She could only manage a crooked schoolgirl smile before having to look down at the small paper plate in her lap.

"What's going on with you two?" Luna asked, observing Tawnyetta's sudden shyness.

"Who?" Tawnyetta feigned ignorance.

Luna rolled her eyes. "You and Laird Michael McDreamy over there. Do you think I'm blind?"

Tawnyetta swept her gaze back to Michael. Bridget had her hand on his bicep as they talked. She noted how happy Bridget looked next to him. Not a care in the world. "Nothing's going on," she lied.

Luna grunted and took a sip of her Irn Bru. They had all become rather obsessed with the bright orange soda since having it at the Games. She observed as Tawnyetta fidgeted on the blanket and tried with all her might not to let her eyes wander toward Michael again.

"Oh, for heaven's sake, Tawnyetta," she blurted out in mild frustration. "You're gonna hurt yourself not looking at him."

Tawnyetta sank into her feelings. One moment she was delighted with Michael's occasional glances and smiles in her direction, the next she was full of dismay over her misunderstanding his feelings, then she swung erratically between being jealous over his attentions to Bridget and then ashamed for wishing to deny Bridget happiness. She didn't eat much. She didn't converse much. She drifted around the peripheral of the happy picnic group and thought about what she should do, coming to no real conclusion.

Flustered by her own inability to make a decision and act on it, not a predicament she was used to being in, Tawnyetta was true to the silent promise she'd made to herself at the previous night's dinner. She did not enjoy the picnic at all. And she especially did not enjoy the tour of the bothy.

The others were so taken with the story of her rescue they couldn't leave it alone. Bridget, Bea, and Mrs. Prescott hounded Michael to give them a tour. Every time they brought it up Tawnyetta's stomach clenched. She didn't want to share her experience with Michael in that place with anyone. It was their moment. It was probably the only moment they would ever share again. Showing the others felt like a violation.

Michael glanced at her a few times during the decision making process as if asking her permission. She looked away each time. Bringing everyone else into the bothy meant the intimacy between them would be laid bare. The fact that he was considering it was upsetting. The fact that she felt so strongly about it was overwhelming. Yet, she didn't know how to stop her feelings or stop the tour from happening.

"It's so tiny," Bridget said as she sashayed into the space and eyed its run down state.

"It's old," Sofia added.

"Dilapidated," Mrs. Prescott chimed in. Her voice sounded particularly nasal and haughty.

The small room with its fat belly wood stove and the crooked bench that they had shared was still charming to Tawnyetta. She felt a lump harden in her chest and move into her throat as she kept silent and listened to the criticism. Every comment pricked at her heart and made her more and more melancholy.

Michael stood stiffly in the corner where he'd found the hidden whiskey. He had remained quiet since they entered the bothy, keeping his head bowed as he stared at the floor. When he finally did look up and catch her eye, his expression was full of apology. She quickly averted her eyes. She didn't want to look at him. Not here.

Tawnyetta noticed the blankets they had worn were still where they'd thrown them on the wire bed frame while dressing to leave the other day. Instinctively she stepped to the cot and folded her blanket. Then she picked up Michael's.

Shaking out the soft cloth and folding it end over end she remembered the way it had slipped off his shoulder when he was lost in conversation. The memory of how soft the blankets felt against her cold, naked skin filled her body with longing. She wanted to return to that day, to that experience.

As she smoothed the top of his folded blanket and placed it next to hers the lump in her throat grew hot and she felt tears pressing at the backs of her eyes. She blinked hard. How stupid. Why would she cry over this? She was being ridiculous.

A warm hand covered hers. She looked up into Michael's concerned face.

"No need to fuss over the blankets, lass," he said softly. When he saw that she was bordering on tears he searched her eyes and furrowed his brow. "Are you all right, Tawnyetta?"

She nodded quickly which forced a tear to drop from her eye and land on the blanket. She shook her head and pursed her lips together, determined to stop overreacting. Michael glanced uncomfortably at the others who were either still busy looking through the cupboards or had already left the cramped interior and were roaming about outside on the porch.

He cleared his throat, uncertain what ailed her. "Do you want to leave? Too many bad memories?"

She braved a look at him and saw the disappointment on his face at that idea. "No, it's not that," she managed. "I'm fine."

Not happy with her response, he watched her for a moment. Then he leaned in so his mouth almost brushed her cheek. When he spoke it was in a whisper.

"I'm sorry for the way I acted yesterday. I shouldn't have said what I said. I would save you again, lass, if saving is what you needed. I will always save you."

All the twisting and turning knots in her heart loosened at his words. Warmth and joy gushed through her as she beamed at him. Relieved at her response, Michael's own countenance relaxed and he leaned more casually against the frame of the cot, settling in for a conversation.

"Am I forgiven then?" His eyes sparkled with delight.

"Yes, you are forgiven," she answered. Her cheeks turned pink.

She loved how he looked at her, how his body seemed to surround her even though they weren't touching, how he made her feel like he was about to take her in his arms. Though he didn't.

"Are you ready?" Bridget interrupted from the doorway.

Tawnyetta jerked at the sound. She looked around the bothy. Everyone had left. She and Michael had been alone staring into each other's eyes for God knows how long. Her blush deepened and she took a step away from him, as if they'd been caught doing something indiscreet.

"Yes, absolutely," she answered. Though, truthfully, she would have rather stayed in this place with Michael forever.

<h1 align="center">Chapter Twenty-Five</h1>

Halfway down the hill Tawnyetta realized she had forgotten her sweater. Not wanting to bother anyone she decided to pop back up to the bothy to retrieve it. She was hanging back behind the others anyway. Nobody would notice.

When she stepped back inside the bothy she was overcome once again by its charm. She took a deep breath and went to the cot where her knobby black sweater lay next to the blankets she'd folded. Despite knowing that she was stuck smack dab in the 21st century, Tawnyetta let her mind wander to the history of this place. What was it like to live in a simple building in these beautiful, wild hills of Scotland many years ago? What would it feel like to hunt for your meat, grow your own food, and be married to a strong, stubborn Scottish Highlander? Her fingers traced the soft threads of the blankets and ran along the unpretentious iron frame of the cot's headboard. Sharing a bed in the Highlands with a man who looked and sounded like Michael would be an epic experience.

She laughed out loud at her train of thought. Then shook it out of her head. She would be flying home to Colorado in less than 48 hours. No time for wild love affairs even if one had ever been fated between her and Michael.

The rays of the early afternoon sun passed into the little room through two small, square windows. They filled the space with a warm glow while pixie dust danced in them. How was it possible that she'd spent more than a week in a luxurious castle, but something about this humble building warmed her heart so completely?

"Have you come back to do more chores?"

Tawnyetta whirled around at the question.

Michael stood in the doorway. One hand held the doorjamb above his head as he leaned into the room. Backlit from the sunshine outside, his white shirt became almost see through. The intensely masculine form of his wide shoulders and muscled chest was undeniable in this position. Tawnyetta's heartbeat quickened at the sight of him—at the look in his eyes.

"What are you doing here?" she asked.

"I could ask you the same thing," he grinned as he stepped inside and approached her.

"I came back for my sweater." Tawnyetta lifted the knobby black sweater off the cot as proof.

He glanced at it briefly before returning his weighted gaze back to her. "I see."

Tawnyetta looked behind him at the empty doorway. "Did anyone—"

"Come with me?" He finished her sentence, making her look at him again. He shook his head. "No."

A thrill shot from her stomach and down. Alone with him again. Her heartbeat grew faster.

"Is that all right with you?" His brow creased with the question. She nodded, unable to speak. One side of his mouth lifted into a sexy smile.

"I could have found my way back on my own," she blurted out, then immediately worried he would take it as an insult.

He nodded, playing at a serious face, "Oh, yes, lass. I have not a doubt about that."

Michael stood directly in front of her now. His body so close she could feel the heat emanating from him. She could smell him. Wild grass wet with rain, cool breezes, and damp earth. She realized he smelled like the Highlands and the skin on her neck and shoulders tingled. Breathing him in, she felt a little dizzy.

"Why–" her voice cracked and she had to swallow before continuing. "Why did you come back for me?"

His smile softened as he let his gaze roam across her face, down her neck and to her chest. He was momentarily captured by the roundness of her bosom moving up and down rapidly underneath her shirt with each shallow breath. Inching his body even closer, so close she had to press her bottom into the edge of the cot to avoid their hips touching, he slowly lifted his right hand. His eyes raised at the same time. Slowly. So slowly.

As his gaze lifted he used it to caress every inch of her neck, her chin, her lips, and her cheek. The whole while he spoke in a deep, rumbling tone, "I wanted to look at you here in the bothy. I wanted to touch your cheek. I wanted..." Here he paused. Tearing his eyes away from the hair just above her ear where his fingertips hovered, waiting to touch, he looked deep into her eyes. The blue in his was intensely dark. "I wanted to kiss you," he said as he bent his head down and softly touched his lips to hers.

Heat shimmered across her skin. His lips, warm and firm, pressed gently against hers and her body rose toward him. Michael pushed his fingertips lightly into the hair just over her ear sending shivers of down her neck and shoulders. He tasted sweet and his beard tickled her lips.

For one glorious moment she was lost in him.

Her hand reached for his cheek where she touched the soft whiskers of his beard, his jaw firm and strong underneath. His free hand slipped neatly around her waist and pulled her to him so their hips were touching. They both paused for a split second, hanging on to the moment as long as possible, then he kissed her more deeply. His fingers moved further into her hair and her senses exploded like a thousand stars twinkling through her body.

So this was what love felt like.

Tawnyetta had never been in love, not truly. She had never completely understood the drive people had for the whole marriage and family thing. But this. This man, this kiss, this moment, made her conscious of a whole new world. If this was how Bridget had felt, Tawnyetta could see why she'd wanted to get married so badly.

Bridget.

With a sudden gasp Tawnyetta pulled away from the kiss and placed both hands on Michael's chest. She pushed him away, still breathing hard from the thrill of their passion.

At first he didn't let go. Still wrapped up in their intimacy, it took him a moment to realize that she wanted to stop.

"What is it?" Michael released his hold on her, instinctively looking around and behind them for some unknown threat.

"Oh, God," Tawnyetta threw her hands over her face. She growled in frustration, "This is wrong!"

Seeing no immediate dangers, he turned his attention back to her. "What's wrong?"

She waved her arms around a little frantically. "All of this is wrong." She flipped her fingers back and forth between the both of them. "We're not supposed to get together. You and Bridget are supposed to get together!"

His confusion was complete. "What are you going on about, lass?"

Tawnyetta pushed past him and went to the corner where the stove sat. Standing right next to him made her dizzy and she needed to think straight. He watched her with growing frustration.

"She's the one who just broke up. She's the one that needs a romance," Tawnyetta tried to explain. It wasn't sinking in.

"Your friend, Bridget?"

"Yes, what other Bridget would I be talking about?"

His eyebrows lifted at her annoyed tone. "Pardon me. I didn't know there was a logical train of thought to this."

She sighed, holding her palm up to him to stop further comment. "I'm sorry. I didn't mean to snap at you. It's just that you are supposed to be Bridget's fun vacation romance, not mine. I didn't even pay for this trip!"

A glimmer of understanding appeared in his eyes. "I've been chosen for your friend? Not you? Is that what you're getting at?" His Scottish brogue was getting stronger, a sign he was getting angry. "And who, exactly, is making these decisions?"

"It's not like that. Not exactly," she tried to backtrack. Her shoulders slumped with defeat. She didn't know how to explain their predicament to him in a way that didn't sound crazy. She decided to just stick with the basics. "You're supposed to like Bridget."

"I don't like Bridget."

The fine hair on Tawnyetta's neck prickled defensively. "What's wrong with Bridget? She's a great person and she's absolutely beautiful. She's loving and would do anything for a friend. You would be lucky to have–"

"Dammit, lass, why won't you stop talking and listen to me!" Michael's voice boomed and his eyes flashed with anger. Tawnyetta froze. He ran his hand through his hair and took a deep breath before continuing. "Your friend is a fine woman, no doubt about it, but it's you, Tawnyetta." He stepped toward her, his eyes burning with longing. "It's you that I want." Tawnyetta's heart skipped a beat. He kept moving closer and closer, holding her attention with his gaze. "You...with the name like a lioness and eyes the color of fine whiskey. You, fighting me at every turn," he sounded exasperated, like someone facing a great challenge and not sure how to proceed. "You've got more than a wee bit of pluck, this is true," he chuckled a little. "You bring light into this ancient place, making it...making *me* come alive." He was in front of her again. She could breathe him in once more. When she did she felt lightheaded. His face softened. His voice followed in kind. "You've been living inside my soul my whole life, lass, and I didn't even know. My world was missing something, someone. And now here you are manifest right in front of me." He reached toward her, but didn't touch her, just held his hand level with her stomach, his fingers trembling, ready to scoop her up if given permission. His voice was gruff, full of emotion. "Sometimes, in the morning, when I see you walking through the mist in the garden I'm not even sure that you're real. You're like a dream. My dream come true. It's you I want, Tawnyetta. It's *you* I've fallen in love with."

His words entered her soul. Ignoring her physical body they implanted deep inside her, piercing places she had never known existed. She couldn't believe this was happening. So many feelings raced to places in her heart that had never been touched. They were too much. They soured in her stomach, turning the joy and happiness into a cynical disbelief.

Tawnyetta scoffed at him and Michael pulled away as if he'd been slapped.

"People don't fall in love in two weeks." Her voice was icy, dismissive. "Not emotionally healthy people, anyway. I mean, maybe you have some co-dependent stuff to work on. I don't know." She laughed and it tasted bitter in her mouth. "A vacation fling is one thing, but love? I doubt it." As the words spilled out of her Michael stepped back, dropping his hand to his side and watching her in disbelief.

Tawnyetta couldn't see straight. She had taken something lovely and twisted it into something embarrassing and awful. All she wanted to do was leave. When Michael stepped away from her, she took the chance to walk past him toward the door, but before she could get through he shoved his arm in front of her, blocking her path of escape.

"Wait," he said. His voice was like gravel in his throat.

She leveled her gaze at him, still upset for reasons unclear to both of them. "Please, Michael, let me leave."

Any hope that had lingered in his eyes dissolved into confusion then drifted away. All that remained were his blue eyes, void of emotion, disconnected. He dropped his arm and she left, because she couldn't stand to look into the emptiness her words had caused for one moment longer.

Chapter Twenty-Six

Tawnyetta burst through the servant's door at the rear of the castle. She rushed by Stewart and the cook, then by Anne, and finally Erin, startling her so badly that she almost dropped a tea tray she was carrying. They all watched her with surprise as she raced by and hurried to her room.

Tawnyetta didn't stop. She barely apologized as she hurried past. It was all she could do to control her ragged breathing as she fought to stop the tears that had been flowing since she left Michael–hurt, confused, and most likely furious.

She wanted to pack. She wanted to leave. Their plane left for home the day after next and it couldn't come fast enough in her opinion.

Tawnyetta managed to open the heavy door to her room. The Queen's room. The room she'd occupied on her own at Michael's insistence since her knee injury. Shutting the door behind her with a satisfying click, she slumped against the dark stained wood and let the tears come full force.

Though the stone walls and heavy door kept all sound out, Tawnyetta was still loathe to make too much noise. She didn't want the staff to hear her or, God forbid, Michael to return and hear her wailing in her room. She left the door and threw herself face down on her bed, muffling her sobs with the pillows.

She had never been in love like this. Never reacted to someone as strongly as she did to Michael, nor felt compelled to repel his advances so strongly either. It was an impossible relationship. She knew this. Surely he must know it, too. Not only were they practically strangers, but they lived an ocean apart. His life here was nothing like the life she had at home. They had so little in common it would be comical if it didn't hurt so much.

Then there was Bridget. She couldn't betray her. Bridget's heart was wounded. She needed love and support and fun, not a self-centered friend who seduced the very first eligible man to cross their path since Bridget's fiasco of a wedding.

Wiping her eyes, Tawnyetta rolled onto her back. The huge bed was remarkably comfortable and she felt guilty for taking this room for herself. As she looked around at the ancient architecture and plush bedding and curtains, she sighed. This life wasn't for her anyway. She was bound for something more rugged, like the Rocky Mountains she'd left behind. Hadn't she told everyone just two weeks ago that her greatest dream was to have an adventure? There was a whole world out there waiting to be explored. She couldn't waste time and energy on a pointless romance.

Tawnyetta sat up and sniffed. Even though her heart felt like it was full of lead and sinking slowly into her belly, she would buck up and move on. First things first, she needed to pack. That would help her get her mind straight and forget about this emotional tangent she'd ended up on. She had only just lifted her biggest suitcase onto the bed to rummage through it and begin organizing when a loud knock sounded at her door.

Tawnyetta jerked her head up, her eyes wide. He wouldn't...would he? Her lead heart thudded hard inside her chest.

"I'll be there in a second," Tawnyetta called out as she hurried into her bathroom and doused a washcloth with cold water. She rubbed it quickly over her puffy eyes and carried it with her back to the door. Taking a deep breath, she gathered herself then pulled the door open.

Her disappointment was sharp.

"Were you sleeping?" Bridget asked as she entered uninvited. Sofia following close behind.

"Yeah, a little," Tawnyetta answered, closing the door and turning toward her friends. Sofia glanced at the open suitcase on the bed. "I thought I would get a jump on packing, then I got really tired," Tawnyetta explained.

Bridget plopped down on the bed. "No packing yet! I don't want to think about going home. We still have the rest of today and tomorrow before we have to leave."

"Yeah, Tawny," Sofia mirrored Bridget's sentiments by closing the top of the unpacked suitcase. "Let's do something fun this afternoon."

"I think we should find the oldest, creepiest room in the castle and do a Ouija board!" Bridget said brightly. Sofia shook her head and mouthed 'no' to Tawnyetta from behind Bridget's back.

Tawnyetta thought about Michael's recently deceased older brother and his parents, not to mention all of the other people who had lived and died in this castle over the centuries. She wasn't one to put stock in silly games like Ouija boards, but she also didn't want to accidentally awaken some ghost that would haunt the halls of this place long after they left.

"I doubt if they have a Ouija board here, Bridge," she said logically. Sofia mouthed 'thank you'.

"Gigi and Lulu went to check," Bridget proclaimed, still holding onto the possibility.

When Angie and Luna arrived soon after they announced that their hunt for a Ouija board had come up empty. Bridget made a long face.

"But," Angie added with a radiant smile, "Dougie's wife is a fortune teller!"

"Dougie the caretaker?" Tawnyetta asked. He had seemed too old to have a wife.

Angie nodded. "She's known all over for being able to tell the future."

Bridget's face brightened. "Really?"

"And she said she had time to tell all our fortunes this afternoon," Luna added with a smile.

The decision was made. Before Tawnyetta had too much time to consider that perhaps she didn't want her future rolled out in front of her for all to see, she was off to see Dougie's wife, Gavina, the fortune teller.

All five friends walked to a small cottage at the edge of the castle woodlands where the caretaker and his wife had lived for decades. They were greeted by Dougie with all of his ancient Scottish charm and shown into a small but comfortable sitting room. There, under a pile of colorful shawls, sitting on a straight back chair in front of a small wooden table, sat his wife. With gnarled, trembling fingers she patted a stack of Tarot cards waiting on the table and beamed a smile at them that was missing one front tooth.

Gavina was tiny and round and as frail as Dougie. Her hair was pure white, braided and pinned in a loose bun at the back of her head. Her eyes were pale blue, but sharp like a bird's when they peered at the group of younger women over a pair of reading glasses.

"Who's first, then?" she asked in a high crackling voice.

Bridget went first. Gavina cooed and clucked over her and

told her all of the nicest things about her future. Wealth, children, and a wonderful home, were just some of the things Gavina let Bridget know she had to look forward to.

"What about love?" Bridget asked, a bit greedily.

"Ah, love," Gavina's gappy smile saddened a little and Bridget took a quick glance at her friends to see if they had also seen the change in the fortune teller's demeanor.

"Is it bad?" Bridget asked.

"It isn't bad," Gavina assured her, though her face was still grim. "Your love is already in your life."

Tawnyetta's heart sank at this proclamation. Unbidden images of having to put on a fake smile and be the maid of honor at Bridget and Michael's wedding flew through her mind. She thought she might throw up.

"Oh," Bridget seemed surprised, then she frowned. "It's not Christopher, is it?"

"You don't see this love, yet," Gavina continued. "But when you do..." the old woman lifted her hands to her ears and wiggled her fingers while widening her eyes until they looked like bug eyes. The effect was both unnerving and silly. Bridget giggled and this sent ripples of slightly awkward laughter through all of them.

It was Tawnyetta's turn next. Gavina stared her down with a piercing gaze for at least thirty seconds after she sat down. So long that Tawnyetta was beginning to wonder if the old woman had suffered a stroke.

"You're a wild-eyed, lass," Gavina told her suddenly. Tawnyetta didn't know how to respond, so she said nothing. The old woman mumbled something under her breath, closed her eyes and patted the Tarot cards with both of her arthritic hands. Then she picked up the deck, pulled a card from the middle and placed it on the table face up. She opened her eyes, took in the image on the card and looked sharply up at Tawnyetta.

"You're a wanderer, are you not?" Gavina asked, her pale eyes glittering.

Tawnyetta gave an uncertain nod, then answered, "I came here so I suppose I am."

Gavina shook her head and when she did there was a tinkling of tiny bells from somewhere unseen on her person. "Not your body, lass. Your mind. Your soul." Gavina tapped the image on the card. It was a drawing of a nude woman who looked to be asleep. She was bound tightly in the roots of a great tree and the roots were lifting her towards a night sky where a huge, white moon looked down, scowling. "You're trapped in your body and letting your mind fall into daydreams all the time. You won't wake up to the truth."

"What truth?"

"That your soul is the real wanderer."

With that announcement Gavina gathered up the card dismissively and waved for Angie to sit down in the chair Tawnyetta occupied.

"But I don't understand," Tawnyetta said. She desperately wanted to ask about her own love life, about Michael and whether or not she would ever find anyone that made her feel the way he did again. But she couldn't bring all that up in front of an audience. However, she could try to understand the cryptic message she had received.

Gavina turned her sharp blue eyes on her again. "Your soul understands, lass. That's all that matters."

When they returned to the castle after having their fortunes told Tawnyetta still had not deciphered the meaning of the old woman's message. Given that the fortunes she'd told the others were almost as strange as hers, Tawnyetta had secretly decided that Gavina was a bit of a con artist. She didn't tell the others, though. No sense in ruining everyone's fun.

"Where is Thomas?" Luna wondered aloud. They had

been so swept away in visiting Gavina that they had forgotten about him.

"Oh, he's running around with his new best friend," Bridget said with more than just a little attitude. She waved her hand around in the air like she was swatting a fly. "They're probably hunting boars or shopping for kilts or something."

In fact, Thomas and Michael were drinking Scotch in the blue parlor. The women stumbled upon them while looking for a quiet place to relax together before dinner.

"Hello Ladies," Thomas lifted his tumbler in a toast to them as he unsteadily got to his feet. Apparently they had been drinking Scotch in the blue parlor for a while.

While the others teased Thomas about being drunk, Tawnyetta gathered up enough nerve to look at Michael. He was glowering at her from a chair in the corner that was very near the statue of Artemis. She remembered the first time she had been in this room and their roles had been reversed. She had been giving him a dirty look that time.

"...Gavina told me all about the love of my life, too," Bridget was filling drunk Thomas in on the details of their afternoon. From what Tawnyetta could tell he was drifting between not comprehending and being annoyed at her chatter.

"Would any of you bonnie lasses like a drink?" Michael's deep Scottish brogue came out of the corner.

The sound of his voice caught her by surprise. Her reaction, actually, is what surprised her the most. She was catapulted back to the bothy this morning and their singularly amazing kiss. The warmth of his hands on her cheek, the heat of his lips on hers, the soft tickle of his breath on her neck. Had all of that only happened this morning? It seemed like a lifetime ago.

"Why, thank you," Bridget said. Dissatisfied with Thomas'

responses she turned away from him and zeroed in on Michael. "I would love a drink."

As quickly as the thrill of this morning had come upon Tawnyetta, the heartache of how they'd ended everything returned. The amazing kiss they'd shared was not to be repeated. Any spark of romance they had shared was doomed and that knowledge filled her with grief.

She accepted the first drink Thomas brought to her and slammed it down. Wiping her mouth with the back of her hand she asked for a second, then a third, but the strong liquor did little to squelch her pain.

Chapter Twenty-Seven

Tawnyetta awoke on her last full day in the Scottish Highlands with a splitting headache. She just wanted to stay in bed in the dark with the curtains drawn and nurse her hangover. Her head hurt. Her stomach roiled. Her spirit was tangled in the sour, damp sheets she had twisted around herself during a night of fitful, drunken sleep.

Tawnyetta squinted at the light peeking around the edges of the heavy draperies and glowered. She dared the sun to shine so brightly over her misery.

As she lay prone on the bed wishing she could magically transport to her own snug house in Colorado and forgo all of the pain and misery this day was bound to bring her, she had a moment of insanity. Thoughts of the greasy sausages that were present at every castle breakfast popped into her aching brain. Maybe, just maybe, they would help.

Bridget, Angie, Luna and Sofia were no better off than Tawnyetta at the breakfast table. They all poured black, black coffee into their mugs and avoided the eggs at the buffet like they were toxic waste. Though they were in bad shape, Thomas was even worse as he stumbled around the table letting out small groans and squinting in agony just to see in the daylight. Michael hadn't even shown his face yet. That's probably for the best, Tawnyetta thought to herself as she sat down at the long table with a plate holding four sausage links and a piece of buttered toast.

Recollections of the night before swam through her groggy brain. How the party in the blue parlor had progressed. How she'd become more and more morose. How Bridget had grown louder and more animated through the evening. How Thomas had been beside himself with the drunken 'I love you's' he was famous for saying. And Michael. Michael, who remained smoldering hot and unbelievably sexy even when he was drunk, hovered around the edges of their group—grim, glowering, and deliberately difficult. That's how she remembered it anyway.

There had definitely been moments between them that were too physical considering where they'd left everything in the bothy. Like when she had swayed a little standing up and leaned into the closest sturdy object, which turned out to be Michael, gripping his iron bicep for support. Or when he had stood just close enough behind her that she could feel the warmth of his body without even having to look. As the evening had gone on and she had gotten more and more tipsy, she honestly didn't know how she had kept her hands off of him.

Unbelievable self-control. Self-preservation. Pride. That's how.

The Prescotts, thankfully, had left on a day trip early in the morning. So the Americans were saved any awkward explanations about their disheveled appearances to the utterly upright and well behaved British family. Upon seeing the six of them stumbling around the breakfast buffet, Stewart very kindly instructed the staff to bring up extra greasy bacon and fried potatoes as well as a silver bucket full of cans of the orange soda drink, Irn Bru, on ice.

"This will set you straight for certain," Anne insisted as she handed each one of them a freezing cold can of the fizzy orange stuff.

Bridget covered her face with her hands at the sight of the food in front of her. "I don't know if I should eat anything."

Thomas moaned, then pushed Bridget's plate closer to her. "Eat. You'll feel better."

"Please," Sofia held her palm up to Thomas. "No shouting."

Angie had her eyes closed and was doing breathing exercises. In through the nose, out through the mouth. Luna watched her with blood shot eyes, unable to stop observing others even when suffering the effects of too much drink.

Thomas moaned again, this time with some measure of relief. He had pressed the ice cold can of Irn Bru to his forehead. "That does the trick," he said.

Tawnyetta took up her own can, placing it gingerly against her temple, and immediately wished she had a dozen of the aluminum cans strapped around her head. The smooth cold of its surface was at once shocking and soothing. She sighed with relief.

Luna looked back and forth between Tawnyetta and Thomas blissfully holding their drinks against their foreheads. She scooped up hers and copied them. The others followed suit until all five women and Thomas were slumped back in their fine hand carved wooden chairs holding iced Irn Bru cans to their foreheads.

Angie looked around at all of them and in her recently perfected Scottish accent said, "Well, isn't this a fine kettle of fish."

Thomas cracked up first. Then the rest of them. Laughing made their heads hurt, which made them laugh harder. None of them removed their can from their head because it felt so good, which was the funniest part.

"Is that even a Scottish saying?" Sofia asked, wiping tears of laughter from her eyes.

Angie shrugged, "I don't know. It just popped into my head."

"It certainly has been a crazy few weeks, hasn't it?" Bridget said. "Starting with the mammoth disaster of my wedding!" She lifted her Irn Bru into the air as if toasting. They all returned the gesture before placing them back against their heads.

"Then we came here on the Not a Honeymoon," Tawnyetta added. Again the mock toast and return.

"Then we surprised you!" Luna said. She raised her can again and everyone returned the favor.

"And then Tawny got lost during the flash flood and Laird MacBrody found her," Angie reminded them. They all toasted Tawnyetta then returned the cans to their foreheads.

"What about when Angie almost drowned and Tawny jumped in after her," Sofia lifted her can.

"And Laird MacBrody saved her," Sofia, Luna, and Angie all said at the same time. Tawnyetta had to laugh at the drama of it all.

"Here, here!" Bridget said as they all lifted their cans high in the air again.

"Here, here!" They responded.

"And then Laird MacBrody fell in love with Tawny!" Thomas called out, caught up in the moment.

The room fell silent.

All arms froze mid-air with the Irn Bru lifted toward the ceiling. All eyes turned to him.

His cheeks grew red and he gave a timid, "Here, here."

"What?" Bridget asked in surprise.

Sofia looked at Luna and said, "You were right."

Angie's face filled with joy and she looked at Tawnyetta. "How wonderful!"

All eyes turned to Tawnyetta and she felt color rising in her cheeks. She fumbled for something to say, but nothing intelligible came out. Her stomach felt sick. Churning from her hangover and a heavy dose of embarrassment and guilt, and something even more sickening, a quavering sensation of hope.

"What is he talking about?" Bridget asked.

"Laird MacBrody has a thing for Tawnyetta," Sofia explained. Luna nodded in agreement.

Bridget kept her gaze on Tawnyetta, trying to understand.

All of them had lowered their Irn Bru's, except Thomas. "More than just a thing," he interjected, closing his eyes once more against the conversation and the too bright morning.

Tawnyetta wished he would just shut up. "It's nothing," she insisted. "Nothing is happening between us." Everybody still watched her, less than convinced. "Okay, well, maybe there was some attraction and...I mean, we were trapped in the bothy for a long time...but I let him know yesterday in no uncertain terms that we were not an item."

Bridget's eyebrows crinkled in confusion. "When yesterday?"

Tawnyetta looked into her big blue eyes. She didn't want to lie. She didn't want to hurt her feelings. But this was Bridget, one of her forever friends. They were all her forever friends. She had to tell the truth.

Tawnyetta drug her gaze away from Bridget and glanced at all of them quickly before looking down at the can of orange soda in her hands. She sighed, then said, "When I went back to the bothy to get my sweater...after the picnic...and he kissed me."

There was a weighted pause as what she said sank in. Her friends stared at her in stunned silence. As surprise slowly registered in their expressions, Tawnyetta sat twisting in discomfort. She couldn't believe she had told them. What did they think? What did she think, really? She didn't know what to think or feel anymore.

When it seemed like she couldn't stand their silence for one more moment and she thought she was going to have to tell them to just say something already, the feeling of uncertainty in the air shifted. In one unified moment the whole room erupted into astonished delight.

Chapter Twenty-Eight

"Oh my God!" Sofia exclaimed.

"Tawnyetta, that's so romantic," Angie said, beaming at her from across the table.

"You called it," Sofia said to Luna again. Luna just smiled and nodded as she watched Tawnyetta react to their overwhelming positivity.

"Tawny..." Bridget searched for the words, then raised her Irn Bru once again in the air to toast her friend for real. "He's totally hot!"

They all laughed, Tawnyetta included. Relief at Bridget's reaction made her a bit giddy.

Bridget turned her attention to Thomas who was the only one of all of them still slumping in his chair. Obviously his hangover had more of a hold on him as he still held his Irn Bru to his forehead. She narrowed her eyes suspiciously. "How did you know?" Thomas squinted at her, looking a little sheepish. He lifted one shoulder and let it drop in an uninspired half-shrug. He opened his mouth to answer when a new thought struck Bridget and she flipped her attention back to

Tawnyetta. "More importantly, why didn't I know?" She looked pained. "Why didn't you tell me?"

Tawnyetta didn't know what to say. Sometimes it was difficult to think when hit with the Bridget spotlight. Especially now. Especially with her body surging with the thrill of admitting her and Michael's secret romantic encounter. She opened her mouth to speak, then closed it again.

"I think she was worried about you," Luna said softly.

Bridget looked bewildered. "Me?"

Tawnyetta nodded, thankful for Luna's words hitting the nail on the head. When she started talking, the whole story spilled out. "I wanted to be there for you, after Christopher and the whole wedding thing." She waved her hand around as if shooing away a pesky fly. "You were all excited about finding the Laird of the Castle and I just...I just..." Tawnyetta couldn't find the right way to say it.

"You were protecting her," Angie spoke up.

Tawnyetta nodded emphatically and pointed at Angie. "Yes, what she said."

Bridget struggled to understand.

"She thought you needed a distraction," Sofia explained further.

Tawnyetta nodded again. "I didn't want to go after the guy you were interested in, especially after what happened with Christopher."

Bridget tilted her head sideways and stuck out her bottom lip, looking at Tawnyetta as if she were a really cute puppy. "Aww, Tawny, that's so sweet." She shook her head and flashed a charming smile, "But I'm not really into him. Not *really*, really."

The weight of the world lifted from Tawnyetta's shoulders. "You're not?"

"I mean, he's absolutely gorgeous and manly, and that accent! Plus he has a castle and everything," her face softened and she reached out to touch Tawnyetta's hand. "But I'm not ready for a relationship right now, you know?" Tawnyetta nodded. "Besides, he's into you! He kissed *you*!" Bridget's eyes flew open as she sucked in her breath and fluttered her fingers on her chest. "Tawny!" Her voice was high pitched and excited. "You could be a princess!"

Tawnyetta laughed, reassured that her feelings for Michael weren't going to ruin her best friend's Not a Honeymoon, a glimmer of true hope lit like a tiny candle in the pit of her stomach. It was immediately squelched by the memory of what she'd said to him in the bothy. Her face fell.

"What's the matter?" Angie asked.

"Do you not return his feelings?" Sofia wondered.

Tawnyetta shook her head, denying that possibility. "It's not that."

"What is it, then?" Bridget asked.

"I told him I didn't want a relationship with him." Tawnyetta looked around at her concerned friends. All except Thomas, who had his eyes closed and head back, were listening intently. The tiny flame of hope puffed out completely as she confessed her mistake. "I was pretty mean about it, too. If there was the possibility of anything between us, I threw it all away."

"Nope," Thomas said, eyes still closed, head still back. All eyes, once again, turned to him.

"What do you mean 'nope'?" Bridget asked, annoyed at what she saw as his indifference to Tawnyetta's plight.

Thomas removed the can and opened one eye so he could squint at Tawnyetta like a pirate. "If you think telling him you're not interested has changed his mind, you're wrong."

"Did he tell you that?" Bridget demanded to know.

"He didn't have to tell me. I can see it on him." Thomas sat up straight and looked around the table at the five women in his life. He sighed as if he was saddened to have to convey some awful truth. "Besides, it's basic human nature. The thing you can't have is the thing you want the most."

They all considered this for a few moments in silence.

"Couldn't you just tell him you changed your mind?" Luna suggested.

Tawnyetta cringed. "I am probably the last person he wants to see right now. We're leaving tomorrow anyway," she said, defeated before she even tried.

"What's the problem? Airplanes stop flying after tomorrow?" Sofia arched her eyebrow at Tawnyetta.

"What's blocking you, Tawny?" Angie asked.

Tawnyetta felt shaky. Like if she tried to stand up she might stumble. "I don't know."

They all waited, watching her, wondering what was wrong and how they could help. Tears pressed at the back of Tawnyetta's eyes. She loved all them so much. They were the best friends anyone could ever have. But there was something deeply sad inside of her, a void, a knowledge that what she wanted could never be.

"What is it?" Luna asked again softly.

A fat tear drop rolled down Tawnyetta's cheek. She wiped it defiantly away. Her bottom lip trembled and she trained her eyes out the nearest window so she wouldn't have to look at them when she spoke.

"I'm afraid," she admitted, her voice quavering just a little. She looked back at them to explain, "I'm afraid it won't work. I'm afraid to be hurt. I'm afraid it's too fast and I'll regret it." Another tear escaped. "I'm afraid I'm giving up my dream of adventure for a relationship."

Bridget looked deep into her eyes. "We're talking about a Scottish Highlander with a castle, Tawny. You're hardly settling for boring suburbia." Tawnyetta laughed at this. "The only thing that would actually missing from your adventure would be dragons! And they're not even real!" Bridget declared.

"Allegedly," Angie corrected her. That made everyone laugh. Still holding all of their attention, Angie leaned forward and focused her mystical dark brown eyes on Tawnyetta. "And, really Tawnyetta, couldn't love be the greatest adventure of all?"

The first place Tawnyetta looked for Michael was in the garden. Her heart sang with the encouragement of her friends. Adding in Thomas' unalterable opinion that she hadn't completely ruined her chances with Michael after all, Tawnyetta practically walked on air as she searched for him. Through the rose garden, into the overgrown Secret Garden, and even through the woodlands right next to the castle, she looked, but to no avail. The only people she ran into were Dougie and the real Shaun who were working on the troublesome fountain in the formal garden.

A chilly mist had moved in and she clutched the front of her sweater close to her body to fend it off. When she returned from the woodlands frustrated at not finding Michael anywhere, she asked Dougie if he knew where he was.

"Could be the Master is in his chambers," Dougie guessed. He said something else, but Tawnyetta didn't hear it because she had already said thank you and was hurrying back to the castle.

As she walked she thought about what she was going to say to him. She hadn't really worked that part through, just took off from breakfast to find him. All she wanted was to see him again, hear his voice, look into his deep blue eyes. Her body ached for his touch, to be close to him and feel his warm strength. Even as she tried to formulate the words she would use to convince him that she was sorry and had been wrong about everything, she couldn't do it. Her heart wouldn't let go of her mind long enough to be that logical.

The halls and walkways of the castle felt like miles and miles of space as she rushed through them, brushing by staff members and completely ignoring all of the architecture and decor that normally caught her attention. Finally she was at the door to Laird MacBrody's private chambers. The very same door she and Bridget had snuck into only last week. It all seemed like so long ago.

So much had passed between her and Michael since the moment they had watched him dancing naked down the hallway to The Backstreet Boys. Though she'd seen all of his amazing body from their hiding place, she hadn't seen his face. The first time she did see him when he'd startled her and she tried to act like he didn't, she had been taken aback by his intensity. His sardonic sexiness.

Admittedly he still had that edge. But since they'd formally met, danced together, escaped torrential rains together, warmed up by the fire and drank spiked tea together, she knew there was so much more of him to explore. So much more of him that she wanted to know. Because every bit of him that she knew so far she loved completely.

Tawnyetta stood quite still at Michael's door. Her breath came shallow and fast. This was it. She was going to lay her heart on the line and tell the man she had fallen in love with that the feelings he'd declared for her were not a mistake. She felt them too.

She lifted her hand to rap her knuckles on the heavy wooden door.

"He's not there, Miss," a man's voice came from directly behind her making her jump and let out a small squeal of fright.

Tawnyetta whirled around to find Stewart standing a few

feet behind her. How long had he been there? How long had she been standing stock still staring at Michael's door? She didn't know the answer to either of those questions, so she tried to regain her composure.

"Who's not here?" That was a silly question. Too late, it had been asked.

Though Stewart's mouth remained in its constant state, which was not quite a frown but not quite a smile, the outside corners of his eyes twitched slightly and moved upward in amusement.

"Laird MacBrody, Miss," he stated without any hint of merriment. His eyes, however, still deceived him.

"And where is Laird MacBrody then?" She heard the slightest tinge of a Scottish accent near the end of her question and felt even sillier.

Stewart gave her a slight bow. "Nobody is quite sure, Miss. He left early this morning and has not been seen since."

Chapter Twenty-Nine

Tawnyetta couldn't go back to her friends. She was too heated, too worried, too flustered. They would be full of questions to which she had no answer and she couldn't face them right now. She couldn't very well stand around Michael's front door waiting for him to return. So she went to the only place she could be by herself and think–the gardens.

The sun had still not come out to burn off the mist or the chill in the air. Everything was damp and green. Leafy vines grew over archways creating the amazing living tunnel she so loved. Little white and purple flowers covered the ground and birds chirped now and then despite the gloomy weather.

Pulling her black knobby sweater even tighter around her for warmth, Tawnyetta walked thoughtfully through the entire Secret Garden then into the woodlands. Nobody in the whole castle knew where Michael had gone to, and though they weren't necessarily worried she could tell there was a growing sense of concern the longer he was away.

The concern was more acute for Tawnyetta. Sharp pricks of panic poked at her heart and stomach every time she let her mind wander to where Michael might be and what he might be doing. Would he stay away until she'd left to avoid any more contact? Was he the kind of man to fall into the arms of another woman for comfort? She didn't know. And there was nothing she could do to find out.

She came to the edge of the woodlands where the path led up and into the hills. There was a cool breeze sweeping down from them. She took a slow, deep breath, remembering how the wildness of the hills had called to her that day. The way each step taking her up to the top had filled her with both a sense of freedom and belonging. As if she'd finally come home.

Another thought struck her and made her stomach twist into a knot. Michael had been drinking last night. Heavily.

He had been downcast and brooding. He hadn't joined in the normal group banter of the party atmosphere, but remained separate and aloof. His brother had died drinking and driving. What if Michael had taken things too far after last night? What if he had put himself in that kind of danger?

"No," she said out loud. Though she was alone, it felt better to speak the word. It had more power that way. He wouldn't do something like that. His brother's death had been difficult for him and he had feelings of guilt, but that was normal. Her rejection wouldn't be enough to send him over the edge into self-destruction. Would it?

A cold gust of air brushed across her face. The fresh smell of the wind, the damp earth below her feet, all of it reminded her of Michael. She closed her eyes and took in another deep breath, missing him, wanting nothing more than to feel his arms around her again.

Suddenly, Tawnyetta knew where he was.

Her eyes flew open. Another gust of wind carried down the steep, wild hills and enveloped her, called to her. As if Michael himself were calling her name.

And just as if he had actually beckoned to her, Tawnyetta answered. "I'm coming."

Without any further thought she took off up the path into the hills, into the deepening mist, as fast as her feet would carry her.

Tawnyetta knew the way with no hesitation. It was as if the hills had imprinted on her mind. She found sure footing with each step. The grass and flowers joined with the rocks that jutted out of the ground and seemed to light her way. Her pace quickened, her heart raced with the exertion and with anticipation. Though the mist grew thicker every moment, she had no fear of what was to come. With everything in her heart and soul Tawnyetta believed Michael was nearby. And Michael would never let harm come to her. He would always save her. He had told her so.

Heart pounding and breathing fast she arrived at the bothy. Ancient and strong, if a little bent and broken in places, it was a beautiful sight. She was so happy to be back that she almost laughed out loud when it came into view. As she grew closer, however, her joy began to dissipate.

There was no sign of Michael anywhere around. No smoke rose from the wood stovepipe. No sound of any living thing nearby. Could she have been so wrong? She had been certain he would be here, that he would have come here after she wounded him. To be alone. To remember her.

She climbed onto the rickety porch and it squeaked. So much for surprising him. There was nothing to worry about, however, because when she opened the door she found only an empty room. Tawnyetta's heart grew heavy. She stepped inside, still not willing to believe that she had been so wrong, but not knowing what else to do or where else to go.

"Michael?" His name came out of her mouth as a whispered question. A small part of her hoped he was sitting in a shadow or standing too far in a corner for her to see him. But there was nothing there. She was alone.

Tawnyetta's shoulders fell and she dropped her face into her hands. She wanted to cry. She wanted to scream. She did neither, just stood there wishing she'd done everything differently.

And just when she thought it couldn't be worse, rain started pouring outside. Pounding on the roof of the bothy it mirrored the anguish in her heart. As the tears broke through and began to stream out of her eyes she thought it fitting that her attempt to find Michael and apologize would end like this. A painful reminder of when they'd fallen in love.

She stayed there in the cool damp air, crying softly into her hands, as the rain filled her with sadness. She didn't know for how long, nor did she care. Everything she'd had at her fingertips washed away with every passing moment and she was at a loss as to what to do.

"Tawnyetta?"

For a split second she thought her ears were playing tricks on her, taking the noise of the rain on the roof and shaping it into what she wanted to hear. But, no. She could sense him in the room. It wasn't her imagination at all. Tawnyetta dropped her hands from her face and turned. And when she finally laid eyes on Michael MacBrody her heart leapt in her chest.

He stood tall in the doorway, dripping wet from the storm, looking just like he did when he scooped her up in his arms and carried her to safety so many long days ago. His dark hair was black with rain and disheveled. His beard was rough around the edges, like he hadn't taken the time to trim it this morning. In fact, he looked like he had been up all night, tension pulling at his rakishly handsome face. But those blue,

blue eyes were still sharp and they pierced right through to her soul.

"Michael," she said again, just louder than a whisper this time.

He stepped into the shack and glanced around, returning his dark look back to her quickly. "What are you doing up here?"

All she wanted to do was fall into his embrace, wrap her arms around his neck and feel his lips against hers. But he stayed apart from her and though there was longing in his eyes, there was also distance and pain. Every muscle in his body seemed taunt, as if he was ready to move lightning fast in one direction or another but had not yet decided which way.

Tawnyetta hesitated. When dealing with an injured animal it was necessary to move slowly and not rush toward them before you knew if they were going to welcome your attention or lash out. And that's exactly how Michael appeared. Like a wounded lion or a wolf pacing back and forth in a cage.

She cleared her throat. "I came to find you."

His expression did not change. His gaze moved up and down her body as if assessing her for weapons. His eyes locked back onto hers, glittering with a challenge. He flicked his hands out at his sides in a mockery of a formal presentation. "Here I am."

This was not going like she had hoped it would.

Making a wide birth around her, Michael moved to the corner that held the secret hiding place. "Were you looking for a wee bit more to drink?" He motioned to the now empty hole in the wall. "I'm afraid you're in for a disappointment."

Tawnyetta watched him as he moved, stung by his sarcastic tone. "No, I wasn't looking for a drink."

"Ah, you had enough of that last night, then?"

Again, sarcasm. She took a deep breath and tried to remain

calm. He seemed in a mood to pick a fight and that's not why she had come.

"What, then?" Michael looked around the humble room. Spying the cabinets he moved quickly to them and opened the crooked door with the tin inside. "Tea?" He yanked the tin out and held it up to her.

She shook her head 'no' but couldn't answer because she was afraid her lower lip might tremble if she spoke.

"Well, what is it, lass?" He dropped the tin down into the sink with a clatter. "Why would you climb all the way up the hill to this pile of ruins?" He threw his arm out toward the door of the bothy. "You have the run of Claymore Castle and servants at your beck and call, do you not?"

He stopped talking abruptly, like he had choked on his own words. His breath was coming fast and hard as he glared at her, eyes flashing.

Tawnyetta wasn't afraid of him. Quite the opposite. With every terse word and violent movement she felt the love she had for him grow. For it wasn't anger that she saw in his eyes, but hurt and fear. Fear of being alone, of loving her and losing her. He was afraid. So was she.

She swallowed hard, trying to ebb the tears that wanted to come. When she spoke it was no longer in a whisper, though her voice quavered dangerously. "I came to find you."

Michael didn't answer, but that didn't matter. She had come to tell him what she had to tell him and she didn't need him to talk her through it. This might be her last chance.

Taking a step toward him she spoke, more firmly than before, "I came to see you."

He flinched. A chink in his fierce armor.

She took another step. He flicked his eyes to her feet then back up. The intensity of his look sent a shiver through her body.

Tawnyetta reached out her hand toward him and was

surprised at how steady it was. "I came to touch you..." The words caught in her throat, stuck somewhere between her pounding heart and a torrent of tears wanting release. She took another step so they were only a few feet away from one another. "I came to tell you that I was wrong."

He searched her eyes for meaning, not trusting the words or gesture just yet. "Wrong?"

Tawnyetta nodded. She gathered all of her courage, took a deep breath and said, "You were right. It is possible for people to fall in love in a few weeks." She held his gaze and watched as the fear in his eyes turned to confusion then to the tiniest glimmer of hope. "I know you were right, because it has been less than two weeks since we met...yet I am, in fact, madly in love with you."

For one moment in time Tawnyetta was not sure what would happen next. She stood on the precipice of this unknown, in love with an unpredictable and powerful man, offering him her heart. As terrifying as this moment was, it also held a priceless treasure. For as she waited for Michael's response, she watched the expression in his eyes and face, his whole demeanor, change before her eyes.

The muscles in his body shifted. They yielded from seeming ready to pounce into a state of relief. The tense lines in his face smoothed. The glimmer of hope in his eyes shone brighter, turning into a look of passion and love that she would remember for the rest of her life.

Suddenly he held her hand in his. Bringing it up to his mouth, he pressed his lips to her fingers, warm and firm. All the while his eyes danced. She smiled and laughed and cried all at once, but only for a moment. For within seconds Michael pulled her to him. His hand on her cheek, his arm around her waist holding her close to him, she fell into the pleasure of his body next to hers with abandon.

"You're certain?" he asked, though she knew he could see

the truth of her love in her eyes, feel it in her touch. She nodded. He traced one finger along her temple, across her cheek and to her lips, tickling her and sending shivers through her body once again. "Because, once I start kissing you again, Tawnyetta Campbell, I'll not be wanting to stop."

She threw her head back and laughed. Then she looked at him and reached both arms around his neck pulling him closer. "Is that a promise?"

"It's a guarantee." He smiled. Then he kissed her. A now and forever kiss that washed away all of her fears and lifted her off the floor until she felt like she was floating.

And he was true to his word. Laird Michael MacBrody didn't let another day go by without whisking her up in his arms for a kiss. And every one of his kisses were filled with so much passion that Tawnyetta never doubted their love, nor her decision to make loving him the greatest adventure of her life.

The End

They were married in the hills.

Michael told everyone that it was because the width and breadth of their love could not be contained in any walls. Not even the walls of a castle. And Tawnyetta was inclined to agree.

This was all much to Bridget's chagrin. As the maid of honor and self-appointed wedding planner, as well as being a lifelong dreamer of becoming a princess, Bridget had hoped Tawnyetta and Michael would have an ultra-grand royal type wedding inside of the castle. This was not to be. So she had to settle for throwing an ultra-grand royal type reception in the castle ballroom instead.

On the day of their wedding the sun shone on the Highlands, as Michael had promised Tawnyetta it would.

"Though I would marry you in the middle of a snow storm, lass, if that's what needed to be," he had declared many times during their engagement.

"No need for that, love," Tawnyetta responded each and every time. Adding, "We'll make sure to have enough umbrellas for us and all of the guests...just in case."

All of the guests included, of course, Sofia, Angie and Luna who had been part of their love story, as well as their families. Even the Prescotts were invited since they were there from the beginning. Bridget stood up with Tawnyetta as her maid of honor and, because they had grown to be great friends over the course of Michael and Tawnyetta's romance, Michael asked Thomas to be his best man.

Michael invited all of the staff and every citizen of Eldin to the wedding as well, making it a true community event. This created a shortage of help for the wedding and the reception, but Bridget faced that problem head on using her event planning wizardry. With Tawnyetta's blessing she hired people out of Edinburgh to help set up the outdoor wedding and a special event company direct from London to handle the reception.

Tawnyetta's parents, brothers, and their families were there. Dougie and Gavina sat in the place of honor where Michael's parents would have sat if they had been alive. Dougie was so overcome with pride over this gesture that he teared up during the ceremony. As did Michael. The sight of his bride walking to him through the green hills painted lavender with heather filled him to bursting.

Tawnyetta's dress consisted of a tight, off the shoulder bodice with long bell sleeves that started halfway down her upper arm and dropped until they skimmed the floor. Her skirt flowed smoothly, and every inch of cloth was covered in handmade Scottish lace that Sadie and Isla at Sadie Sews had been saving for just such a magnificent occasion. Tawnyetta's hair was swept up and she wore the Peridot and diamond tiara that had belonged to Michael's mother, Lady Margaret MacBrody. The golden amber of Tawnyetta's eyes glowed with love and contentment.

Michael wore his formal kilt, of course. Standing proud under an archway woven with white ribbon and the grey and black of his tartan, the bagpipes played, and Michael was every bit the Laird of Claymore Castle. He was also the man that she loved. He waited for her impatiently, her handsome groom. And as Tawnyetta walked toward him she felt like her soul was blooming. The love in her heart could not be contained, it poured out of her to Michael, to all of her friends and family, and to everyone in her presence. And this overflowing love made her, in Michael's words, the most bonnie bride in the history of Scotland.

In fact, all who were present that day told stories for years to come of how brightly the new Lady MacBrody shone on the day of her wedding, and every day thereafter.

Sofia...

Sofia moved confidently through the crowded ballroom on her stilettos. For the wedding she had chosen a sleeveless black sheath dress with a plunging neckline to make the most of her cleavage. The dress was made of taffeta and hugged every curve in her exceptionally curvy figure. The hemline ended just above her knee and over the top of the dress hung a long, loosely crocheted sheath of black lace. Her dark skin peeked out from behind the lace making her feel feminine and just a little naughty. Nothing like feeling ultra-sleek and sexy at one of your best friend's weddings.

Sofia had straightened her long black hair, painted her nails in the deepest red she could find, applied the same color lipstick, and added her highest black stilettos for the final touch. Granted, her look might feel a little dark for the occasion, but that was her style. Sleek and smart, with an edge. Besides, she wasn't a bridesmaid in this wedding. For that much she could be grateful. She was free to wear what she chose. And Sofia with her emerald green eyes and deep brown complexion felt comfortable in black.

Tawnyetta and Michael's wedding had been gorgeous.

Watching her friend marry the love of her life was a particularly pleasant and joyful experience. Add on top of that the fact that the reception was being held in a castle with the finest music, wine, and food served by waiters in tuxedos where most of the male guests were sporting formal kilts and, for sure, it was an impressive event.

Tawnyetta deserved to be happy and Sofia was so glad that her friend had found such an amazing man to marry and was off on the adventure of her lifetime. It made Sofia's soul smile, but it also made her a little sad. Not that she wanted to be married. No way. She had bigger goals than just finding a husband. But it made her a bit sad that Tawnyetta would be living her beautiful new life so far away from all of them back home in Denver.

Sofia grabbed another glass of sparkling champagne from a waiter. Her deep red polished nails made a satisfying clicking sound on the fine crystal. She took a sip and some of her waxy red lipstick left an imprint of her bottom lip on the rim. The crisp champagne popped and fizzled in her mouth.

The room was thinning out. Many of the older wedding guests were taking their leave to drive home or retire to their rooms if they were staying in the castle. The excellent, if rather formal, orchestra had played their last song a few minutes ago and packed up their instruments. A mixture of pop and rock music pumped through the tastefully hidden speakers that were placed throughout the ballroom. Sofia sipped her champagne and watched as a group of decidedly less formally attired men set up a drum set and other makings of a rock band on the stage that the orchestra had vacated.

"You're going to love these guys," Bridget said as she sidled up to Sofia with her own glass of champagne.

"You think?"

Bridget took a sip and nodded, her blonde curls bouncing

chaotically. "They're called The Robot Tellers. I picked them." She grinned at Sofia.

Bridget had been Tawnyetta's ever helpful and sometimes overbearing maid of honor and wedding planner. But Tawnyetta herself admitted she welcomed the help and the whole wedding and reception had been so lovely, going off without a hitch. Sofia was sure this late night entertainment band would be everything Bridget promised.

"I'm sure they'll be great...despite that name."

Bridget chuckled and took another sip of champagne. Her eyes roamed around the room taking in all of the smiling faces and twinkling candles and lights.

"I love weddings," Bridget said with a sigh.

Sofia gave her friend a knowing look and felt a stab of pity for Bridget's failed wedding. She leaned over slightly, giving Bridget's shoulder a soft bump with hers. "I know," she said.

"Good evening, ladies and gents," a smooth male voice with a British, not Scottish, accent came over the hidden speakers. Sofia and Bridget both looked towards the stage.

A ginger haired man was at the microphone. He was tall, fair skinned, and wore a black long-tailed tuxedo jacket over a pair of worn jeans and faded Joy Division T-shirt. Sneakers, or "trainers" as they called them here, topped off the look of who Sofia determined must be the lead singer of The Robot Tellers.

"First of all, congratulations to the bride and groom." The lead singer was adjusting his electric guitar as he spoke. His mouth was so close to the round surface of the microphone it appeared that he might try to eat it. He remembered something, bent down and picked up an open bottle of beer that was sitting at his feet. He stood and lifted it into the air toward Tawnyetta and Michael who were closer to the stage. "To Laird MacBrody and the new Lady MacBrody!"

The guests cheered and Michael leaned down to give

Tawnyetta a kiss. It was all very sweet, but Sofia wasn't paying attention. She could not take her eyes off the lead singer.

His hair was deep red, cut short and sticking straight up off of his head in messy spikes. Angular cheekbones, a square jaw, and a sprinkle of freckles across his nose and cheeks gave him an interesting look. He was handsome, quite handsome. When he took a swig of his beer, the sleeve of his jacket rode up his arm revealing a colorful twisting pattern of tattoos that started on his wrist and looked like they continued up his whole arm. She was too far away to make out what the tattoos were, but Sofia found herself wondering about them—and him.

"So now that the formalities are out of the way..." He placed the beer bottle back at his feet and took hold of the guitar hanging around his neck. "I'm Ian Law." He strummed the guitar with that announcement, sending the electric sound through the speakers. Ian grinned at the sound, nodding his head a little as if appreciating the acoustics. "This is Danny." He turned and looked at the second guitarist, a small wiry guy with long, wavy blonde hair. "Hugh." He looked at a tall black man holding the bass guitar. Hugh played a short rift on his bass in response. "And on the drums." Ian put his back to the crowd so he was facing the drummer as he shouted, "George!" The drummer hit a few loud beats and Ian turned back to the crowd. He leaned into the microphone again and Sofia was surprised how much the move seemed sensual, his lips so close. "But we call him Charlie," Ian said. The sound of his voice reverberated through the room.

The crowd clapped and cheered and the band played a few seconds of the beginning of a song she didn't know. Sofia's stomach fluttered. It wasn't that she'd never been to a rock concert, but there was no denying that Ian Law put out some serious sex appeal on that stage.

"We are The Robot Tellers," he said, his voice rising to be

heard over the growing sound of the song intro. He looked sharply around the room. Sofia couldn't tell what color his eyes were from where she stood, but they glittered with that look musicians have when they are about to sing. The look that says they know they are about to become the most important person in the room.

Ian's gaze fell on Bridget and he gave her a little nod of acknowledgement. Then his eyes locked onto Sofia's and the flutter in her stomach went wild.

Ian leaned into the microphone. Reading his body language, the band lowered the volume of their playing so he could speak. He did not break his eyes away from Sofia as he said, "And we are gonna rock your world."

The crowd around her cheered, but Sofia remained still. Held by his attention as the song began, she felt everyone around her begin to move as one to the rhythm of the music. Ian's eyes remained laser locked onto hers, refusing to look away, refusing to let her escape. Then, to her surprise, he gave her a wink and like a 13-year-old girl she felt a rush of heat flush through her body and fill her cheeks. Ian grinned and ducked his head, confident he had made an impression. Then he closed his eyes, put his mouth against the microphone, and sang.

The next book in the Dream Come True series, Her British Bard, is available!

Also by Darci Balogh

<u>Dream Come True Sweet Romance</u>
1. Her Scottish Keep
2. Her British Bard
3. Her Sheltered Cove

<u>The Mighty Aphrodite Writing Society</u>
1. Beach Retreat at Turtle Cove
2. Beach Wedding at Turtle Cove

<u>Lady Billionaire Series</u>
1. Ms. Money Bags
2. Ms. Perfect

<u>Sweet Holiday Romance Series</u>
Holiday romances for Halloween through New Year's Eve!
1. Enchanting Eve
2. Love is at the Table
3. Mistletoe Madness
4. New Year in Paradise

<u>Sugar Plum Romance Series</u>
Christmas, cooking, and chefs falling in love!
1. Charlotte's Christmas Charade
2. Bella's Christmas Blunder

~

<u>Love & Marriage Series</u>

Steamy, emotional, relatable characters, these older woman, younger man love stories are both racy and romantic.

1. The Quiet of Spring

2. For Love & For Money

3. Stars in the Sand

About the Author

Darci Balogh is a writer and indie filmmaker from Denver. She grew up in the beautiful mountains of Colorado and has lived in several areas of the state over her lifetime. She currently resides in Denver where she raised her two glorious, intelligent daughters to functioning adulthood. This is, by far, one of her highest achievements.

Darci has a love-hate relationship with gardening, probably should dust more, adores dogs and is allergic to cats. She has been a writer since she was a child and enjoys crafting stories into novels and screenplays. Big surprise, some of her favorite pastimes are reading and watching movies. Classic British TV is high on her 'Like' list, along with quietly depressing detective series and coffee with heavy cream.

For more romance books by Darci Balogh, go to www.knowheremedia.com/books